"Let me go!" Persephone struggled in the grip of whoever, or whatever, it was. The grip didn't loosen.

She writhed in his arms and pummeled him with her fists. Persephone was a country girl, used to working in her mother's garden and catching wild goats for amusement. She was nearly as strong as any boy in the village.

Her mind filled with pale wraiths brushing by her as they passed, ghostly fingers ~~~~~~ cloak; and that seeme~~~~~~~~~~~~~~~~~~~~~~e was going. The air ~~~~~~~~~~~~~~~~~~~~~~~. Her arms and legs ~~~~~~~~~~~~~~~~

They passed ~~~~~~~~~~~~~~~~~~~~ and Persephone bega~~~~~~~~~~~~~~~~uld never find her way ou~~~~~~~aze. And the pale, dark-bearded man who was plainly Hades himself would rape her or eat her or suck her soul away or all three, and she would never see her mother again. She burst into a despairing howl just as the sheeplike servants stopped at a doorway with a wooden door in it instead of a tapestry. The door had a large bronze bolt on the outside.

The largest sheep servant patted her shoulder clumsily. "No one will hurt you."

"Then what does he want with me?" Persephone demanded, sniffling.

The servant opened the heavy door. "Marry you, I think," he said, and pushed her inside.

"*Marry me?*" The door closed behind her and she heard the click of the bolt. Their footsteps padded away outside it. . . .

# THE GODDESSESS

# LOVE UNDERGROUND

## *Persephone's Tale*

## Alicia Fields

A SIGNET ECLIPSE BOOK

SIGNET ECLIPSE
Published by New American Library, a division of
Penguin Group (USA) Inc., 375 Hudson Street,
New York, New York 10014, USA
Penguin Group (Canada), 90 Eglinton Avenue East, Suite 700, Toronto,
Ontario M4P 2Y3, Canada (a division of Pearson Penguin Canada Inc.)
Penguin Books Ltd., 80 Strand, London WC2R 0RL, England
Penguin Ireland, 25 St. Stephen's Green, Dublin 2,
Ireland (a division of Penguin Books Ltd.)
Penguin Group (Australia), 250 Camberwell Road, Camberwell, Victoria 3124,
Australia (a division of Pearson Australia Group Pty. Ltd.)
Penguin Books India Pvt. Ltd., 11 Community Centre, Panchsheel Park,
New Delhi - 110 017, India
Penguin Group (NZ), cnr Airborne and Rosedale Roads, Albany,
Auckland 1310, New Zealand (a division of Pearson New Zealand Ltd.)
Penguin Books (South Africa) (Pty.) Ltd., 24 Sturdee Avenue,
Rosebank, Johannesburg 2196, South Africa

Penguin Books Ltd., Registered Offices:
80 Strand, London WC2R 0RL, England

First published by Signet Eclipse, an imprint of New American Library,
a division of Penguin Group (USA) Inc.

First Printing, July 2005
10  9  8  7  6  5  4  3  2  1

# AUTHOR'S NOTE

The country of myth is not the world that we inhabit, but an older place, next door to the land of fairy tale. Like fairy tales, myth is peopled with the stuff of legend; however, while fairy tales tell the small domestic legend—the wicked stepmother, the younger brother who finds his fortune—myth tells the wider story—how fire came to mankind, why the winds blow, how the crops and animals were tamed for our use. All these great steps toward civilization took centuries, with small discovery after small discovery. Myth compresses that history into story, which is always more powerful and memorable.

In Greece, in between the grandeur of the Minoan civilization of Crete and that of the Mycenaeans of the mainland, from about 1600 B.C. to 1200 B.C., and the age of recorded history, which began in about 750 B.C., there was a Dark Age, a long period of wars and invasions during which those older worlds crumbled. Technology and knowledge were lost, and many of the refugees of those wars scattered to the islands of the Aegean. Such are the dark times when myth is born, when we yearn for the adventures of heroes in a greater, brighter time. That is the time into which I have put this tale of Persephone and Demeter and Hades.

As well as its own time, myth has its own landscape, and so this story, which is halfway between the tale as the Greek bards told it, and the account that history and anthropology would give us, is set in that Dark Age, when old skills were lost and later regained, on an unnamed island of the Greek archipelago.

# I

❧

## Stepping Across the Border

When Persephone was small, her mother taught her how to plant seed in the ground and wait patiently, absolutely not digging it up to see how it was coming along, for it to sprout. The process was beautiful: First, two fat leaves would appear, then green tendrils promising beans, or the curly leaves of cabbage, or the slender shoots that would grow to tall bristly heads of wheat. She took her first steps in Demeter's garden, following her mother down the rows while Demeter hoed the weeds away with a pointed stick and cut stray branches from the fig tree with her small bronze pruning knife.

Persephone thought of her mother as a melon, her head topped with a leafy crown, her green body rounded at the hips like the statues of Earth Mother, which women kept in their houses to bring babies. She padded through the garden at Demeter's heels, talking to the bees, and the mantises with their cocked triangular heads and bulging eyes. As she grew older, she took to the woods with her cousin Hermes, bringing back armfuls of flowers and clay jars containing toads and newts for further study in the brook that ran behind the garden. Persephone was aware, without quite knowing why, that most people in the village were a little afraid of her mother. That offered a certain immunity when she stole honey from someone's hives or lay on her back in the sunny grass and sucked the milk from someone's goat, but it did not keep Demeter from smacking her. No one else was allowed to except for Great-Grandfather Aristippus, who was the high priest of Zeus and therefore in direct communication with the gods.

The girls of her age, Echo and Narcissa, who were her particular friends and somewhat more strictly supervised, could be counted on to take part in her tamer adventures. Only Hermes, however, would take risks with her, as when they climbed to the top of Aristippus's goat shed to spy on Great-Grandfather, who liked to hide in there with girls while his wife, Bopis, was looking for him. Only Hermes would help her set a snare for a wild goat and then try to tame it with offerings of cabbage from Demeter's garden. Like all island children, they took to the water early. It was Hermes who tried to make a boat of her goat cart, and set them adrift so that they had to swim back when the goat cart sank.

It was also Hermes who convinced her when they were eight to show him what she looked like naked.

"Only if you do, too," Persephone said. She was curious. She had caught a glimpse of Great-Grandfather once, and of course she knew what male goats looked like, but it was hard to picture, all the same. She was unimpressed with Hermes and said so.

"It gets bigger when you get older," he said indignantly.

"Will mine?" She peered down.

"I don't think so. I've never heard of that happening. Let me look. Hmmm . . .

At that point Demeter had caught them. She came in from the garden, where they had thought she was planting beans, and chased Hermes from the house with a rake. He took to his heels naked and laughing, while Persephone pulled her dress back on, and fled into the woods.

"You stay away from that boy!" Demeter yelled at her daughter. "You stay away from all boys! They will give you nothing but grief."

Persephone learned to be more wary of Hermes as they grew older. He was precocious and, she discovered, he made things up. Even though he was fun, you couldn't ever quite trust what he told you.

By her sixteenth summer, Persephone knew a few things about her world: The earth was flat. At its center was Hellas, comprising the island on which she lived, and a surrounding archipelago of other islands large and small. The River Ocean flowed around the world, and through its middle ran the Sea where Hellas stood with its roots in the bottom of the world. In the North lived the Hyperboreans, a perpetually happy race who existed in inaccessible bliss behind the mountains. Their icy winds brought winter to Hellas. In the South lived a legendarily virtuous people called the Aethiopians, whose behavior was generally cited to Persephone as an example when she teased the goats or made a dam in the brook and flooded the beans. In the West lay the Elysian Fields where those favored by the gods went to share their immortality without dying first. No one seemed to know what was in the East. Persephone guessed the Sun's house was there, as each morning the Sun drove his fiery chariot out of the Ocean, across the sky, and down into the waters in the West. Great-Grandfather said at night the Sun traveled around the back side in a winged boat.

When Demeter was Persephone's age she had gone away somewhere, but no one knew whether it was to the happy Hyperboreans or the virtuous Aethiopians, or maybe even inside the borders of the Elysian Fields. She was gone for several years and was presumed to have been eaten by lions, until she reappeared with a child on her hip and the knowledge of how to tame the plants that grew wild on the island. She knew how to grow them for her own rather than just pick them where she could find them. Teaching this to the people of her village, mainly goat herders, had given Demeter her reputation. They decided that wisdom had to come from the gods, in whom they believed implicitly, although no one had actually seen one, but there was no other accepted explanation.

Persephone had asked her mother several times who her father had been, but Demeter would never say. No one else had the nerve to ask, and all Demeter told Persephone was, "Watch out."

"Watch out for what?" Persephone had asked her when she was eight.

"For strangers," Demeter had answered.

"What kind of strangers?" Persephone had asked her when she was twelve.

"Men," Demeter had said and wouldn't say anything else.

It was clear to Persephone at sixteen that her mother's order was not going to be difficult to obey. All the boys in the village were too afraid of Demeter to court Persephone. The exception was Hermes, who still wasn't afraid of anything because he didn't have enough sense to be. Hermes had thought he could ride old Leucippus's big ram, and it had tipped him off and butted him into the river. This did not stop Hermes from bragging about it afterward. He had convinced the smaller boys to climb a wild bee tree and bring him down the comb. When they were stung, he had advised them to run for the village rather than the river with a cloud of bees behind them. Hermes liked to stir things up just to see what would happen. He courted all the girls indiscriminately, and he was not the faithful sort.

Persephone and her friends would see him hiding in the rushes while they bathed in the river. They would throw stones at him for spying on them, but Hermes would just laugh and run away. An hour later he would be back, his pointed face peering at them from between the gray leaves of an olive tree.

"Go away! You nasty boy!" Echo shook one small fist at him and pitched a rock from the pool's bottom into the branches with the other.

Hermes slid down the tree, his red hair a flash like a russet fox among the olive leaves, and then he was gone, bounding over the hillocky bank and into the woods, leaving his cackling laugh hanging behind him in the still, hot summer air.

"Ooh! And I saw him with Clytie just yesterday, crawling all over her, the slut, after he asked *me* to go walking last full-of-the-moon!" Echo balled both fists up and pounded them on the water.

"And you trusted him?" Narcissa shook her head solemnly, wet dark hair dripping over bare shoulders.

"Echo, you know he always lies." Persephone paddled in the slow water where the stream widened into a bathing pool. Her chin skimmed just above the surface, and her long hair floated around her like gold seaweed.

Echo pouted. "Well, of course I do, but this was different. He *said* it was different. And anyway, what was he doing with a cow like Clytie? Honestly, that girl will go with anyone, so I don't see that she really counts. Except of course, she does count because he *promised me*. Anyway—"

Echo was the shortest of the girls, and she was standing on a rock embedded in the bottom of the pool so that her breasts just bobbed on the surface. They reminded Persephone of figs and she watched them idly to see if they were going to sprout leaves and split open while Echo nattered on. They didn't, so she lay back in the cool water, paddling with her fingers just enough to keep her from drifting downstream. Their shucked dresses lay on the bank. No boy except Hermes would have the nerve to come near the pool after seeing those dresses. If Demeter didn't curse him so that his penis withered like an uprooted stalk (it was rumored that she could do so), the girls would heave rocks at him and tell his mother. Girls in Persephone's village didn't lie down with boys when they didn't want to. Persephone was not aware, and nor were they, that this was not the case elsewhere. There was something in Demeter's garden that protected women.

"So anyway, Harmonia wanted to go out after the spring bonfires with Tros, and her mother wouldn't let her because his people are so poor. . . ." Echo had taken a new tack.

Narcissa grinned at Persephone and lay back in the water, too. They watched a dragonfly skim over the pool. It was blue with emerald wingtips. Echo liked to talk even when you weren't listening. Sometimes you found out something interesting from her, such as the fact that Glaucus, who was as old as dirt, was finally dying, and his daughters were fighting over who would inherit his house and his sixty goats, and one of them had tried to cut another one's fingers off with a cheese knife. Or that Dryope, Glaucus's third wife, had run away and was hiding from the daughters, because she was afraid they would come after her next. What the daughters didn't know was that Dryope had all of Glaucus's gold.

"Glaucus has gold?" Narcissa sat up in the water, paddling with both hands.

"Yes, and no one knows where he got it. His daughters don't even know he has it. I heard it all from Dryope because I gave her a cake and some milk when she came to our house. Mother wouldn't let her stay; she's afraid of those old women." Glaucus's daughters were nearly as old as he was.

No one in the village had any gold to speak of, except for those few who had been off the island. There was no reason to leave. Anything you might want was right here, which made gold fairly useless, although coveted just the same. Demeter had said once, darkly, that people were not rational when it came to gold.

"Well, where is she staying?" Persephone asked.

"I don't know," Echo said regretfully. "She wouldn't tell me where she was going when she left."

"She probably wished she hadn't told you about the gold," Narcissa said. "You can't keep a secret."

"I can so!" Echo looked indignant, her freckled face squinched in outrage.

"Oh, you can't," Persephone said lazily. "You know you can't. You told Tros when I said that Harmonia could do better than him."

Narcissa pointed a finger at Echo. "Then you told her mother she didn't come home all night after the equinox bonfires, when her mother thought she was in bed."

"I didn't mean to!" Echo clapped her hand to her mouth.

"And then you told *my* mother that Arachne finished my weaving for me. You know I hate weaving, and she made me make two whole blankets as punishment."

"I didn't mean to!" Echo wailed. "It just slipped out!"

Persephone grinned. "Everything slips out. Echo, you cannot keep a secret. You had better try to keep your mouth shut about Glaucus and Dryope and any gold, or everyone in the village will be in a buzz over it, and someone will come after *you* with a cheese knife."

Echo pouted, arms folded across her breasts. "Well, if you're going to be like that, I just won't say anything else."

"You've already said it," Narcissa said.

"Don't be cross, Echo," Persephone said, ducking under the water. She surfaced just behind the shorter girl, spouting river water at the back of her head.

Echo turned and dove at Persephone's legs, pulling her under. They wrestled, shrieking, while Narcissa watched primly. When Echo, who was stronger than she looked, had ducked Persephone three times, they paddled to the riverbank and lay panting in the shallows.

"Something's going on," Narcissa said. "You two were making too much noise to hear it, bellowing like cows. Listen!"

They cocked their heads toward the path that ran away over the tree-dotted hillocks toward the village. The sound of wailing and the shrill of pipes hung in the air.

"Glaucus has died," Persephone said. She heaved herself out of the shallows and picked up her dress.

"Maybe it's pirates!" Echo said.

"Then *everyone* would be screaming," Narcissa pointed out. "That's mourning. We'd better go. It's not respectful to be lolling here in the pool." Glaucus was older than Persephone's great-grandfather and so was due some honor, even if he had been nearly as unpleasant as his daughters.

"Do you suppose Dryope can hear it?" Echo said.

"Probably," Persephone said, her head muffled by the folds of her dress. She pulled it down and pinned the right shoulder. "Sound carries up into the hills."

"I bet she doesn't come down," Echo said, drying her feet with her hem. "If I were Dryope I'd be looking for a nice boat on the other side of the island. One with a handsome captain."

"He was her husband," Narcissa said. "She owes him something even if he was an evil old toad."

"Well, I think she paid her debt," Persephone said, tying her sash. "Living with him all those years. Ugh. Would you marry someone like that just because he had sixty goats?"

Persephone was in her sixteenth summer, the eldest of the three, and even fourteen-year-old Echo was of marriageable age. It was a topic they discussed at some length almost daily, while floating in the pool, or cursing their weaving in the flat courtyard in front of Narcissa's mother's house.

"You wouldn't have to," Narcissa said. Persephone was by far the most beautiful girl on the island, and Demeter had no need to marry off her daughter for goats.

"I'll be lucky if I get married at all," Persephone sighed. "Mother says men aren't worth the trouble."

"Glaucus had all that gold, too," Echo pointed out.

"Even gold wouldn't be enough to marry him." Persephone shuddered pointedly. "And anyway, no one knew that. Unless he told Dryope's parents, to convince them to let him have her."

"No, he didn't," Echo said. "She found it in a trunk. It was locked, and she broke the lock off with a rock."

They set off up the stony path to the village, contemplating Dryope's ingenuity. It was the most interesting turn of events that had happened locally in a long time, and they were gratified by the idea that they knew more than anyone else.

"She must have had some reason for marrying him," Persephone said. "He was awful."

"Her family was very poor," Narcissa said, "and

he wasn't, even without the gold. Sometimes that's all it takes."

"Oh, poor thing. Well, I hope she gets away."

They crested the last hill and came down into the village through the olive grove that Demeter had planted fifteen years before. Just in the last year the trees were beginning to hang heavy with fruit. Olives gave the people of Hellas light, food, and soap, and they took a long time to mature. The wild ones were jealously guarded from outsiders. Beyond them lay Demeter's vineyard, another ingathering of the wild, with the grapevines arranged in neat rows and pruned to bear the most fruit.

They could hear the pipes and the wailing clearly now, with the high notes of a lyre in between. As they came through the vineyard, a procession wound out from among the mud houses and into the agora, the dirt courtyard that was the heart of the village. At its center grew a single ancient olive tree, and the ground around it was packed as hard as stone from decades of feet. The agora was the daily marketplace, where anyone with something to say stood and harangued the village, where marriages were solemnized and deaths mourned, and where the village elders, all men, sat in the evening and drank wine and discussed matters of great importance.

Glaucus's daughters, draped in black, were howling and pulling at their veils, while Glaucus lay on a litter, wrapped like a cocoon in his shroud. Great-Grandfather Aristippus was there, leaning on his staff, nearly as old as Glaucus had been, his white shock of hair standing up as if on fire in the late afternoon sunlight. His wife, Bopis, was there, too; she narrowed her eyes when she saw Persephone.

Bopis didn't like Demeter or Persephone because Demeter's mother was a daughter of Aristippus whom he had got with another woman. Persephone saw her mother and scooted through the crowd to her, pulling the folds of her mantle up over her wet hair in respect. Great-Grandfather Aristippus was invoking the gods, asking them to take Glaucus down the river of the dead into the land of spirits and look on him kindly there. Hades, the deity who ruled the Underworld, lived in a cave at the foot of the cliffs that lined the island's southern shore. Beneath the shroud there would be two copper pennies on Glaucus's eyes, to pay the invisible boatman who would row his ghost downriver to Hades's dark realm.

Demeter put an arm around her daughter. "You're wet," she whispered. "You were supposed to be pruning the grapes."

"It was hot," Persephone said. "We went swimming."

"We?"

"Echo and Narcissa and me. Hermes was there, hiding in a tree. We threw rocks at him."

Demeter snorted.

"He gives himself airs because he's my cousin."

"Second cousin," Demeter said. "My cousin Maia never did have any sense, and that boy is proof of it. She claimed he was fathered by Zeus."

"Right. And Zeus wore a shepherd's cloak and snuck into her bed at night disguised." Persephone chuckled. She knew things, even if she wasn't married. Any country girl did. Demeter herself had never made any claims about Persephone's father, but Persephone privately thought that if anyone had had an affair with a god, it was more likely to be her mother than Cousin Maia, who had buck teeth and was nearly bald from a rash.

"Well, you're not going to marry him."

"Mother!" Persephone whispered, indignant. "I wouldn't want to!"

"You'll want somebody. I know girls," Demeter said sharply. "You're too pretty."

Persephone shrugged. So far she hadn't seen any boy she would be willing to marry.

Demeter poked her. "Now, be quiet. People are looking at us."

Persephone shrugged again. Her mother had been both a scandal and a minor deity herself since her return with the gift of gardening from wherever she had been. Persephone was used to people looking at them. She turned to watch the procession, with Great-Grandfather Aristippus, Bopis, and the wailing daughters at its head, snaking its way along the edge of the goat pasture toward the rocky cliff that rose behind the pasture's western edge. It mirrored the one that dropped down to the sea on the southern shore. Here the village dead were laid to rest, in chambers carved out of the rock, with things beside them they might need for their journey. Glaucus had been provided with a jug of good wine, a slab of goat cheese, and a loaf of bread. His best knife lay beside him, along with a herd of small clay goats. Two of the daughters had wanted to give him the best cookpot, as well, but they had been overruled by the third daughter with the cheese knife.

The passage to Glaucus's family tomb sloped downward into the mountainside, a stone-lined corridor wide enough for only one at a time. Most of the village

waited respectfully outside, but Demeter and Persephone followed the wailing daughters, Phaedon the
doctor, Aristippus, the priestess of Hestia, so old she
had to be carried chair-fashion by two young men, and
others who represented power in the village.

Glaucus's young wife was nowhere to be seen, a
circumstance that was commented upon in a low
murmur throughout the funeral.

"She was a slut anyway," the youngest daughter
said.

"No worse than some," the middle daughter muttered, nursing bandaged fingers and casting a baleful
glare at her elder sister.

The eldest turned on her, and they fussed among
themselves like a trio of weathered black crows, eyes
beady beneath their black veils, voices rising until Aristippus stomped his staff hard on the rocks and
coughed, and they settled down again, rattling feathers.

Persephone giggled, and Demeter tweaked her ear.

They stood in the tomb's antechamber while Glaucus and his grave goods were laid in the round rock-
cut tomb at the end of the passage. Two smaller
chambers held his first two wives, and Persephone
privately thought that Dryope was better off wherever she was. Despite his wealth, Glaucus had
worked his first wives to death, and only his final
demise had prevented the same thing happening
again.

Now the boatman would come for Glaucus and
demand his pennies, with which Persephone imagined he would be reluctant to part; then he would
leave his body behind, and the boatman would row
the ghost of Glaucus down the rivers that ran inside
the earth and deposit him in the realm of Death.

By the time the proper prayers had been said, the stone tomb had begun to close in on Persephone, or seemed to. She felt as if the bones of those wives might rise and pull her into their chambers with them. She was relieved when they turned around and filed up into the light again. As she reached the passage's mouth, she gasped and took deep breaths of the sunlit air.

The men of the village filled in the passageway's opening with rocks, and the procession wound its way back to the village. No one heard any more of Dryope, and Persephone imagined her sailing away in a boat with a red sail, her arms glittering with gold bracelets. She thought no more of death until the next week when Narcissa's father, Echemus, capsized his boat while fishing for tunny and was brought home nearly drowned.

At first it was thought he would live. He had retched up seawater and then more seawater and blood, but he was breathing; however, his breathing grew labored, and there was a pain in his chest that would not subside, so that each breath cut him like a knife. He was laid on a bed where Narcissa's mother hovered over him. The village doctor boiled herbs in a cauldron and had him breathe the vapors. Bopis offered advice about the dangers of seawater and the evil eye. Apollo was prayed to, and Narcissa's mother sacrificed a kid, but Echemus only grew worse. His breathing sounded dark, as if it came whistling laboriously from inside a cave. Narcissa clung to Persephone and Echo and cried, while her mother sat stoically by the bedside, losing hope.

Persephone always associated a terrible or a great

event with the smell of cooking meat. Meat was scarce—if you ate your goats and sheep they couldn't give you milk and wool—and animals were almost always killed only to give some meat to the gods. After that, however, someone had to dispose of the actual meat, since the gods ate only the vapors rising from it, its essence, its other self which traveled to their world. You didn't waste things, not in Persephone's village, where there was very little to waste, so the living people ate the meat that stayed behind in this world.

Persephone kept watch with the rest in Narcissa's house, gnawing a rib bone with one hand, the other arm around Narcissa's shoulders. Narcissa wept quietly, her share untouched, while Bopis bustled about, organizing things.

"I said that was a bad day to sail," Bopis said, carrying an armful of soiled bed linens. "And with a red sky. Father always warned me, and of course I listened, not like the folk today. The young ones are the worst, but that Echemus didn't even stop to listen to me when I told him his boat needed caulking. Of course it didn't actually leak. I believe it capsized, but these things go together. Careless is as careless does, and now poor Irene . . ."

"Eat," Echo said on Narcissa's other side. "You don't want the gods to think we don't appreciate what they give us back."

"I can't." Narcissa looked at the collop of meat in her bowl with revulsion. "It looks like the inside of something."

"It *is* the inside of something," Echo said. "It was inside the goat."

"He's going to die. Mother talked to Aristippus

this morning about sending him down to . . . down to the shore."

The other girls drew in their breath. Persephone felt the fine gold hairs on her arms rise. "To—to *him*?"

Narcissa nodded miserably. "Mother doesn't want to. She's afraid. But Aristippus says sometimes people with what he has have lived."

Echo's eyes grew wide. People sent to the shore either came back living or didn't come back at all. Their bodies went into the house of the dead with their souls. And you never knew, you just never knew what had happened.

"Sometimes he gives them back," Persephone said, trying to comfort Narcissa. She laid her gnawed rib across the edge of her bowl and wiped her hands with some water from the clay jug that stood among the cookpots. The goat smell still drifted from the hearth in the Temple of Apollo across the agora.

Echemus was a well-off man, not so well-off as Glaucus had been, but enough to have a stone floor to his house and a bed apiece for his family. He lay behind a hanging woven by Narcissa and her mother, while Aristippus talked softly and insistently with his wife. Narcissa buried her face in her hands.

Sometimes when a villager was wounded too badly to recover, or in unbearable pain, or near death from disease, the village gave the person to the dark shade at the foot of the cliffs. Once in a while, the person would return healed, possessing only dim, dreamlike memories of the Underworld; most often, however, that person was never seen again. It was there that Aristippus proposed to take Echemus and give him to Hades alive.

Narcissa's mother came wailing from behind the curtain, and all three girls stood up.

"Irene"—Aristippus put a hand on her shoulder—"Be quiet now. We are asking a great gift of him."

"He will take him!" Irene wailed.

"Hush! He will have him anyway soon enough," Bopis said. "I've seen that look in his eyes before. Do you remember that child who drowned on the other side of the headland?"

Phaedon, the doctor, emerged from behind the curtain, as well, scrubbing his hands on the hem of his robe. "He has a fever in his lungs from the seawater," he said. "My diagnosis is definite." He held up one finger for emphasis.

"I don't want you to tell me what he has!" Irene turned on him. "I want you to heal him!"

Phaedon regarded her haughtily, a mere woman. Irene returned a furious glare. "Proper diagnosis is the heart of medicine," Phaedon informed her. "Only then do we know how a cure may be effected."

"Then effect one!"

"In this case, there is none," Phaedon retorted.

Aristippus took her by the arm and steered her away from Phaedon. The doctor picked the biggest piece of goat meat out of those still left in the big bowl by the hearth and departed.

Aristippus turned to Narcissa. "Help your mother get him on a litter." Narcissa whimpered. He looked at Persephone. "Go ask Demeter to come and help."

Bopis snorted, but she didn't offer to help get Echemus on the litter herself. Death was catching; everybody knew that.

Persephone gave Narcissa a squeeze and darted out the door. The whole idea of handing someone over still alive to the dark presence at the foot of the cliff, sacrificed like the goat, made her skin crawl. She took a deep breath of fresh air as she came out of the house, but the smell of goat meat still hung in it. She could see the smoke rising from the temple where the bones were burning. The temple complex was a small collection of huts at the east end of the village, with separate altars to Apollo; to Hestia, the keeper of the hearth; and to Zeus who ruled the gods on their mountaintop. Great-Grandfather oversaw the Temple of Zeus and Apollo; Hesperia, who was a crone so old that no one remembered her being a child, or even a young woman, tended the Temple of Hestia where the sacred fire of the village burned. Persephone darted past the temples, making a quick bow of respect at Hesperia, who frightened her, and who was sitting nodding in the sun outside her door.

Hermes watched her go from his perch in the olive tree in the agora. After a moment he slid down and followed her. She jumped when he popped up in front of her on the path.

"You scared me. Don't pop out at people like that!"

"Old Echemus is dying, isn't he?"

"Yes, they're going to give him to . . . you know. Great-Grandfather says people with what he has sometimes live."

"Great-Grandfather ought to know. He's older than that olive tree." Aristippus was Hermes's family patriarch, as well. His mother, Maia, was the granddaughter of Aristippus and Bopis. "Where are you off to?"

"To fetch Mother. Irene needs her."

"Aha." Hermes grinned at her conspiratorially. His eyes were interested, gray green and slightly slanted under a shock of unruly hair. "They'll all be wailing and carrying on at the cliff. Never miss us."

"I'm not going anywhere with you," Persephone said severely.

"I'm more fun than a trip to the land of the dead!"

"Barely," Persephone said, but she chuckled in spite of herself. Hermes was maddening, but sometimes he made her laugh.

He slid an arm about her waist as they walked, and she pushed him away.

"What we ought to do is get married," Hermes said seriously. "Then I wouldn't have to try to lure you off into the woods."

Persephone thought maybe he really meant it, but he couldn't keep his hands off the other girls, and that wouldn't change if she married him. She wasn't going to have that; she wasn't going to be Bopis.

He slid his arm around her waist again and nuzzled her neck. A shiver of pleasure ran through her, and she pushed him away again, harder. "No! Now go and annoy some other girl! I have to find Mother." She began to run, and he dropped behind.

"You'll be sorry!" he called after her. "When you're an old lady, married to some lout, you'll think to yourself, 'Ah! I could have had Hermes!'"

"Mother!"

Demeter was cutting the first of the wheat to ripen, her bronze sickle in one hand, the other wrapped around a sheaf of waving stalks. She straightened at Persephone's footsteps.

"Mother! They're going to take Echemus down to

the coast—you know, to *him*." No one liked to call Hades by his right name, lest they summon him by mistake. "And Great-Grandfather wants you to come and help. Irene and Narcissa are frightened." Persephone was frightened, too, but Demeter nodded briskly and tucked her sickle in her sash.

"Very well. I'll come. You stay here. I don't like you going near that place."

Persephone didn't want to go, either, but she thought of Narcissa's pale miserable face and frightened eyes. "Mother, I have to come. I promised Narcissa." Everyone was looking out for Irene. No one would pay any attention to the daughter.

Since her return to the village with a child, Demeter had not known what it was like to have friends, as her daughter had. Women who had been girls of her age now gave her nervous respect but not friendship. Still, she could remember a time when they had, and so she nodded again. "But you must stay well back, with Narcissa. Irene and Grandfather and I will take him to the cave mouth. You are not to go near it. Understood?"

"Yes, Mother."

They had already loaded Echemus on a litter when Persephone and Demeter arrived. He was pale and sweating, and his breath rasped like a saw. His eyes were open, and Persephone could tell by the panic shown in them that he knew where they were taking him. She put her hand to her mouth. She wondered if the goat had known, too.

The little procession wound through the village much as Glaucus's funeral had, but this time it ran to the south where a path followed the river toward the coast. At the cliffs it zigzagged down along steps

that had been cut in the rock, through the sea spray
that blew up around them. Gulls squawked overhead
in the blue, and Persephone could see boats like
small dark toys on the sea beyond the harbor. Along
the cliff top above them, poppies grew, blooming a
deep blood scarlet, their heads nodding in the sea
breeze.

Hermes trailed them at a distance, waiting to see
what would happen next. He liked it best when upheaval was in the air. It made life interesting. Persephone's hips swayed as she walked, her arm about
Narcissa, and he grinned as he felt himself stiffen,
watching her. Eventually he would have her. All the
girls gave in eventually. Persephone was the most
important of them, and so he could afford to wait.

It was slow going, carrying a litter down the steep
trail, and Persephone held her breath as Irene stumbled. Demeter, at the head of the litter beside her,
righted it swiftly, helped by Aristippus, who carried
both poles at the other end. There were younger,
stronger men than he in the village, and certainly
stronger than Irene (Demeter was another matter),
but it was important who brought a patient to the
god of Death. If the sick soul didn't seem to matter
much to its bearers, then he might not be so inclined
to give it back.

At its foot they crunched over sand and small
stones, and bits of dried seaweed left from the high
tide. The gulls circled overhead, interested, to see if
there was something to eat. When it became clear
that there was not, they squawked and flew toward
the harbor.

Demeter and Irene set the litter down beneath the
slanted stone that overhung the cave mouth. Perse-

phone could see that the cave ran deep into the cliff, dark and mysterious, its floor also littered with the scraps of the last tide. She wondered if anyone would watch to be sure that someone came for Echemus before the water rose again. But maybe he wouldn't come if there were watchers. Maybe you just had to trust him. The thought lifted the hair on her arms again.

Aristippus raised his staff. "Lord!" he called in a booming voice that echoed back at them out of the cave mouth. "Lord! We have laid a soul at your doorstep."

Nothing stirred inside the cave, but Aristippus motioned to Demeter and Irene to come away and leave the litter there. Behind them on the sand, the men of the village had gathered, and now Persephone saw that one of them carried a black sheep on his shoulders. She turned her head away as they cut its throat. Of course, there would be a gift for this god, too.

Irene wailed one more time, stuffing her black veil into her mouth with her fist, as if Echemus were already dead. Demeter took her by the hand and pulled her away. They started up the cliff path again, no one looking back. That was another of the rules. If you looked back, it was said, he might keep you, too. By the time the last villager reached the top to stand amid the blowing poppies, Echemus and the sheep were both gone from the sand below.

The sea brings things to those who live along its shore: small bits of smooth glass rounded from broken bottles sunk leagues away; the outer husks of creatures unimaginably strange; wood from what was once a boat; drowned sailors. All were collected, taken in, as were the offerings left by the living in the village on the headland.

Two shadows came out from the cave mouth, smoky forms scuttling crabwise along the sand, lifting the litter by its poles. They disappeared into the depths. A moment later two more, or perhaps the same ones, emerged again, and hoisted the sheep by its feet.

Hades watched the procession of the living climb the cliffs, knowing they would not dare look back at him. He stared into the bright mist that blew around the cliff, squinting his eyes at the light. The girl with gold hair was at the end of the line, arm around her weeping friend. She looked like a piece of floating light, the corporeal embodiment of the scent of flowers. Gold hair was rare in her village. Hades had noticed her before, picking flowers and playing like a child in the river. She was past marriageable age, but he thought her mother had something to do with that. Demeter had the kind of power that you could feel at a distance. Now he watched the daughter until she passed from his sight. When she was gone he could still see her outline, bright against the poppies.

# II

❧

# *Under the Earth*

Echemus did not come back. Narcissa and Irene haunted the top of the cliff path as if sheer will could make him materialize. By late in the month of Gamelion, they knew he would not come, and men began to court Irene, a widow with a fine house and sheep and goats.

"Two have come from over the mountain," Narcissa said with disgust, "and wanted to marry me and Mother both. They said they didn't care who married which—we could choose."

"Oh, you don't want to marry someone from the north island," Echo said. "He'll take you away there, and they eat their meat raw and keep their women in cages. I've heard that."

"They do not," said Persephone. "They're just like us. Mother said. And anyway you've been to the big market there. You bought red sandals."

"That doesn't mean it wasn't all for show," Echo

said darkly. "Don't you do it, Narcissa. I heard once of a girl who went there to marry and—"

"I'm not going to," Narcissa said. "They're both ugly."

"Imagine marrying someone who didn't care which one he got," Persephone said, but she knew that Narcissa was bound to marry someone soon. And then Echo. And she would be alone. The other two were hiding from their mothers, for whom they were supposed to be weaving and making cheese, respectively, to pick flowers in the meadow on the headland with Persephone. The flowers weren't for anything in particular, not for a festival, or a wreath for the statue of Hestia. They were picked solely for their loveliness, so the girls could put them in a jar at home until they faded. A woman couldn't do such a thing when she married. She couldn't run away from a husband and babies and wash and weaving to pick flowers like a child. The older women in the village told Persephone this often, shaking their heads. Bopis, Great-Grandfather's wife, in particular predicted ruin. Persephone privately thought that Bopis wouldn't be so sour if Great-Grandfather wasn't *still* chasing after other women. Sometimes they even let him catch them.

Persephone gathered her armful of white daisies against her chest and breathed in their summery tang. The iris and jonquils that bloomed in spring had better scent, but Persephone loved the flowers of summer with their sharp dusty smell. In a corner of her mantle was a handful of pale pink peroukas. At the edge of the meadow the poppies that grew on the headland waved their bloodred heads. Persephone bent to add them to her gleanings.

"You know those won't keep," Narcissa said.

Persephone smiled. "They'll last a little while. Till evening anyway. There are so many of them." Enough to waste, she thought, pulling them into her arms. Their scarlet heads made the daisies blaze whiter than ever. The sky above was the deep hot blue of midsummer. The sunlight, dusty white, bounced off the limestone walls of the village and off the bright, glassy surface of the sea below. Tiny black boats, like dots, marked the fishing fleet. Above them in the tawny hills, they could hear the baaing of sheep and the bleating of goats. The whir of insects in the meadow grass was a hot, sleepy lullaby.

Persephone sat down in the grass, her flowers in her lap, and yawned. She unslung the goatskin wine bag from her shoulder. Echo produced a half loaf of bread and a piece of cheese wrapped in cloth from the folds of her mantle, and Narcissa a handful of dried figs. They shared them between them, sighing in contentment.

"Bopis is coming to see Mother again tonight, with some horrible old man she's found," Narcissa said. "With Father dead, everyone thinks we need marrying off right away."

"Make her find you a handsome one," Echo said sleepily.

Persephone plugged the wineskin and lay back in the grass with her hands behind her head. "Tell her to find one for me," she murmured.

"You know you don't mean that," Narcissa said. "Your mother hates men."

"I know," Persephone murmured. "So she isn't going to find me one, is she?" Lately it had begun to seem to her that running wild wouldn't be quite so much fun once she found herself doing it alone. But she wasn't sure she had really meant what she said. When she thought of Echo's older sister, with a baby on her hip and one at her heels, her figure and three teeth gone already, the alternative didn't look all that enticing, either.

They awoke to the sound of footsteps, and Persephone's shrieks. There were dark shapes everywhere, their shadows black across the wildflowers as if they had emerged suddenly from the ground. They made muffled grunts but spoke no words, and their footsteps made the earth thunder. One of them had Persephone in his arms, her gold hair flying around her as she struggled, her spilled flowers a red and white carpet at her feet.

"Let her go!" Echo leaped at him, and one of the black shadows sent her flying back with a blow from its fist. Narcissa stood clutching her mantle to her chest, frozen, her face as pale as ice. A shadow came toward her, too, but a shout from the one holding Persephone called it back. They started toward the cliff's edge with her.

Echo sat up among the trampled flowers, her head spinning. The dark, terrifying shapes wheeled in her vision and dropped out of sight. She staggered to her feet. "Run!" Echo grabbed Narcissa by the wrist and yanked. They turned and raced across the meadow for home.

"He came up out of the ground!" Echo said. "With black horses and a black chariot! The ground just opened! We saw it!" She looked at them, wild-eyed, while Narcissa sat shaking on a bench under the olive tree.

"Who came out of the ground? Calm down, child." Irene took Echo by the shoulders. She looked around her at the crowd. "Someone go and fetch Demeter."

"I always said it was a mistake to let that girl run wild," Bopis said. "Mark my words, I said."

"I'm here," Demeter said quietly behind her. No one ever knew quite how she did that. "Who has taken my child?"

"I don't know!" Echo said. "He was black, and he drove enormous black horses, and they had teeth like fangs! He came out of the ground!"

"Oh, indeed?" Hermes shook his russet head scornfully. He could be counted on to appear wherever there was any trouble brewing, Echo thought. "And I suppose the ground closed up again after him? Or did you fall in the hole?"

"Be quiet!" Demeter snapped at him. "Narcissa?"

"They must have. They were just there all of a sudden, and Persephone was screaming, and they had her."

"Where did they take her?" Demeter's jaw was clenched so tightly no one was sure how the words came out.

"Over the cliff!" Narcissa said, trembling.

Bopis made the sign against the evil eye, and everyone else did, too.

"In a chariot?" Hermes raised an eyebrow.

"They flew!" Echo said. "I saw them! They went over the path to the caves."

Irene drew her breath in. She looked despairingly at Demeter. "We should never have let them go down there. Never have let him see them!"

"We don't know it's him yet." Phaedon, the doctor, held up a finger. "We have not yet ascertained the full facts."

"Who else could it be?" The villagers asked themselves the question and argued the evidence.

"In a chariot?" Despite Hermes's skepticism, they were all willing to believe in the chariot; the ground opened all the time—this was earthquake country.

No one in the village drove a chariot; horses were expensive to keep up. A chariot was a rich man's conveyance. And one that could go down a cliff? Well, that settled it.

"It was only to be expected," Bopis pronounced.

Irene began to weep, clutching her daughter to her.

Aristippus spoke for the first time. "If *he* has taken her, she won't come back." He looked at Demeter.

Demeter's feet were planted wide apart, as if she braced herself for some struggle. The village watched her uneasily. "I will find her," she said and turned on her heel. The implication that someone would be sorry hung in the air.

"Let me go!" Persephone struggled in the grip of whoever, or whatever, it was. The grip didn't loosen. She could feel him staggering a bit under her weight, and she swung her head around and sank her teeth into the arm that gripped her. It was enveloped in a dark material that left a taste of salt in her mouth.

"Ow! Stop that!" He staggered a bit, and she felt them both tipping. "Do you want to go down the cliff on your head?" He righted himself, and they kept going down. Persephone's mantle was tangled around her face, and she shook her head to free it.

The cliff face swung into view and bobbed in her vision as they staggered down the narrow steps. She caught a flash of blue sky, a gull's interested face, the pale pink blossoms of peroukas growing between the steps. She began kicking her feet, hoping to hit something tender. The voice was male.

More dark forms clambered down the cliff below and above her. They moved with the agility of mountain sheep. Her captor seemed equally sure-footed, but he said, as she struggled, "If I drop you, you'll break your head."

"Let me go!" She writhed in his arms and pummeled him with her fists. Persephone was a country girl, used to working in her mother's garden and catching wild goats for amusement. She was nearly as strong as any boy in the village.

He stumbled on one of the steps, but he didn't loosen his grip. "There's no point in your going on saying that; I'm not going to." The voice was panting a little, however.

Persephone began to kick again. The grip around her waist made her frantic, until she didn't care if she fell, if she could just make him let her go. Her captor lost his footing, and they began to slide, bumping over the steps in a fashion that was probably more painful for him than for her. At any rate, she hoped so. He kept his arms locked tightly around her, and they slid in a heap to the bottom.

"Take her," he said, gasping, and two of his dark servants appeared and gripped her by the arms and feet. The grasp around her middle loosened, and they hefted her like a freshly killed deer. She thrashed her arms and legs.

"Quit it, or I'll have them tie you up," her captor

said ominously from behind her. "And I ache like Typhon, you witch."

Persephone's last glimpse of him as she hung upside down caught him rubbing his backside ruefully. He was tall, with curling dark hair and a dark beard, his skin milky pale as befitted someone who lived underground. His tunic was of dark wool that she could tell was good cloth even at a distance, and his cloak the same, although just now ragged with their descent and studded with burrs and dry twigs. He inspected his shins and glared at her as they dragged her into the cave.

The roof was low and the initial opening merely a slanted outcropping of rock that looked as if its shade might provide shelter for some weary traveler. The sand on the floor was damp, and a tidal pool scent rose from it. She wondered desperately how far the water traveled at high tide. If everyone was dead here it might not matter. The floor was strewn with huge boulders as if some god had flung a handful of marbles, and she saw that the cave's depth was deceptive. Persephone's captors wound among the rocks and squeezed through a narrow gap, banging her head against the stone as they went. She heard him yell "Watch it!" behind her, and the servants made apologetic noises. His voice boomed and echoed in the rock. They turned abruptly, dodging another outcrop, and she saw the real cave mouth, a dark opening in the earth wide enough to drive cattle through, four abreast.

"No!" she said pleadingly, and then she screamed, "No!" but they paid her no heed. They ducked their heads and plunged into the mountain.

Persephone closed her eyes in terror, still screaming "No!" but her mind filled with pale wraiths brushing by her as they passed, ghostly fingers tearing at her cloak, and that seemed worse than seeing where she was going. She opened them again. There was no one to be seen but her bearers, and the passage walls made her blink in surprise.

The passageway went into the earth as Glaucus's tomb had done, but seemed to wander up as often as down, its walls lined with smooth dressed stone and lit with oil lamps set in niches. Off it branched other passageways whose windings she could just glimpse as they passed. In the pools of light the walls were carved with images she could barely make out. She stared at them as they passed, and sometimes a carved face stared back. The air was dank this far below the sun. Her arms and legs ached like fire.

"Put me down and I'll walk," she said finally.

They stopped, apparently considering this. "Might run off," one of them said at last, startling her. She hadn't been sure they could speak.

"How could I, with both of you here?" She tried to sound dignified, despite her terror and the stone walls closing around her the way they had in Glaucus's tomb. Their voices were deep and sepulchral. They considered her request, while she hung from their grip like a deer.

Finally the one at her head said, "Arms. One each," and they set her upright. A huge hand closed around each arm.

Persephone rubbed her wrists and eyed them warily. They were tall, as tall as her captor had been, and like him, dressed all in black. The hands on her arms looked human. Their faces were human too, probably—long and mournful and vaguely sheeplike.

They made her think uneasily of the black rams sacrificed at the cave mouth.

"This way," one of them said, prodding her with his free hand, and they set off down the passage. Now that she was upright, she could see that the stonework here was indeed much finer than Glaucus's tomb, where the rough stones had jutted from the passage walls and snagged her mantle. Here the stones were cut flat and dressed so that the joinery was almost invisible. The carved faces were of people all hurrying along, walking endlessly toward the same destination, some with servants behind, some with a child by the hand. The lamps that sat in the niches along the walls were of fine pottery painted with sea creatures, shells, and waves. An octopus goggled at her, round-eyed, as they passed. More passages branched off the main one, and they took first one and then another. Persephone tried desperately to fix the way in her head, but they all looked alike, and she lost count of the doorways as they went. She thought of the tales of heroes and heroines who had found their way out of labyrinths with a ball of string, and wondered if they habitually carried string here, just in case.

They came into a large room and she stopped, goggling at it, before they hurried her through. Around the raised hearth in the center, tiles gleamed blue and yellow, making a pattern like waves all around the base. It was lit, warming the dank air, and smoke rose from it into a vent in the stone roof, going somewhere. Around the walls were couches and benches covered in embroidered fabric, interspersed with life-size statues in marble and bronze—youths with a spear or discus, maidens virtuously spinning. Persephone thought suddenly of the souls who came here. Was that where they went? Into bronze and stone? The dark sheeplike servants hustled her across a smooth stone floor covered with thick weavings laid down on top, and out a door at the far end. She tried to look back at the great room as the hanging in the doorway brushed her head, but they tugged her onward.

They passed no one else in the cold corridors, and Persephone began to weep silently. She would never find her way out of this maze. The pale, dark-bearded man who was plainly Hades himself would rape her or eat her or suck her soul away or all three, and she would never see her mother again. She burst into a despairing howl just as the sheeplike servants stopped at a doorway with a wooden door in it instead of a tapestry. The door had a large bronze bolt on the outside.

The largest sheep servant patted her shoulder clumsily. "No one will hurt you."

"Then what does he want with me?" Persephone demanded, sniffling.

The servant opened the heavy door. "Marry you, I think," he said, and pushed her inside.

*"Marry me?"* The door closed behind her, and she heard the click of the bolt. Their footsteps padded away outside it.

Marry her?

The room was larger than she expected, with a tiled hearth like the one in the great room. Its warmth was inviting, and she sat on its edge, pulling her mantle around her. As in the great hall, the smoke went up through a vent into somewhere she couldn't see. There were two couches, an armchair, and two of the small backless benches most Hellenes used when they wanted to sit down, these with luxuriously padded seats. A loom and a basket with raw wool, a spindle, and a distaff stood in opposite corners, and on a three-legged table near the hearth was an array of food: wine and water in silver pitchers, a silver goblet, a plate of figs and cheese, a loaf of bread, a cruet of olive oil, a bowl of pastries, and another of mutton in a mint sauce. Persephone looked at the mutton and her stomach flipped over.

She got up and banged on the door, but no one came; she hadn't really expected them to. She was plainly being left to think things over and appreciate the luxury he was offering. She glared at the loom and the basket.

There was another door at the other side of the chamber, this one hung with only a tapestry. She explored, pushing the tapestry aside, and found a second chamber behind it, dominated by a huge bed hung with red curtains. Persephone stared at it, and in spite of herself, pressed the mattress down with one palm. It was soft, as if it was stuffed with down. Her bed at home was stuffed with straw. She sat on it gingerly, and leaped up again. Oh no, he wasn't going to entice her into bed with goose feathers!

She prowled about the rest of the room, discovering a vanity table laden with a seemingly endless array of pots of bronze and alabaster and painted clay, holding creams and unguents and rouges enough to paint an entire brothel. Persephone poked indignantly at a pot of rouge with one finger.

Another door opened off this room, too, and she followed it to find a plastered chamber painted yellow and containing a five-foot terracotta tub with bottom and sides adorned with leaping dolphins. For some reason the dolphins made her want to weep. They looked joyful, as if they had no idea they were painted here on the bottom of a tub inside a mountain, not frolicking in the waters off the headland. Persephone had never seen a bathing tub before, but she had heard of them. They were such things as rich men had, richer than Glaucus, men who lived on the other side of the mountain. A three-legged stool held a flask of oil, a bowl of sponges, and a strigil for scraping oneself clean. An open chest beside it offered piles of folded clothes. She turned from the chest and found herself face-to-face with a marble servant holding a towel over his arm. She shrieked and clapped her hand over her mouth. Behind the marble servant an arch opened onto yet another chamber, this one nearly entirely filled with a pool of water tiled in more blue and yellow, with a painted squid at its bottom. Hangings depicting sea nymphs splashing in a cove covered the walls. At the pool's center was a bronze drain, and at its end a clay pipe dribbled a musical stream of fresh water. Persephone put a toe in the water and jerked it back again. It was hot, as if it came out of the boiling heart of the earth.

Beyond the pool was yet another arch, this one with a discreet tapestry across it. She peered into a small stone room and found a stone seat with a hole in it. The sound of flowing water came from somewhere, and a ewer of water sat beside the seat. She sniffed cautiously, and her eyes widened. Hades was so rich his guests need not even leave his halls to shit.

Persephone backed out of the little room and sat

down by the pool to think. After a few minutes she got up and came back with the tray of food. She set it on the pool's edge, took her sandals off, and put her feet in the water. The pool had steps at this end, and she rested them on the highest one. The warm water bubbled around her ankles. She ate a fig and thought.

Item one: She wasn't dead, so far as she could tell.

Item two: She hadn't seen any dead people, except maybe for those carved into the walls.

Item three: Unless you counted the statues.

Persephone ate a pastry and licked the honey and fine flakes of dough from her fingers. It was important to be logical. Hellenes valued logic. It was what made them civilized, so Aristippus said. He had told her this when she was small, when the sun was in her eyes and she had demanded petulantly that he move it. The sun went one way, he said, because that was how Apollo drove his chariot. No one had the power to make him move it for their own ends, and if he did it would likely set the world on fire, so there was no use asking for things you couldn't have. Ask instead for what you might get. He had said that with a nudge and a wink at her mother taking bread from the oven in the courtyard, and Demeter had given her a piece of it hot with a bowl of olive oil to dip it in. There, said Aristippus. See?

Persephone wasn't certain how to apply this logic to her current situation, but at any rate (see item one) she wasn't dead. She ate another pastry, filled with crushed nuts and honey, the kind that were so tedious to make that they were kept for weddings and feasts. Hades (she named him firmly to herself) must be rich enough to have a kitchen full of cooks. He probably had a hunchback or a wall-eye, she thought moodily, some excellent reason why he would have to kidnap a wife. Unless of course he really was Death, in which case she could see that courting would be difficult. She ate an olive and another pastry.

Item four: There was no sunlight here. How did anyone live without sunlight? Even with enough money to afford to keep lamps lit all day and all night.

Item five: How did you tell whether it was day or night?

Persephone was running out of numbers that she knew, and couldn't feel that she was any farther along with her problem.

Item six: If you eat in someone's house you bind yourself to them. That idea came to her, and she put down the bowl of olives. Mother had said that, and so had Aristippus. Food was what kept everyone alive, so naturally sharing it with someone meant something. Did it count if no one knew? Did it count if the other person didn't need food because he was Death? She rearranged the pastries in the bowl to look as untouched as possible and took the tray back to the central chamber, her wet feet leaving footprints on the cold stone. She thought with longing of the carpets she had seen in the great hall and went back for her sandals. While she sat on the goose-down bed tying them, she heard the bolt rattle in the chamber outside. She got to her feet, faced the doorway, and braced for whatever was going to happen to her.

A sheeplike face poked its long nose through the far wall instead, around a curtain she hadn't noticed before, and she screamed.

"Master sent you a present." He held out a folded carpet of the sort she had seen in the great hall, laid across his arms like the statue with the towel. "Master forgets that the floors are cold for young ladies from the upper air."

"How did you get in here?" Persephone backed away.

"Chamber is a spiral, madam. Like a seashell. Many doors." He laid the carpet on the bed and lifted the hanging he had come through with one hand. Persephone could see that the unnoticed door opened on the chamber with the pool. She had not thought to look behind the hangings on its walls, but she could see now that the pool was the chamber's true heart. All doors except the one to the outside world opened onto it.

The servant hefted the carpet again and disappeared back into the wall. She heard movement in the outer chamber and lifted the hanging to see him laying the carpet on the floor beside the hearth. He bowed toward Persephone. "I will bring more. Master says not but one of us at a time, so as not to frighten the young lady." He bowed again, backing through the door into the corridor, and slapped it shut briskly. She heard the bolt slide.

A few minutes later he was back, with another carpet. He laid it on the other side of the hearth and bustled out, returning with a third. All the carpets were blue, woven with shells and tritons riding fish. Persephone began to feel as if she were drowning in so many fish. The octopi would inhabit her dreams, driving out the ghosts she feared, only to replace them with bulbous heads and goggling eyes, tentacles plucking at her bedclothes.

"No more fish," she said when he came back a fourth time.

He looked disappointed. "Master is very fond of fish."

"Well, I'm not. And I'm not fond of your master either." Persephone stamped her foot and pointed at the tray of food. "And take that away. I won't eat it and you can tell him so."

"Very good food," the servant said hopefully. "No fish."

"Take it away!"

The servant sighed and hefted the tray. This time he was gone a long time. When he reappeared he bore a red carpet, rolled up on his shoulder. He took it into the bedchamber and unrolled it with a flourish. "No fish!" he announced.

There was a restrained design of waves around the edges, but as he said, no fish.

"Thank you."

The servant bowed. "One more thing." He popped out the door and back in with quick snicks of the bolt. He was stooped and elderly, but surprisingly agile. Persephone suspected that if she raced him for the unbolted door, she would never make it. He unfolded a cloth package and shook it out. It was a gown, already pinned at the shoulders with pearls. The cloth was pale blue and finer than anything Persephone had seen. He draped it across the bed, gesturing to it enticingly like a salesman selling goods. He laid a mantle of deeper blue beside it, with an ebony box containing six more pearl pins. "Finest quality. From my master." He looked hopeful. When Persephone didn't answer him, he said, still hopeful,

"Young ladies like these things." Finally he sighed and bowed himself out.

When she was sure he had gone, Persephone touched the cloth gingerly. It felt like milk beneath her fingers, cool and slippery and with a faint sheen. The edges of the mantle were embroidered in gold thread. Persephone's own gown, which had been her second best, was covered in mud and burrs and stained with grass on the backside. Persephone sighed and pulled it over her head. She turned it to the other side, refolded and repinned it with her own bronze pins. Both women's gowns and men's tunics were made from a single sheet of cloth folded over the top and wrapped around the body. One pinned it at the shoulders and open side, and arranged the folds with a girdle tied at the waist. If one was wealthy, embroidery might decorate the hem. The pins that held the shoulders might be made of precious stones or artful twists of bronze. Village fops like Hermes spent hours achieving the perfect fold. The pearls in the ebony box were worth a fortune. Persephone snapped it closed.

Item seven: honor before greed.

No one came back for hours, until she had slept her way in the goose-down bed into what she thought must be the next day. She awoke, burrowed into the soft folds of a mountain of blanket, which had not served to keep out the dank cold or the dreams of pale ghosts riding the wind that blew into the cave mouth and down the long corridors. No octopi, but the sound of the sea was all around her, not quite heard, like the whushing in a shell. The oil lamps had been freshly filled. She got up and used the room with the stone seat, wondering where it *went*.

Her skin felt gritty and itched, and she oiled it and scraped herself down with the strigil. Someone had filled the bathtub while she slept (she thought uneasily of a parade of soft-footed sheep servants trotting past her with ewers) so she got in it and sank to her chin. The water was still warm—it must have come from the pool—and soothed the bruises she was just beginning to feel from yesterday's fall.

She got out of the bath, wrapping herself in one of the soft towels from the chest (she couldn't bring herself to take the one the statue held out to her). When she walked into the bedroom the sheep servant was standing there. Persephone screamed, and he winced.

"Madam need not make that noise every time," he said reproachfully.

"Then don't keep sneaking in!" Persephone said, teeth chattering with the cold.

"Master sends something to break the fast." She could see a tray of wine and water and figs on the table by the bed.

"Take it away!"

"Madam will grow thin."

"Good. Then he won't want me."

The sheep servant shook his head. "Oh, I don't think so. Master is in love. He said madam is 'like a piece of sunlight.' He sent madam a present."

Persephone snatched the ebony box, twin to the first one, from the tray and threw it against the wall. A spill of polished stones and gold fell out and lay winking in the lamplight. "Get out!"

The sheep servant bowed himself out, and she sat down weeping on the bed, her face in her hands.

Persephone was not a girl who spent much time crying, even as a child. Generally, after having a good howl, she had trotted off and done something. It was not always something anyone liked very much, but she had taken action. When Hermes had painted mustaches on all her dolls, she had lain in wait for him in the branches of an oak tree and dropped a bag of sheep manure on his head. When her mother had refused her the wherewithal to buy a pair of green sandals with red embroidery from a peddler, she had traded him Demeter's best copper pot for them. When Bopis had complained that Persephone was allowed to run wild like a savage and set other, well-behaved children a bad example, she had danced through the agora, wearing nothing but a wreath of grape leaves, and stuck her tongue out at her. All three instances had brought swift punishment from Demeter—the first because she had ruined Hermes's tunic, the second for stealing, and the third for disrespect—but Persephone had considered them all well worth the paddling.

Now she remembered the jackal pup she had wanted to keep for a pet. Demeter had told her that it would not be happy, and Great-Grandfather had told her it would eat their chickens. Everyone else had told her it would bite her. All three had proved true, and she had set it loose again near the den where she had stolen it. So now she sat up after a middling cry, and tried to think what would annoy her captor the most.

*     *     *

Hades himself came to see her on the third day. Perhaps the old sheep servant had told him that he was getting nowhere with his gifts when Persephone dropped the gold and aquamarine necklace and matching earrings down the hole in the stone seat and sent something unsavory after them.

He found her sitting on the edge of the hearth in her old gown, now more repulsive than ever, her hair a tangle of snarls and mats.

"I did give you a comb," he said mildly.

Persephone inspected him from slitted eyes, like a cat. He looked to be her mother's age, or maybe younger. It was very hard to tell. His pale skin was nearly unlined. His nails and heavy beard were neatly trimmed, and the dark curling hair on his head was held in place with a silver fillet. Dark eyebrows slanted over startlingly blue eyes. He wore a brown tunic embroidered with pale acanthus leaves around the borders and a mantle dyed with the dark purple that came from sea snails. This dye was so costly that even Glaucus had had only a band of it around the hem of his best tunic. Hades's sandals were soft dark leather with bronze buckles. He was tall. His head nearly bumped the ceiling.

When Persephone didn't say anything, he drew up a stool and sat down. "I brought you some food." He gestured at the tray he had set on a table.

Persephone pressed her lips together.

"You must be hungry."

The smell of an omelette of eggs and cheese drifted from under the cover on the tray. She ignored it resolutely.

"You know I won't hurt you."

Persephone sniffed.

"You look a mess."

"I'm not going to get better looking."

"You could get cleaner."

"But I won't."

Hades sighed. "It's a shame. They say that filth affects the mind. Pretty soon a person goes raving mad. Then they're seen running on all fours and grunting like a pig. I've seen it happen."

"Then no one marries them," Persephone pointed out.

"Oh, I have a great tolerance for that sort of thing," Hades said. "Living down here as I do."

"With dead people." Persephone shuddered.

"Very few of them are dead," Hades said.

"Then where is Echemus?"

Hades sighed. "He *is* dead, I am afraid. They don't understand what sort of ailments to send me. There is not much I can do for pneumonia."

"Great-Grandfather said that sometimes people with what he had have lived," Persephone countered, interested in spite of herself.

"Indeed. But not through my agency. In those cases, the body heals itself, or it does not. All I can do is give it rest, and hope. Or ease the passing," he added.

"Where is he then?"

"Dead, as I told you. I buried him."

"Where is his spirit?"

"Gone, I suppose, on its own errands." He saw Persephone's perplexed expression, and said, "You think they all live with me, don't you? Maybe they do. Sometimes I think some of them are still here."

Persephone looked around her as if something had brushed her hair.

"I have given my servants instructions not to let any spirits in here with you," he assured her solemnly. "However"— he took the cover off the plate—"if you don't eat, you're likely to be one yourself."

Persephone leaped from her seat on the hearth and snatched the plate. He looked gratified for a moment until she flung it at him.

Hades sat very still for a long while, while Persephone considered that she might have overdone it. Finally he brushed the omelette from his beard and said carefully, "Don't you think that I might grow on you?"

"No!"

He stood. "In that case, I shall go and have a bath." He eyed her appraisingly. "You might do the same."

# III

§

## Fire and Rain

When Demeter was angry someone was generally sorry afterward. Now that she was angry at Death no one knew quite what she might do. At first she had climbed down the steps from the headland to stand outside the caves and shout for Persephone. When there was no answer she had shouted his name instead and blundered about the dank stone chamber while the sea washed her ankles, trying to find the way in. Whatever way he had taken was sealed, or hidden by magic. She had stayed there all night, pleading with him, but no living thing had come out.

Now she stalked up and down the rows of her garden, her white gown a flash in the sunlight like an angry heron. The village watched her at a respectful distance.

"No good is going to come of this," her cousin Maia said, pulling her mantle around her head and shoulders as if whatever was going to happen might drop out of the wild blue sky on her. "That child was allowed to run around like a wild goat, and now look."

"We all said so," Bopis said with satisfaction.

"I feel responsible." Irene sighed. "I let the girls go down there with poor Echemus. And all for nothing anyway. I haven't even a body to bury." She sniffed loudly at all of it.

"It was Persephone he took," Maia said. "Narcissa and Echo were with her, and nothing ran off with *them*."

"Persephone's prettier," Hermes said. "I would have run off with her if it was me. Echo has freckles, and Narcissa's nose is nearly as big as Echemus's was."

"It is not!" Irene rounded on him. "Narcissa has an elegant profile, just like a painting on a vase!"

Maia took her son by the arm. "This is women's talk. Go and see to the goats. Two of them were in the vineyard yesterday. I told you to keep better watch on them."

"Yes, Mother." He bowed low at her and ran off, chuckling.

Doris, Echo's mother, glared after him.

The sun burned down on them like a bowl full of brass, and only Hermes, bathing in the river, was cool.

Demeter knew they were watching her. How on earth did you talk to women who had never been out of the village and tell them all the things there were on the earth that could swallow you whole? The gaping jaws of Death and Mischance and Vengeance? They had no idea. She had been Persephone's age when she had fallen off the edge of the world.

That had been chance, too. She had gone down to the beach alone, to a rocky cove where no one ever came, to see what the tide had brought in. That particular morning it had brought a young man mending his boat. He was from Eleusis on the mainland, which no one Demeter knew had ever seen. They had talked all morning about the things that lay over the horizon, and when he sailed in the afternoon she had sailed with him.

It hadn't been a kidnapping exactly. Village life was dull, and so were the men courting her, presented by Grandfather who had raised her and wanted her well situated, and Bopis, who hated her and just wanted her out of the house. Triptolemus, on the other hand, had been handsome, with a head of gold curls, merry blue eyes, and muscular shoulders. She had gone with him willingly, lured by tales of wonders. He spoke of five-storied houses with painted walls big enough to hold her village, ships with hundreds of oars, chariots with silver wheels, and tamed trees arranged in rows.

It hadn't been quite like that. The wonderful cities were dead, torn apart by wars and rebellions. The silver chariot wheels he had stolen out of an ancient grave. And the peaceful hills he had described—a sailor's homesick vision—were infested with bandits. They arrived for the funeral of his brother.

Demophon had been alive the first time Demeter saw him and in flames the next. He had welcomed Triptolemus home with a brotherly arm about his shoulders and an appreciative glance at Demeter, although the parents had been less pleased and the two sisters looked at her with suspicion. But there had been a feast all the same, with a great deal of wine, watered less and less as the evening wore on, and much singing and boasting. By the end of it, the men could barely walk, and Demeter's head was spinning, too. Triptolemus's father, Celeus, was nodding on his couch, and his mother, Metanira, and her daughters had gone to bed. Demeter wanted to go to bed, too, but didn't know where she was to go.

"That's a fine piece of sea glass you picked up," Demophon said, slapping his brother's shoulder. "Give her to me, and I'll give you my best ram."

Triptolemus laughed. "She's worth more than that, you young fool."

"My best ram and four jars of oil."

Demeter's eyes widened. "I am not a slave!" She looked at Triptolemus, horrified.

Triptolemus nodded drunkenly. "You're my woman. Worth more than that anyway."

"My best ram, four jars of oil, and an ox. How about that?" Demophon flopped on the bench beside Demeter. "You'd like me, wouldn't you? I'm handsomer than Triptolemus anyway." He tried to kiss her, his breath heavy with wine and garlic, and she shoved him away.

Demophon lurched and lost his balance. He toppled, slowly, like a tree being felled, while she watched, and he landed in the hearth. It was sheer evil chance that his fall swept a clay lamp off the table and into the fire with him, where it broke on the coals. His oil-soaked mantle had tangled around his right arm where it lay in the flames, and as he struggled, a gout of flame shot up from the hem of his tunic. He tried to stagger to his feet but fell again with his face in the heart of the fire, and his hair caught.

"Get him up!" Triptolemus leaped from his couch, and Demeter helped him tug Demophon from the flames.

"Father!"

Celeus jerked awake, rubbing sleep and wine from his eyes. They rolled Demophon in his mantle and doused the flames, but he was horribly burned. Celeus shouted for Metanira, who came screaming from their bedchamber.

Metanira and her daughters cut away the charred cloth and rubbed his burned skin with unguents. They sent for the village doctor, who gave them a poultice of herbs and shook his gray head despairingly. Everyone knew that no one that badly burned ever healed. Metanira had Demophon taken to his chamber, and she and her daughters sat with him through three days. Demophon's skin peeled away in horrible strips, and the red raw flesh underneath it oozed yellow fluid. Gradually it hardened and turned black. His breathing grew labored, and the burned flesh on his lips and mouth fell away.

When Demeter tried to bring them food, Metanira's eyes flashed and she shrieked at Demeter, "Get out! This is your doing! Get out of my sight!"

Demeter hid, weeping, while Demophon died. Triptolemus told her it wasn't her fault, but he, too, spent most of his time at his brother's bedside. By the time they buried Demophon, Demeter felt like a ghost in the house herself, and hid most of the day in the olive orchard.

The tame trees Triptolemus had told her of were actually there. Triptolemus had laughed at her on their arrival when she had run into the olive grove and stared in wonder at the trees, dozens of them lined up in straight rows like game pieces.

"You are an ignorant islander," he had said, shaking his head.

"Teach me to plant trees," she told him the day after the funeral.

"That isn't women's work," Celeus said.

"Let the whore plant trees," Metanira said. "I don't want her in my house."

Demeter had known then she couldn't stay. She wasn't even sure why she had come, other than impulse, and the fact that Triptolemus was so handsome; but it was clear to her now that he would go only so far against his parents' wishes, and that he would not marry her. Maybe he never would have. She was reasonably sure that he would not have sold her to Demophon, but she was increasingly aware that he could probably do what he wanted to with her in this foreign country.

While Metanira glowered at her from her chamber window, spindle and distaff in hand, Demeter followed Faunus, Celeus's gardener, who practiced a skill she had never heard of before. On her home island, the men and boys went into the hills at the start of winter and beat the nearly ripe olives out of the trees with flails. The women gathered grain in May from wild wheat that grew on the hillsides and valley floor, and figs in summer and grapes in autumn. Here in Eleusis, Demeter followed the plow that Faunus drove behind an ox, and sowed the wheat in rows. She helped him prune the grapes, and he showed her how to take cuttings from the vines. Together they planted beans and cabbages in neat rows and tied the trailing pea vines to trellises. He was a slave and treated her as if she must be one, too, although at night she slept with Triptolemus and ate with his family, while Celeus, despite his sorrow, tried jovially to be kind, and Metanira and the daughters shot her poisoned looks. Demeter bit by bit stole seeds from the gardener's store and hid them in a little jar in a hole she dug behind the goat shed.

Demeter lived with Triptolemus in Eleusis through the cycle of one year. Midway through she knew she was pregnant. While the garden grew, she grew, and Metanira announced that she had known the girl was a whore. Triptolemus was pleased, when he was not hunting or fishing or taking the wheat crop to market in his boat, and had time to think about her. For the sake of what they were sure would be Triptolemus's son, the sisters grew somewhat kinder.

The baby was born in the spring, a year to the day after Demophon's death. Metanira, prepared to forgive all if it was a boy, held up a small squalling girl by the feet and dropped her in Demeter's bloody lap.

"It looks sickly. It ought to be exposed," she said vindictively, while Demeter looked pleadingly at Triptolemus.

"No need to talk of that tonight," Triptolemus said cheerfully, ushering his mother out of the chamber. "Give her one night with the babe, can't you? We'll talk tomorrow."

"The child is an ill omen."

Triptolemus didn't sleep with her that night, and before daylight Demeter got out of the bed, washed herself and the baby with water from the pitcher in their chamber, and dressed. She packed the clothes that Triptolemus had given her into a sack and stole the gardener's pruning knife from the potting shed. By moonlight she cut shoots from the best grapevines and unearthed her jar of seeds, digging into the dirt behind the goat shed like a dog, while the baby watched her, eyes bright as silver coins under the moon. Demeter scooped up baby, cuttings, seeds, and sack and stole Triptolemus's best boat.

How could she have explained all that to Persephone? Told her how her mother had sailed away with a young man just because his hair was gold and his eyes were blue? She had never told even Aristippus what had happened, but Demeter had come home armed with new knowledge and planted her garden. When the village had seen what she grew, they had asked no more questions for fear that she would take it all away again.

And what did it all matter to her now if her child was gone? And who could go down into the earth and get her back? Demeter went into her house and closed the door behind her.

The sun blazed just a shade brighter, as if in sympathy with her anger. It had been a hot summer, and the sky was the deep clear blue of a bird's egg. Its heat shimmered on the sea and on the white limestone walls of Demeter's house. When she emerged it was only to pace wildly up and down the headland, shouting at him, calling for Persephone. Nothing ever answered her but the white gulls wheeling in the sky overhead. Summer in Hellas is always hot, but now it seemed as if Apollo had halted his chariot stock-still in the noon sky. The irrigation channels that brought water from the river to the garden cracked and dried out, and Demeter didn't come out to tend them. The bean vines withered, and their leaves turned brown. The cabbages, even under their shade-cloth, wilted and then desiccated so that there was left only a ragged spiral of transparent green leaf that crumbled when touched.

The grass turned brown underfoot, and the poppies on the headland withered, leaving only their tall brown stalks and urn-shaped seedpods rattling in the wind.

The sheep and goats foraged farther and farther up the mountain for graze. The village boys scampered after them, with what food could be spared, half a loaf of bread and a bag of dried fish to see them through. More often than not they slept in the hills with the flocks. The river ran lower, and the water in the well came up muddy. When the breeze blew, the agora disappeared in a cloud of dust.

"It's her!" Phaedon, the doctor, said coughing, his mantle to his mouth. He pointed at Demeter's house, sitting silently in the heat. "Look at her garden!"

The brown bean vines rattled to dust on their trellises.

"It's the heat," Maia said.

"She brought it," Bopis said.

"We've had hot spells before," Phaedon said. "She's let those channels she dug go dry."

"Do you suppose it's cursed the whole island?" Hermes asked.

"Well, of course it has, boy! You can't have a place like that"— he nodded at the garden—"and not have it spill over."

Magic leaks. Everyone knew that. When you lived

near a place of magic, near anything touched by the gods, you felt its vibrations in your skin. When there was upheaval there, it was mirrored in the world outside and around it. That only stood to reason. Demeter's garden was dying, and it was taking the island with it.

"The whole village is suffering." Aristippus thumped his staff on the tiles, but Demeter didn't look up. She sat with her face to the window, staring out at the sea off the headland. "Pay attention to me!"

"They managed before."

"That would be very true if the whole island were not drying up like a slug in the sun." Aristippus thumped his staff again. "You changed things with all your new ways. They can't go back to the old ones. The island can't."

"I don't care. I want my child back." Demeter's pale brown hair was unkempt, and she hadn't bothered in a moon to wash her clothes in the river that now was sluggish and dark as mud anyway.

"Sulking won't bring her back."

"It gives me pleasure."

"It does not." Aristippus got between her and the window. "He will give her back or he won't. Won't, most likely, since he stole her." He glowered at Demeter. "She would have married sometime. Gone away."

"She would not."

"Maybe you should have let her," he said.

For three months Demeter did not go into her garden, and no one saw her except as a wild form pacing on the headland. Weeds, which do not mind drought, overran the garden, swallowing up the dried husks of her vegetables. The bug people, unmolested, came out and ate the rest. The wheatfields, harvested in the month of Maimakterion, were tinder dry, and a spark from the temple hearth caught them on fire. The men of the village fought it through the night with jugs of water, shovels, and blankets, but the fire ate the whole field and singed the olive grove before they stopped it. A stray spark ran along the grapevines, and a whole row blazed and crackled into cinders. The glow of the flames lit the night sky.

Demeter, watching from her window, thought of Demophon.

At the start of the month of Elaphebolion the village scoured out the wine vats with boiling seawater and harvested what was left of the grapes.

"You will come to the agora for the pressing," Aristippus said to Demeter, and this time she nodded listlessly. She had combed her hair and put on a clean gown, but it was like watching a walking corpse, to see her coming softly along the path from her house to the agora where the winepresses had been set up. Scrubbed and dried, they held promise each year of a new vintage, but this year the festival had lost its heart. Everyone was just slightly hungry, and half the grapes had gone bad on the vines for reasons that no one could explain.

The islanders had dragged benches out of their houses into the open for the old people to sit on and watch the pressing. Demeter sat down on one, listlessly as if she had been dropped there accidentally by someone who was carrying her somewhere.

The old men on either side of her edged away, but Demeter didn't seem to notice.

Hermes danced past her, playing his flute, a jaunty tune to accompany the grapepickers coming single file down the path from the vineyard in the morning sun, baskets on their shoulders. Demeter should have been at the procession's head, but she didn't look up.

The harvesters dumped the grapes into the biggest vats, where it was the job of the young people to dance the wine out of them. Three or four boys set the tempo with their flutes, and the rest climbed into the vat, laughing and pushing each other, dancing for the attention of the girls who had hiked their skirts over their knees to dance beside them.

The pressed juice ran in a red stream out a spout at the bottom of the vat, into a smaller tub where it would be left to ferment until spring. Through the morning the men brought the grapes in baskets and dumped them beneath the dancers' feet. Under Bopis's supervision, the women carried plates of dried fish and cheese and cups of last year's vintage, well watered, and handed them around. The dancers leaned over the edges of the vat to grab a cup and drain it.

"Hey ho, Echo." Hermes flicked a piece of grape pulp at her. "Want to watch the moon come up with me tonight?"

Echo considered him, remembering their last moonlit walk. He was handsome—something about him made you want to abandon caution and dance through the field with him—but completely unreliable. The number of girls who had thought he would marry them could not be counted on both her hands. "Mother says I am not to," she said primly, and sought refuge next to Harmonia and Tros, who were dancing hand in hand while Harmonia's mother glared at them. They would be married soon, despite Tros's lack of wealth. He had almost earned enough for the bride price that her father had set, in the assumption that it would be beyond him. Tros was a faithful sort—Harmonia wasn't even more than passably good-looking.

What made love? Echo wondered. Bopis was a sour old busybody just because Aristippus wouldn't leave other women alone, although to give him his due, he didn't chase young girls anymore. Widows were his specialty, and no wonder Bopis wanted to marry Irene off. And look at poor Persephone, snatched up in the arms of a fearful being, not even human. He probably loved her. Persephone, so far as Echo knew, had never loved anyone, but Echo thought she had wanted to. It was the one indulgence that her mother had denied her. Persephone could have had anything else—freedom to roam the hills playing with the wild goats, to spend her days picking flowers and romping in the stream, pleasures that her friends had to filch time for from their other duties. But not love. No young men. No old men, for that matter. Demeter hadn't even dedicated her to Hestia, or to Artemis, the goddess who roamed the countryside hunting and indulging in other sports reserved for men, always virgin and untouched; however, there had been no men allowed to come courting and offer a bride price. After the first one or two, no one had even tried. It was as if Persephone's virginity was Demeter's offering to avert from her whatever fate had befallen Demeter so long ago.

Echo wondered what that had been. It must have

been a man, that stood to reason, or she wouldn't have had Persephone. She had gone somewhere over mountain, over sea, who knew, to the gods, people said, and been given gifts. Apparently a child had been one of them. The gods were like that, just ask Maia, although Echo didn't think Hermes was a god's son, despite Hermes's insistence that he was. "A child of the god" was a euphemism for a baby got in unorthodox ways: in the hayfield on solstice night, for instance.

But something else had been given to Demeter, along with the child. It had been impossible to tell Demeter from her garden. When you saw her in it, it seemed as if her feet went into the earth and her fingers ended in sprouts of green leaves. She was the garden. No wonder that a child who had grown up in it would appeal to a man who lived down in the darkness; but child and garden and mother had all been one in some way, Echo thought. When she saw Demeter sitting lifelessly now while life danced around her to the flute song, she thought of bean pods stripped of their seed or wheat chaff when the grain has been threshed out of it. There was something gone out of Demeter now, and the absence made Echo want to cry.

They danced in the vats until the noon sun tilted and slid down the western sky. The air was hot and sticky with juice. Insects buzzed around them, and the vintner's boys fished them out of the vats with a scoop. Dogs trotted between the legs of the watchers, seeing if anyone had dropped anything to eat. A cat, unnoticed, slunk along the windowsill of Narcissa's house and began licking a cheese on the table, the gift of Narcissa's mother's suitor, another from the north island. She would have this one, Narcissa had told Echo, and he had a younger brother also in the market for a wife. This was the last year she would dance in the vintage with Narcissa, Echo suspected.

The sun dropped farther, burnishing the water to copper in the west. Echo's legs ached. Her dress was splashed with juice from hem to shoulders. It was the old one that she always wore for the vintage, splotched with wine of other years. She could trace the history of her girlhood in the faded stains. The pale one at the hem, bleached with much subsequent washing, was from the first year she had been allowed to dance in the vats. She had been so short she had sunk into the grapes up to her waist. Persephone and Narcissa had each taken one of her hands and held her upright until she got her footing. Persephone should be here now, dancing beside her. Echo felt a hole in the air between herself and Narcissa.

"Hey ho, Echo." Hermes was there again, cavorting beside her in the vat.

"Go and dance somewhere else," she said irritably.

Hermes's mouth was red with wine stains, and he handed a clay cup to her. "Here. Keep your strength up."

Echo took it and drank. It was the last of the wine from four years ago, just on the edge of going bad. She swallowed and handed him back the cup. Hermes handed it to Narcissa, and Echo knitted her brows to see Hermes in Persephone's place.

Hermes seemed to catch her thought from the air; he had an unsettling way of doing that. "I could bring her back," he said, grinning as he danced.

"Go down there?" Echo snorted.

"You would pee all over yourself just thinking about going into that cave," Narcissa said.

Hermes looked offended. "I go down there all the time. He's old. I will wrestle him for her and pin him on the first try!"

"He'll feed you to his dog," Arachne said from the other side of the vat. She was a slender girl with long dark ringlets. She swayed gracefully as she danced, like a stalk of grass, never seeming out of breath while everyone else huffed and puffed.

"What dog?"

"Haven't you seen it? Since you go down there all the time?"

"No, I haven't." Hermes narrowed his eyes at her, as if trying to decide whether she was making that up.

"Just at dusk," Arachne said dreamily. "I've seen it twice. It comes out to play in the surf. It has three heads," she added.

Hermes looked unnerved.

Echo giggled. "Great big heads." She snapped her teeth at him.

"With green foam," Narcissa said knowingly. "We've seen it, too."

"No foam," Arachne said. "Just teeth. I made a weaving of it. I'll show you."

Narcissa sighed. Arachne's weavings were magical. It was as if she just painted things on the loom. Narcissa's mother was always asking her why she couldn't weave like Arachne, which was a silly question because no one could.

"Never mind," Hermes said. "You'll change your tune when I go down there and bring her back."

"Then why haven't you?" Echo asked him.

"Demeter has to promise her to me. I'm not going to go fight a dog with three heads just to be kind."

"And you just asked me to watch the moon come up with you!" Echo threw a handful of grapes at him. "Faithless! Faithless!"

They all started shouting "Faithless!" at him and threw more grapes. Hermes vaulted over the side of the vat in a shower of juice.

"Be careful, you cursed goat!" The vintner shook his paddle at him.

Hermes dodged between the vats and climbed into another one.

"That one won't do anything," Arachne said with a sniff.

"No, but somebody had better," Echo said, watching Demeter. She hadn't moved since the morning. She sat on the bench as if she were a pile of laundry.

When the last juice had been run into the tubs, Demeter stood finally and looked around her as if she had been asleep. She walked back to her house, leaving the village to dance out the rest of the evening on the packed dirt of the agora. Aristippus saw her go and knew there would be no more to be got from her tonight, so he gave his attention to dancing in the wine, which was a matter of some importance. He joined the end of the line as the dancers flew by him, taking the hand of Irene, still a passably attractive widow, while the onlookers clapped out a rhythm to flute and lyre. Nearly everyone in the village played one instrument or the other, although the lyre was considered somewhat more respectable. In their midst Bopis stood stiffly, watching Aristippus to be sure he didn't disappear with Irene as the moon rose.

The vintner's boys dumped the juice into the press and hung on the end of the heavy beam until the juice flowed into the storage vats and left the pulp behind. The dregs of the old vintage were handed round. The fermentation process never really stopped, and it spoiled if you left it too long. Four years was elderly, so it needed to be drunk.

"I'm elderly," Phaedon said with satisfaction, pulling on his cup. "I need to be drunk, too."

"Get up and dance, you old goat," Echo's mother Doris said, prodding him with her sandal. They were brother and sister, and she felt entitled.

"Bah, woman. Dance yourself." Phaedon settled back on his bench. Doris grinned and sat down next to him. "I paid good money in my youth to study with a man who studied with a man who once studied with Asclepius. I have no need to cavort like a ram in spring. It is undignified."

"You mean your bones ache," Doris said. "Mine too. There is a bad winter coming."

Phaedon sniffed and flicked a small grasshopper out of his beard. "No one but gods and soothsayers know what the weather will be," he said. That was a proverb, but the truth was that everyone generally knew what the weather would be: hot and sunny in the summer, mild and sunny in the winter, occasionally with a bit of rain.

"This will be different," Doris said. "You mark my words."

The dancers snaked past them, feet skipping to the flutes, clothes flying, bare feet stained red to the knees. Some of the girls, despite Bopis's orders, still had their gowns hitched up, as if they just hadn't remembered to let them down.

"Shameless," Doris muttered.

Phaedon took the knot of hair on the back of her neck in his hand and gave it a shake back and forth. "Old women forget things. Men have much better memories. I, for instance, remember quite clearly pulling you out of the dance at the vintage when you were sixteen, on Mother's orders, because your skirt was up to your backside."

"Nonsense," Doris said primly. "I don't remember anything like that at all."

"All the men of that year do," Phaedon said, chortling.

Doris ignored him, watching the sky.

Phaedon elbowed her, to see if she had got the joke, and saw what she was watching.

To the west, where the sun was sinking in the water, dark clouds were boiling up, lit from below by the sun, like fire in a forge. As they watched, the clouds rose like a dreadful being climbing out of the sea. The sun dropped below the horizon and the air darkened suddenly about them as if a door had shut. The dancers hopped uncertainly on one foot and stopped while the flutes and lyres jangled into silence. The sky rumbled, and they saw a distant flash of lightning on the water.

Before the tubs of new wine could be sealed and rolled away to the cellars where they were left to age, the sky opened. Water poured down on them as if out of a bucket, and the agora filled with mud. The vintner's boys slipped and slid as they rolled the tubs away. Echo pulled her mantle over her head and took her mother by the hand.

"Get out of this! You'll catch your death!" She could feel the cold rain plastering her mantle to her hair, and the sticky hem of her gown to her shins. Her sandals, retrieved from under a bench, were sodden with mud.

They ran for home, tugging the benches they had brought from their house and sliding in the mud.

When the storm stopped, the wind and rain had knocked down half the unripe olives and had broken whole branches from the trees. The storm had also torn a hole in the thatch roof of the Temple of Hestia and put out her fire. The whole village stood wailing outside the temple. The fire on Hestia's hearth was the heart of the village, daughter of the sacred fire of the ruined city on the mainland from which the ancestors of these villagers had fled generations ago, carrying their hearth fire in a clay pot. To allow the fire to go out was sacrilege. Hesperia, Hestia's ancient priestess, stood wavering in the temple courtyard, her thin arms shaking as if a sea breeze might blow her over.

"What are we to do?" Phaedon asked her. He attempted to look businesslike, but his eyes were uneasy. Bopis, quiet for once, shivered in her wet mantle.

Hesperia mumbled something no one could understand.

"The goddess must tell us," Aristippus said. "The priestess will go into a trance, and the goddess will speak." He seemed to be talking to Hesperia more than to anyone else. She nodded, her chin trembling, and shuffled back into the temple.

Echo clung to her mother's arm. This was bad. It was bad to let your own hearth fire go out, your own little offering to Hestia. To let the village fire go out . . . well, who knew what might happen if the goddess was not placated. The hearth fire was where anyone could go for refuge, where no one could kill you without sacrilege if you sought its asylum. Without it the village itself was naked, unprotected by any power.

Phaedon and Nicias, Irene's new suitor, brought a young goat and killed it in the temple doorway, cutting its throat and letting the blood pour into a bronze bowl. They put the bowl on the altar and the bones in the cold hearth. Over them they laid all the dry tinder that could be found, liberally sprinkled with oil and herbs, and set a torch to it. Old Hesperia came forth, leaning on Aristippus, and stood in the smoke, arms outstretched.

At first Echo thought she would choke. She began to cough, and Aristippus thumped her back. Her eyes bulged, and Echo looked uneasily at Phaedon, the doctor. If they killed the priestess of Hestia trying to get a divination from her, surely that would not be good.

Hesperia coughed again and stepped back from the smoke. She looked wild-eyed, like a sheep caught in briars. "There is worse to come," she said, which was not what anyone wanted to hear. "The sky will freeze."

"What must we do?" Aristippus asked her.

"Take back that which is lost." Hesperia sounded puzzled, as if that wasn't what she had thought she was going to say.

A murmur rose from the crowd. Demeter was not among them. Demeter was sitting in her house, where the rain had washed mud all over the floors, and she hadn't even cleaned it up. Doris knew that;

she had been to see her, to make sure she wasn't drowned. Echo thought privately that Demeter was the cause of the storm, and not likely to be its victim, but that was not a thought she wished to speak aloud. She did wonder, if mother and daughter and garden were all one, what effect that was having on the man who ruled the caves underground and had stolen the daughter.

"Take her back, lest the sky freeze," Hesperia said again. She began to shuffle away. "And sacrifice two more goats," she added, over her shoulder. She disappeared behind the hangings at the back of the temple.

The goats were not a problem, although there was some discussion over the question of *whose* goats. But the taking back of that which was lost—that was another matter. Hermes rather abruptly stopped boasting that he was the man for the job in case that someone decided he might be, Echo thought. Demeter said nothing. Irene told her of the divination, but Demeter only nodded, as if waiting for them to do it. The village waited, too, torn between anger at Demeter whose grief, they were sure, was the cause of theirs, and fear of provoking her further.

In Thargelion, the month of the olive harvest, it snowed. In all of Hellas snow fell in any strength only in the mountains. The sea moderated the climate, and the valleys might get only a dusting of frost, or a thin blanket of white, no more than would hold a footprint, in a cold year. Now the sea itself seemed to have frozen and fallen from the air, breaking more olive boughs and filling the agora up to men's calves. The olives still left on the trees were spotted and half gone bad. The houses, built to keep cool in a warm climate, were chambers of ice, badly lit by coals in bronze braziers set in every room by those who could afford them. Those who could not huddled together and froze. Glaucus's daughters, who were rich enough to actually own a slave, were too afraid to take him into the house with them, and he was found dead among the goats.

Tros and Harmonia's wedding was stopped in midbanquet because a snake fleeing the snow was found like an evil omen coiled among the wedding cakes. Harmonia went home weeping with her mother while a delegation of the village elders conferred. At the end of their conference they set out grimly for the cold, silent house where Demeter lived.

# IV

§

## Souls in Jars

"Madam must be very uncomfortable like that.
Lack of hygiene causes rashes of the skin."
The old servant peered down his nose at Persephone.

"Madam is," Persephone said grumpily, sitting on
the edge of her bed and resolutely ignoring the
freshly filled tub of water just beyond the hanging.
She had lived underground for a week now. "But *he*
won't like me this way."

"He will not wish to make love to you perhaps,"
the servant said, considering that, "but he appears to
like you in any condition." He sighed.

"Why?" Persephone demanded.

"Madam, who knows? What makes love?"

"He can't love me. He doesn't even know me. I
throw things at him."

"Ah, yes. He hopes that will pass."

"Then he is crazy. I'm not going to marry Death."

"Oh, it isn't as bad as all that," the servant said.

"And what are you? And those others? Where do you come from?"

"I am Lycippus. I am from Thrace."

"Then you're not . . ." Persephone looked uneasily at the roast mutton with rosemary on her tray.

"Perhaps madam should eat," Lycippus said. "Madam can't go on like this."

Persephone knew she couldn't. She hadn't eaten in six days. Her head was swimming, and she was never sure if she really saw the things that floated past her peripheral vision, or the pale wraiths that seemed to hang in the corridor outside when Lycippus opened the door.

"If madam wishes to try this nice dish of squid with fig sauce . . ." Lycippus appeared to notice her aversion to the mutton. "Or we have a nice pheasant pie." He bent down toward her with an avuncular expression. "If madam wishes to eat just a bit, I shan't tell him."

The pheasant pie was hot, and its odor circled her head. Starving herself was probably a bad idea. If she died, she would have to stay here, anyway.

"Just a bite," Lycippus said, cajoling her as if she were a wayward child.

"If I eat will you let me out?" she asked craftily.

"Oh, that would be a very bad idea. Madam would get lost in the caves."

"I wouldn't go anywhere."

"Well, perhaps we might take a stroll. If madam eats a bit. And stays with me."

Persephone grabbed the pheasant pie, just big enough to fit in her hand, and sank her teeth into it. It was wonderful, savory and delicate, baked in a light crust with onions and peas. She would have just one bite. Maybe two. She gobbled it down, and Lycippus patted her on the head.

"Madam will feel much better now."

Persephone wiped her fingers on her grimy gown. "Now we'll take a walk. You promised."

"If madam will be careful . . ." Lycippus opened the door, and Persephone darted through it. "Madam, wait!"

Persephone fled down the corridor and dodged through the first doorway she saw. It opened into another corridor that slanted upward a bit, so she took it. She could hear Lycippus puffing and calling behind her. His voice grew fainter as she ran, taking any turn that led upward. The walls were lit by oil lamps in their niches (he must be wealthy beyond belief, or else it was magic oil that never burned up) making intermittent pools of light on the gray stone. She couldn't hear Lycippus any longer, but she thought she heard voices raised somewhere, shouting back and forth to each other. Her corridor ended and branched three ways, all going down. She stopped, gasping for breath, and took a frantic step into each one. She hadn't realized how weak she had grown in just a few days. her head was spinning. She leaned against the stone wall. There were no carvings here, just blank stone. Behind her she could hear more shouting. She fled down the middle corridor.

The walls grew rougher, the stone unfinished, and the lamps were farther apart. She stumbled over the uneven floor, and something scuttled past her feet. She ran from it. This had been the wrong way. It was going down. She took another opening on her left that went up again, but the path was still rough, plainly not the way they had come in. She saw a dimly lit room filled with dusty wine jars. Farther on there were bones, a white tumble on a bier. Persephone fled back the way she had come.

Her heart was hammering in her chest so loudly she grew frightened and stopped. She crumpled onto the rough stone, weeping, her head buried against her knees. Lycippus had warned her. She would never find her way out, and they would never find her here, either. She had run too fast for the old servant to keep up. She thought they could search for weeks in these corridors and not come upon her.

She was cold in the dank passageway and thirsty, her tongue dry in her mouth. After a while she pushed herself to her feet and tried to find the room with the wine jars. It wasn't where she thought it had been, nor could she find the chamber with the bones again. She sank down on the stone and closed her eyes.

A rat went over her feet, and she sat up shrieking. Her voice echoed in the stone corridor under the earth, and nothing answered her. She wondered how long it would take her to starve to death. Surely she was halfway there already. Wispy shades appeared to flutter around her head, ready to take her hand. She closed her eyes despairingly, and then opened them again when she heard more rats. Could she follow the rats? Surely they were going somewhere. If anyone could find food, it was a rat. She got to her feet and propped herself against the wall until she was sure she wasn't going to faint. She would wait here until a rat went by and then she would follow it.

Something was coming. She could hear movement

in the corridor. She flattened herself against the wall and stood perfectly still so as not to frighten the rat back the other way. The corridor made a bend where a lamp sat in its niche, and the thing she had heard came around it. Persephone stuck her fist in her mouth to stifle a scream when she saw it, her heart pounding against her breastbone. It wasn't a rat.

It was a huge beast, as black as the depths of the cave. The light caught its eyes, and they glowed green, like a lamp under seawater. Its mouth was open, and she could see the saliva hanging in ropes from its jaws. She stood frozen. There was no point in fleeing from it. Its huge paws would run her down in seconds. She whimpered and waited for it to leap at her throat.

It padded closer, tongue lolling, and gave a deep sonorous bark. Then it sat down on her foot and leaned its huge, hideous head against her.

Persephone shuddered. It drooled, dripping saliva on her foot.

"Good boy!"

His voice rang in the stone corridor, and Hades came around the bend behind the dog. When he reached them, he patted the dog's monstrous head and regarded her with curiosity. "What made you do a foolish thing like that? If Cerberus hadn't tracked you, you could have died down here. It's happened."

She didn't have any answer. Her leg muscles quivered with the effort of standing.

"You're done in," he said. He scooped her up before she could protest and carried her down the corridor. She tried to struggle, but she was too tired. And there was the dog looking up at her, jaws agape. If Hades dropped her, the dog would probably swallow her. She tried to pull her feet up out of its reach.

"He doesn't bite people unless I ask him to," Hades said.

He carried her to her chamber by a route that she was fairly sure was not the one she had taken in her flight, and set her down. "Please don't do that again. It's very hard not to get lost down here. It takes a long time to train servants when I hire new ones."

"You hire them?" She saw Lycippus peering out at her from the bath, a jug in his hand.

"Did you think they were ghosts?"

"Of course not," she said uncertainly, because he sounded so amused.

"I don't buy slaves, either. I prefer people who are motivated to stay by me. They don't get lost in the caverns, for instance."

"Then why did you kidnap me?" she demanded.

He raised dark eyebrows. "Frankly, it never occurred to me that you would come willingly."

"I wouldn't."

"There. You see?" He put his hand on the door. "I'll stop locking this if you'll promise not to do that again." He closed the door behind him, but she didn't hear the bolt slide.

"Perhaps now madam would like to bathe," Lycippus said.

"Why couldn't I get out?" she demanded. "I went up every time the corridor branched."

"We are inside the cliff, madam. Many corridors go up. To go out you must go down. Up a little, too. Sideways a bit."

"Oh." In spite of herself, Persephone looked longingly at the bath.

"The dog has soiled your gown, madam," Lycippus said tactfully. "There are clean ones in the bathchamber."

"Is the master certain that it was wise not to lock the door?" Lycippus poured a silver goblet a third full of wine and added water to fill it. The master was a man of moderate habits, despite his reputation. Stealing that girl from the upper air was the worst thing Lycippus had known him to do. Of course she was probably going to cause more trouble than she was worth.

"She knows she can't get out now," Hades said. "She won't try it again. She's a fast learner."

Lycippus thought that she would more likely try something else, possibly even more ill-advised. "Perhaps the master is not taking the right approach," he offered.

"Indeed? And in your vast experience of courtship, what would you suggest?"

Lycippus sighed. "It is possible to buy a bride. It is also possible to court a woman before taking her home with you."

"And how close do you think she would have let me get to her, to start courting?"

Lycippus sighed again. "I was thinking of women in other places, Lord. Areas less . . . primitive. Master has traveled widely."

Hades reclined on his couch. The dog, who had been sprawled on the floor by the hearth, came and put its head into his hand. He scratched its ears. "This is the one I wanted," he informed Lycippus. "So if you are going to be helpful, concentrate on that."

"If master will permit," Lycippus said, "Master will have to let the lady get used to him." He tutted. "These people are not widely educated. One must give her time. Bring her presents, perhaps."

"I sent her an extremely valuable aquamarine necklace," Hades observed, "and she threw it down the commode."

"Ah, exactly. Master *sent* it. Perhaps master should try bringing his gifts himself."

Hades eyed him consideringly. "If you will recall, I took that advice two days back, and she threw eggs on me."

"One must be persistent in wooing." Lycippus bustled about, tidying the hall. "These things require time," he offered, a pair of wax tablets tucked under his arm, and Hades's stylus in one hand. He balanced a draughts board and a bag of game pieces in the other.

Hades stood up and paced, wine cup in hand, while Lycippus sprinkled sand and dried herbs on the rugs and swept it up again with a broom, dodging around the master's feet. The huge dog paced after him.

"Go and sit down!" Lycippus said to the dog and he flopped on the floor again in the pile of sand and sweepings. "Tsk! Take the dog to see her. Women like dogs."

"She didn't appear to."

"She doesn't know him well." Lycippus prodded the dog with his foot. "Move!"

"Do you think I should take her the same necklace again, or another one?"

Lycippus paused in his sweeping. "The first necklace is in the drains."

"Well, I'm not going to leave it there. I thought I mentioned that. Get it out."

"I shall delegate the task," Lycippus said gravely.

"Wise man."

"And I should take her another one, if I were you. That one will have associations difficult to remove."

Hades smiled. "Then we shall sell it, when next you take ship for the mainland. Give me that." He held out his hand for the draughts board. "I shall teach her to play."

"A happy thought, Lord."

"Indeed. And the pieces are small enough not to hurt, should she throw them at me."

The door swung open. Persephone, who had been driven by boredom to begin spinning the wool in the basket, dropped it lest anyone think she was going to do that sort of thing here. Without turning her head, she slewed her eyes around to see who it was: Hades, bearing a tray of food and wine. The dog paced at his heel.

"I am told you enjoyed the pheasant pie," he remarked, setting the tray on the three-legged table next to her seat.

"It was passable," she said icily, but her eyes dropped to the tray.

"You might as well eat. If you don't, Cerberus will be into it as soon as you turn your back. He's very badly trained, I'm afraid."

"You said he only bit people when you told him to," Persephone retorted, eyeing the dog warily. It waved a plumed tail and sighed at her.

"He loves you, too," Hades observed.

"He is drooling. He wants my dinner. And you don't love me."

Hades sat down on a bench opposite her. "I do. I find it very odd."

There didn't seem to be a good answer to that, since she found it extremely odd herself. If Death was in love with you, what on earth did that mean? She gave in and reached for the tray. If you ate in someone's house you couldn't kill them, but she doubted that being dead would have much effect on Death. On the other hand, they couldn't kill you. That might be important, since she wasn't sure what a marriage ceremony with Death involved. And there were honey and nutmeat sweets on the tray.

"I brought you a gift," he said. "I don't think it will fit down the commode."

Persephone looked up at him, her mouth full of nuts and honey. He held out a silver mirror, polished to a high shine. Persephone stopped chewing and stared. She had never seen herself in a good mirror before. Her mother owned a bronze one, rather elderly and scratched, and her only other reflection had been in the pool or the still surface of a basin of water. This one had a stand to hold it upright, cast with silver deer supporting it with their hooves on each side. Hades set it on the table before her. She put the sweet down and licked her fingers, and the girl in the mirror did the same. Her hair was pale, like ripe wheat, and her eyes, seen clearly, were a blue green like the sea in shallow water. Her face was triangular, wide at the forehead and narrow at the chin, with arching brows and thick pale lashes. There was a mole just at the corner of her left eye.

It was pale and flat, and she hadn't even known it was there. She put a finger to it, and then to her mouth and small, curled ears.

"You are very beautiful, you know," Hades said.

Persephone turned away from the mirror. "I might be a shrew, you know."

"You are," he agreed.

"Then what do you want with me?"

"You bring me light," he said. "It's dark down here."

Persephone thought about that over the next weeks, trying to discern what it was that he thought she could give him. He came regularly to bring her meals and left the door unbolted behind him, but she didn't leave. She knew now she wouldn't find her way out of the caverns, and to go to him in the great hall, where Lycippus had offered to escort her, smacked of giving in. Instead, she waited for him to come to her, and spun the wool to keep herself from screaming, although she hid it in the basket whenever she heard footsteps.

While she spun, she thought of what was happening in the upper air, about the wine making in the fall, and the olive harvest at the start of winter, and whether Narcissa or her mother, Irene, was married by now. She lost track of time, with no way to mark the days as they came and went, and no way to be sure when a day had gone by in the first place, except by the appearance of Lycippus or her captor with her meals. She imagined Echo and Narcissa dancing the vintage out of the grapes without her, the sun hot on the rocks by the headland. In her mind she saw the olives, dark greenish black, tumbling from the heavy branches as the boys beat them with their flails, and the littlest ones climbed to the highest branches to pelt the others. There would be singing and dancing and much foolishness at the pressing as the men, five of them at a time, took turns working the lever that squeezed the oil from the olives.

The summer solstice must be long gone by, she thought, the season turning toward the equinox when night and day stood balanced. Then came the long cool slide toward the winter solstice, when the sun shone for the shortest, heart-stopping day in the sky, and you were never really sure that this year it would turn around and creep northward again into the lengthening days of another spring. All that was happening in the air above her, but like the shades of the dead who lived here, she had no way to know it.

"What are you thinking?"

His voice startled her out of her reverie, and she looked up quickly, stuffing the skein of spun wool behind her and sticking herself on the spindle.

"I hate spinning," she said.

"Really? Some women find it soothing."

Persephone looked at it with loathing. "It's only something to do."

"Well then, I have brought you something more interesting to do." He set the draughts board on a table. "Only you have to do it with me." He shook the bag of men into his hand.

Persephone watched him suspiciously as he laid them out on the board. They were carved in the shape of owls and made of onyx and some green stone she didn't recognize.

"Do you know how to play?"

"I have played with Mother." Persephone eyed him thoughtfully. "She is going to be most awfully angry, you know."

"I'm sure she'll get over it," Hades said, arranging the draughtsmen. "I will be an admirable son-in-law." But Persephone thought he looked just a little uneasy, as if Demeter was something he hadn't considered—or had thought of and decided to ignore.

"Mother makes things happen," Persephone said.

"Women do." Hades moved one of his black owls toward her green ones.

"She made Glaucus get boils all over his backside once, when he beat his wife," Persephone offered.

"I shan't beat you."

"They were large boils, filled with pus."

"I'm sure they were a coincidence."

"Nothing of the sort."

"So far my backside is intact."

"Just wait," Persephone said darkly.

Hades smiled. "I don't think you're afraid of me anymore."

Persephone pushed a green owl toward his. "That doesn't mean I am going to marry you."

"Noooo," Hades said, considering his next move, "but you have figured out I'm not going to rape you. That seems an admirable beginning."

"If you did that, it would fall off," Persephone informed him. "Mother can do that, even down here." She wasn't entirely certain of that, but she wouldn't have been surprised.

"I thought, actually, that it didn't seem the foundation for a happy marriage," Hades remarked.

"I'm not going to marry you."

"What are your plans, then?"

Persephone narrowed her eyes at him. "I'm going to wait until you get bored with me."

Hades pushed an owl forward and deftly removed one of hers from the board. "I am a patient man. And you look very nice in that gown."

"My old one was spoiled by your dog." Persephone pushed the dog's head from the lap of the new gown and smoothed the shining folds. They rippled and shimmered like blue water. "What is this made of?"

"It is called silk," Hades said. "No one knows where the fiber comes from. They make it in another world."

"In the Underworld?" What else did he have here, where she had never been? The idea of exploring his kingdom was intriguing and terrifying.

"No, in the East. A long way east."

"There is nothing in the East but the Ocean."

"With all due respect, you are an ignorant child." He glared at her as she captured one of his black owls. "A good draughts player, however. There is a whole world beyond what you know of here in Hellas. There are things you never imagined."

"Tell me some of them." She put her chin in her hand, bored with the draughts already.

"Elephants."

"What are elephants?"

"Animals as big as your house, with ears like monstrous fig leaves and a nose like a snake which he blows through like a flute."

"I don't believe that. Where do these miraculous elephants live?"

•

"To the south," Hades said. "Among the Aethiopians."

"Have you seen one?" Persephone asked him suspiciously. They sounded like gorgons or chimaeras, which everyone was fairly certain didn't exist, or had died out.

"I have." Hades twisted a bracelet off his wrist and handed it to her. It was made of silver embossed with strange animals. One appeared to be an elephant.

She turned it over in her hand. Like all his possessions, it was richly made, of fine workmanship and finer materials, and just a little odd. His clothes, for instance—the fabric of his tunic was embroidered with a border of scarlet poppies against a golden background. They shimmered so, it must be made of the strange otherworldly silk. His cloak was black wool (she thought of the sheep again) caught at the shoulder with a heavy gold pin shaped like a pomegranate. The fillet that bound his dark hair was a golden snake that clenched its own tail in its mouth.

The world contained more than she had imagined. "Tell me more," she said to him.

"About what?"

"About the world. About things like elephants that live outside of Hellas."

"There were miraculous things inside Hellas, too, but they are gone now for a while," he said. "Whole cities crumbled to dust and bits of painted clay. The palace of King Minos at Knossos where they danced with bulls."

"How could you dance with a bull?"

"Very carefully. It was dangerous. They were a sacrifice to their gods."

Persephone had never known of any sacrifice but the goat kids they gave to Apollo and Zeus, and to Hestia in her temple, and of course the black ram they gave to Hades when they took someone to him. "What happens to them?" she asked.

"The dancers? They used to die when they grew too big to flip between the horns."

"No, the sheep we bring you. That my village brings you."

"We eat them. What do you do with all the other sacrifices your people make?"

"We eat them," she said, "but the gods don't. They eat the smell of the burning bones."

"We are usually hungrier than that, down here."

She studied him across the draughts board. He didn't look like a god, who she had always imagined would have fiery hair or burning eyes or smoke issuing from the mouth, or some other indication of divine status. Hades—no one at home liked to call him by his actual name, but she found that she had got used to it—merely looked like a human man of somewhat indeterminate age. Up close she could see fine lines around his eyes and the corners of his mouth. His hair and beard were dark brown, not the blue black she had at first thought they were, and they curled, so that he looked a bit like a faun— something else she had never seen, but everyone knew what they looked like. The woods were full of them.

"How many of you are there? Down here, eating sheep?" There must be more. Someone was doing the cooking and the laundry. Her soiled clothes disappeared and came back clean.

"Quite a few, actually. I haven't sent anyone else to you because I didn't want to frighten you."

"That might have suggested to you that it wasn't a good idea to grab me and leap off a cliff with me," she retorted.

Hades smiled. "I couldn't see a way around that." He inspected a plate of fresh fish on her tray. "This is very good. The cook simmers it with olive oil and leeks." He picked up a piece between thumb and forefinger and offered it to her.

"Thank you. I can feed myself." She took a bite of fish in her fingers and glared at him.

Hades popped his bite into his own mouth.

"How do you know all these things?" she asked him. Persephone had always thought that her mother and her great-grandfather between them knew all there was to be known. Clearly she had been mistaken.

"I have been places," he said. "Not all places are Hellas."

"Tell me about them," she demanded.

Hades considered, eating fish as he thought. "In Mycenae there was a palace where they buried their dead wrapped in gold. They worshiped a scared snake and lived by the thousands in a city with houses five stories tall."

"What happened to them?" Persephone tried to imagine people like that. How had they made those houses stay up?

"They liked to make war. They besieged Ilium for ten years over a woman, and the war ruined them. War has a way of doing that. You who live in these islands and on the mainland now are their heirs."

"I've heard that story," Persephone said. "They must have been very stupid in that city. Who would believe that a giant wooden horse big enough to hide an army was a goodwill gift from an enemy?"

"People stupid enough to kidnap a king's wife and fight over her for ten years. They sacrificed their children after it was ended, to seal the peace. A thing like that lays a shadow on a land."

"What happened to all their gold?" Persephone wanted to know.

"It lies buried in the ground with their dead."

"Is that where you get yours?" No wonder the god of Death was rich, if people buried themselves wrapped in gold.

Hades looked indignant. "I am not a grave robber."

"Well then," Persephone said, plainly waiting for an answer.

"I have ships that go out to places you haven't seen. To India, for instance, where there are big cats, like lions, that are striped red and black. And monkeys."

"What are monkeys?" she wanted to know, distracted from the subject of gold.

He chuckled. "They are much like people. Like little hairy people, with tails. They have hands, and they throw things at each other."

"You should bring one back." Persephone wanted one immediately.

"I did. It got into the kitchen and opened all of Cook's stores and strewed flour everywhere, and ate the mussels he was keeping for dinner. Then it caught its tail on fire in a lamp and set the hangings alight before Lycippus dunked it in the pool in this chamber."

Persephone laughed, clapping her hand over her mouth. "Oh, I want to see it!"

"You can't. I sold it to a man who had sold me bad wine. For all I know the beast sank his ship."

She laughed again, and he thought he saw light pour from her face. It turned his heart over.

"Get me another," she said. She thought with glee of turning it loose in Bopis's kitchen. It would annoy her worse than Great-Grandfather chasing women.

"There are some creatures who should not live in houses," Hades said.

"I tried to keep a jackal pup once," she said.

"There. You see. I will get you anything else that you want."

Persephone thought for a long moment, more somber now. "I don't know what I want," she said finally. "I thought I did."

"And what did you think you wanted?"

"Just to go on as I had been. Playing in the woods. Running after my friends. But all my friends will get married."

"Aha."

She regarded him darkly. "I didn't say *I* wanted to." She breathed deeply, a long breath of the dank air, not quite dried by the fire in the hearth, not quite scented enough to mask the faint smell of mold. "But I miss the sun."

"I will give you all the lamps you want," Hades offered.

"Lamps are not the sun."

"What if you went back to the upper air," he said, "and nothing was the same? What if time slows here in these caves, and not in the upper air? What then?"

"Does it?" Fear ran down her back. What if her mother and everyone she knew were dead already?

"I don't know," he said finally. "It is different here. I know that. And I know this: Once when the world was young, everything was different sizes. Dogs as big as horses. Horses as small as cats. Their skeletons are buried in the earth. It happens sometimes that someone digs them up. I have seen them. If the animals can change, then anything can shift."

"Where are all those animals now? Do animal souls come here?" If her mother and her friends were dead, wouldn't she have seen *them* here? Was he hiding them? "Where do you keep the human souls?"

"I don't keep souls; it's not like putting them in jars. I don't know where souls go," Hades said. "That is as truthful an answer as I can give you."

"They must go somewhere."

"The Aegyptians actually do put theirs in jars, or they think they do," he said.

That didn't seem helpful as an answer, but the notion intrigued her. "Who are the Aegyptians?"

"They live to the east of here, not as far east as the people who make silk. They embalm their dead with spices so the bodies will never decay and store their internal organs in jars. One of their gods is a jackal, and one of their goddesses is a cat."

"How much of this are you making up?" Persephone demanded. It sounded like the nursery tales that Bopis used to tell her to frighten her as a child.

"Practically none." Hades smiled. "You have no idea how odd the world really is."

"What's in the West?" Persephone demanded.

"A great ocean. I have heard that there is another

land on the other side of it, but I have never had the courage to try to cross it."

What kind of ocean would halt Death? Persephone put out two careful fingers and laid them on the back of his hand.

"Seeing if I am alive?"

She jerked them back. He was much too able to read her thoughts. She returned her attention to the draughts board and extracted one of his men with a move that hadn't occurred to him.

Hades chuckled. "You seem to have won." He sounded appreciative. "Would you like to see the rest of my kingdom? I promise you I shan't let you get lost."

She stood up and looked him in the eye. "Are you really Death?" His hand had been quite warm.

"Your people think so."

Persephone considered that. "Not everything they think is true. That's what *I* think. About Mother, for instance—I think most of the things they think she can do happen because they think she can. Not all," she admitted.

Hades grinned at her conspiratorially. It was a nice smile, rather like the dog's, toothy but friendly. "I'm sure the falling-off part is among the ones that are true."

"No doubt," Persephone said. "Some things are." She looked up, as if she could see through the stone roof to the upper air, smell what was in the wind. "I don't quite understand how."

"No one does," Hades said. He was serious now, dark brows solemn. "It's all part of the dance. That's what they call it where the monkeys live. The dance of life, and death. It's all a great circle. It . . . carries things with it sometimes, from one world to another."

Persephone thought about that, thought that here beneath the earth they were in a different world from that of the air above them. The thought, circling around on the wheel he had spoken of, came to her, quite clearly: *Something is wrong up there.*

# V

### ❧

## *Bridal Feast*

Narcissa stood on a stool while Bopis and her mother arranged the yards and yards of pale veiling in which they were going to envelop and deliver her, a moth in a cocoon, to her husband. Echo thought she looked stunned, like a goat that someone had knocked in the head. Outside, torches went back and forth in the falling snow as guests gathered for the wedding.

"He's very rich," Bopis said, tweaking folds into place. "Such a good match, I told you, Irene, and how nice for the two of you to be married and live so close by, especially when Narcissa starts to have her babies. Of course *you're* too old for such a thing. Such a blessing Nicias already has children from his first wife, poor girl, and won't want more, but Narcissa has good big hips. She'll have easy babies—not like the trial I had when I was young. It was dreadful, but then I've always been so small. . . ."

Echo caught Narcissa's eye and winked at her, but

Narcissa didn't blink. Weaving the crown of olive leaves for Narcissa's head, Echo thought, *I'm not going to let any of the old biddies in the house with me when I'm about to get married. They're enough to scare anyone.* She wrinkled her nose at Bopis. Bopis's big cow eyes were damp with the emotion of the moment, or with relief at getting Irene married off, too, the next day. Bopis spent her life in a constant frenzy to run everything in the village and to keep Aristippus from straying. Echo had seen the old man with Clytie in the woods, just past the lower goat pasture. She had been feeding him grapes, the two of them bundled in one cloak. Clytie would go with anyone.

Echo was beginning to think that maybe being a slut was not such a bad idea. No one expected Clytie to get married. She could feed grapes to old men behind their wives' backs if she felt like it, and not if she didn't, which wasn't the case if you were married to the old man. Narcissa looked as if this was dawning on her, although at least Nicias's brother Phitias was young, no more than five-and-twenty.

Echo could hear flutes now, escorting Phitias through the gently falling snow to his bride. The snow really was beautiful, even if it was bad for the trees. Echo had heard that people in the mountains of the mainland, when caught in storms, often felt very warm and happy just before they died. Maybe this was like that. After the disaster of Tros and Harmonia's wedding—finally held after an extra sacrifice had been made to Hestia because of the snakes— everyone with an opinion on the matter had gone to talk to Demeter in her cold house, where she sat beside the unlit hearth looking as if she were made of snow herself.

Of course Echo hadn't been allowed to come—she was much too young and unimportant—but she had eavesdropped and watched from outside the window, nose plastered against the limestone sill. Demeter had offered no help, but had just huddled into herself, pouring her grief into the weather while lightning crackled over the gray water. Echo thought she had been out on the headland again; her hair was dark with rainwater.

"No good will come of it. I said so at the time!" Bopis's voice was shrill and vengeful.

"We were happy enough here before *you* came with that child and no father." That was Glaucus's eldest daughter.

"Hush!" Irene said, shocked.

"Things like this didn't happen then," Glaucus's daughter sniffed. "Strange weather coming from Hestia knows where."

"Hestia was quite clear about it," Aristippus said. "We are to retrieve that which is lost. And Demeter must make up her mind to help us."

"If Demeter wanted the girl back, she'd have had her by now, if you want my opinion," Bopis sniffed.

"No one does!" Demeter spun around on her seat, and they all gasped. She hadn't moved since they had come in. She narrowed her eyes at Bopis. "If I knew how to get her back, I'd have her by now, *Grandmother*."

"That's what we have come here to take counsel on," Aristippus said, stepping between Demeter and Bopis.

Echo thought for a moment that Demeter was going to launch herself at Bopis. She looked like a wildcat ready to spring. "It was *your* idea to send Echemus

down there," Demeter said to Aristippus. "*Your* idea,"
she said to Bopis, "and my girl went with us, and he
saw her! *You* tell me how to get her back. *You* go
down the cliff and knock on Death's door."

"Oooh yes, send Bopis!" Hermes said, crouching
under the window beside Echo. "Please!"

"What are you doing here?" Echo hissed.

"Same thing you're doing—eavesdropping. But old
Cow Eyes is right—this sort of thing never happened
before *she* came back."

"And how would you know?" Echo asked him
scornfully. "You were a baby."

"Mother remembers," Hermes said.

"I say she ought to leave," Bopis said from inside
the house. Her voice carried an awful satisfaction.
"My own granddaughter—I never thought I would
be forced to such a choice, but it's for the good of
all. If Demeter can't control the consequences of her
emotions, and everyone knows how vengeful a woman's rage is"— She glared at Aristippus—"Well then,
we have the children to think of."

There was a murmuring of cautious agreement inside. "Harmonia may be pregnant already. What if
something should mark the baby?"

"My aunt's cousin saw a snake once, and her
baby's teeth came in like fangs. They had to file
them down."

"I heard of a woman once who had a child with
three arms. She had eaten squid."

"*I* ate squid," Irene retorted, flapping her arms at
them. "My children are all normal. Have you lost
your minds? Demeter, they are fools, but you *must*
stop grieving so."

"Then bring me back my child," Demeter said softly.

Aristippus knelt in front of her, his white-bearded face near hers. In spite of his age, and lascivious nature, he was still the most powerful figure in the village. Any other old man would be a laughing-stock, Echo thought, but somehow women *wanted* to go with Aristippus. He bent close to Demeter, blue eyes grave under bushy white brows. "How, child? That's what we need to know."

Demeter's tears filled her eyes and spilled over onto her hands. "I don't know," she whispered. "Who can give orders to Death?"

"See now," Hermes said outside the window, in Echo's ear. "That's just the problem. No one knows how to get in there and out again. In is the easy part. It's the out, you know, that's hard. Better to send her on her way and let it be someone else's trouble."

Echo crouched under the window, glaring at him. "Then tell me, Most Clever, if Demeter is causing this awful weather, what will happen, do you think, if you *do* drive her out of the village? Do you really think it will just go and snow someplace else, wher-ever she goes? *I* think we'll have an earthquake if she gets any madder or sadder, and it won't be some-where else."

Hermes sniffed, adjusting the folds of his mantle where it had trailed in the mud and snow. "What a lot of worry over a girl who probably ran off with the man of her own accord," he said sulkily. "That one wasn't any better than she had to be. Any of the boys can tell you that."

Echo leaped on him, rolling him in the mud. "Take

it back! Yah, you coward! You said *you* could go and get her if you wanted to. I heard you!"

Hermes writhed in her grasp. His red hair was splotched with mud, and he spit dirt out of his mouth. "I did not. I said it would be a hero's task."

"And you said *you* were the hero! I heard you. At the grape pressing. So did Narcissa and Arachne! You said you would go and get her if Demeter would promise her to you! You goat's backside!" She took him by the ears and tried to pound his head in the snow.

"Ow!" Hermes howled and shoved her off him, twisting her wrist.

"You aren't any hero, you lying, braggy goat's prick! Go stick it in a knothole!" She swung at him and connected her fist with his ear.

Hermes howled and smacked her in the nose.

Multiple heads popped out of the window, with Aristippus at the center. "Silence! You are a disgrace!" He pointed at Hermes. "What are you doing?"

Hermes rubbed his ear. "She hit me."

Echo glared at him, her nose bleeding. "He's a liar! He bragged at the wine pressing that he could get Persephone back, and now he won't admit it."

"Are you five years old?" Echo's mother Doris pushed her head through the window next to Aristippus. "Fighting with boys?"

Aristippus raised an eyebrow at Hermes. "*Did* you say that?"

Hermes lied with agility and abandon to everyone else, but he found it hard, for some reason, to lie to Aristippus. "Well, sort of, Grandfather. Not exactly."

"Yes or no?"

"Well, in a way. Maybe. I said I thought it could be done."

"You said you would do it if Demeter promised you Persephone," Echo interrupted. "You thought you were safe, because you knew Persephone wouldn't have a braggy little prick like you if you were the last man on the island!"

"Echo!" Aristippus pointed his finger at her now. "Be quiet."

Echo subsided and packed a handful of snow against her bleeding nose. The argument inside seemed to have quieted, as well.

"Demeter has asked the proper question," Aristippus said when they were silent. "Who can give orders to Death? That is a question we must ask the gods, I think. And since it is Hestia who has told us we must seek our lost one, then we must also ask her how to do it. Demeter will ask, because it is her child." He looked her way, ignoring the two in the snow outside.

Echo crept to the window again and saw Demeter nod her head.

"And you will light a fire in here," he ordered.

"It won't do any good," Demeter whispered. "I have tried."

"Tchah!" Bopis sucked on a tooth and sent someone for a torch and dry kindling, but Demeter was right; it wouldn't light.

Aristippus scratched his head.

"Demeter." Irene knelt down by her. "You must let the fire kindle."

"It won't." Demeter shook her head. She was wrapped in furs in that icy house. "It never lights."

Echo wondered what it would be like to have that

kind of power, for things to happen just because you felt them. Blood from her nose dripped into the snow, making splotches like poppies. Maybe it wouldn't be a good thing. Who knew what would grow from your blood, for instance, if you were a person like that.

While Echo was thinking, her mother emerged from the house and took her by the arm, rolling her eyes. Doris dragged her away, and Echo stuck her tongue out at Hermes as they passed.

"Tomorrow," Doris said, "tomorrow, Demeter will go to ask the goddess what to do next, and there is no telling *what* she will say. You know how priestesses are when they're in a trance. Half the time you can't figure out what they mean; it's all riddles. Then there are two weddings to get ready for, if we don't all freeze, and you've spoiled your mantle with blood. Why did I have children?"

"To be a comfort in your old age," Echo said, and Doris snorted.

The next day Demeter went in the dawn light through the snow to the Temple of Hestia and offered a goat kid, cutting its throat herself in a spray of blood that showered over her feet. The temple was old, the oldest thing in the village, and dim and smoky with age and the fires of many sacrifices. Only the new thatch on the roof was clean. Hesperia shuffled up out of the chair in which she usually sat propped, and rolled her eyes back in her head.

They waited, breath held. Finally Hesperia opened her mouth. "You have asked an unlucky question," she told Demeter. "You must ask it again on an auspicious day. At the next dark of the moon you may ask."

That was all she would say, no matter how many

further questions they put to her. Echo privately suspected that the goddess—or Hesperia—wanted time to think about the matter. But the snow lessened then from a steady sleeting downpour to a light falling dust, which everyone decided was a good omen. The village turned its immediate attention to the weddings of Narcissa and her mother.

"Echo, I can't do it." Narcissa looked out at Echo from the leaves of the olive tree where they had hidden from Narcissa's mother in the blue dusk. The faint veil of snow drifted and caught in the leaves, powdering them white.

"We could run away to sea and be pirates," Echo said. It was their childhood game. Persephone had been the captain, Echo the first mate, and Narcissa the rich merchant sailing to the mainland to buy gold and fine clothes for his daughters at home. The pirates captured the merchant and sold him into slavery until he escaped, or ransomed himself with wine and figs.

"I would if I could," Narcissa said. "If I had known, I would have asked Dryope to take me with her. I could have been her servant and companion, and we could have had adventures." She sniffed dolefully. That had been their other game, in which they slew monsters and rescued lost heirs, who often proved to be themselves.

"Oh, Narcissa," Echo said miserably, "I'll come visit."

"If your husband will let you," Narcissa said. "Persephone's gone, and in a year they'll make you marry, too; then I'll never see either of you anymore."

Echo wrapped her mantle more tightly around her shoulders. It was cold in the snowy branches of the olive tree. She could hear Narcissa's mother calling. When the three of them had talked about getting married this summer, it hadn't seemed real—just something to speculate about in the meadow while the bees buzzed around their heads in the sun. Now Narcissa was actually going to be taken off by a man to his house. Echo was a country girl; she knew what would happen next. For herself, Echo thought that didn't sound so dreadful as long as you liked the man—the dogs and the goats obviously enjoyed it, and it must be fun or Clytie wouldn't do it—but she thought Narcissa was terrified.

"I can't do it," Narcissa said again. "I have nightmares about it. He puts his hands on me and he turns into a snake, or it's bigger than my arm, or something awful. I've thought about hiding a knife in my gown."

"No!" Echo said. "Narcissa, it won't be that bad. You can't!"

"It will be that bad," Narcissa said with conviction. "If I could just stay with you, maybe Persephone would come back, and it would be just the three of us again."

Echo blinked at her. "Narcissa, it doesn't work like that. Life doesn't."

"I asked Mother to give me to the goddess, so I wouldn't have to, but she said it's too late. I'm already betrothed, and we can't insult Phitias or Nicias, not if Mother is going to marry Nicias."

"Give you to the goddess?" She knew Narcissa meant Hestia; there wasn't any temple to Artemis on the island. Irene would need Narcissa's bride price, and a temple paid that when it took in a new virgin. "Oh, Narcissa, no. Look at poor old Hesperia. She's never been allowed to do anything in her life but sit in that temple while her joints stiffen."

"She's fed," Narcissa said. "She's respected. She doesn't have to go with men."

"Oh, darling, it won't be that bad." Echo scooted a bit down her branch and put her arms around Narcissa. "It won't be, and you'll have babies to take care of you when you're old."

Narcissa buried her face in Echo's shoulder and howled.

Now Echo watched Narcissa being made ready for her wedding and wondered if maybe it was going to be that bad, after all. The snow was still falling in a thin veil, and Narcissa's friends ducked in and out through it all morning, bringing presents: a mantle of deep scarlet wool woven with pale green acanthus leaves from Arachne; a bronze mirror with poppies around the edge from Echo; a bronze fillet for her hair from Demeter in Persephone's name. Clytie brought a painted clay box of dried figs and sweets, and Harmonia a carved wooden box holding a painted distaff and spindle. Irene gave her a cameo ring that had been her grandmother's, and Phitias sent a necklace of pearls. Everything that could be worn, she put on dutifully, looking like an advertisement at a merchant's stall. Bopis and Irene took the scarlet mantle and bronze fillet off again ("Another day, dear, they'll be lovely"), painted her lips and cheeks with rouge, and pronounced her ready.

Narcissa stepped down off her stool with Bopis holding the folds of her veil so that they kept their

careful arrangement. Beyond the hanging that
shielded Narcissa's preparations from the wedding
guests, Phitias waited by the hearth with his brother.
Echo could feel him there, and she thought Narcissa
could, too. Narcissa's hands shook, but the rest of
her was perfectly still.

"Come, dear." Bopis prodded her gently between
the shoulder blades. Narcissa threw a stricken look
at her mother and Echo.

"You look beautiful, darling. Everyone is waiting
for you." Irene took her hand and led her into the
outer room while Bopis held the hanging to one side.
On the threshold, Irene gave over Narcissa's hand
to Nicias, who as her own betrothed constituted the
family's only male relative. Nicias smiled and patted
Narcissa's fingers. Narcissa didn't move. He tugged
at her hand a bit. Narcissa took three steps to the
hearth where Phitias waited for her.

Phitias wasn't bad-looking, Echo thought, with a
handsome nose and stocky, muscular body. His
hands were nice, too, long-fingered and shapely. He
smiled at Narcissa who looked as if she couldn't see
him. She looked through the crowd of guests as if
they weren't there, either, as if she had just come to
stand by the hearth for no particular reason. A fire
blazed at its center, and coals glowed in bronze braziers in the corners of the room. Irene's house was
crowded with well-wishers. Nearly everyone in the village was there, those who couldn't fit into the house
standing patiently under a canopy outside the open
door. Echo saw Hermes leaning against the doorpost,
and she made a rude gesture at him when she
thought her mother wasn't looking.

Doris was looking and cuffed her gently behind the ear. "Do you want to bring bad luck to your friend's marriage?"

"I don't think I could make it worse," Echo whispered to her mother. "She doesn't want to do it. She told me last night she'd rather go to the goddess."

"She'll come around," Doris said with conviction. "Girls don't know what they want. Look at me. I wanted to marry a pig boy. Luckily for me, my parents had sense enough to give me to your father."

"We never see Father," Echo protested. "He's always on the other side of the island, selling goats." And drinking in the tavern there, but she didn't say that, since her mother already knew it.

"Well, then, see? We have a fine house and a good life here."

Echo wondered if her mother counted her father's absence as a factor in that equation. Probably. Maybe Phitias would go away and sell goats, and Narcissa would be able to breathe. Right now she looked as if she were suffocating.

"Hush now; they're starting," Doris said.

Nicias had killed a fine ram in honor of the occasion. He and Phitias laid the thigh bone on the hearth, and the elders asked for Hestia's blessing on the match.

Nicias said, "Grant to Phitias love and tenderness toward this young bride, that he may instruct her with understanding and kindness, and train her to be the guardian of his house and the mother of his children."

Irene said, "Give to Phitias and his bride long life and contentment in each other's company." For ei-

ther sex, marriage was as inevitable as being born
and dying. There wasn't anything you could do
about it, so you had best hope for contentment.

Phitias said, "I pledge to you dominion over all
my household and all my goods."

Narcissa said nothing. No one expected her to.

The wedding guests exploded in whoops and
cheers. Irene, Doris, and Bopis brought out plates of
sesame cakes and pitchers of bridal wine. Demeter
was not there, but they hadn't expected her to be,
and were all rather relieved that she wasn't. Bopis
poured a few drops of wine into a cup and spilled
them on the floor for the gods, then Nicias superin-
tended the mixing of the wine with water in silver
ewers (borrowed for the occasion from all households who possessed them), and cups were handed
round. Hermes took a tray of them outside to the
well-wishers waiting in the snow, and Echo followed
him with a plate of cakes.

"Yes, it was a lovely ceremony," he was saying to
Glaucus's youngest daughter. Funny how all three
were still called "Glaucus's daughters," Echo
thought. They were all older than dirt and widows
who were so cross no one would marry them, but
still they had to take their identity from a man. Echo
shrugged. It was the way it was. She threaded her
way through the fading afternoon light with cakes
and smiled and nodded while everyone told her how
happy Narcissa was going to be. She was afraid to
go back inside and see Narcissa herself with her frozen smile and blank eyes.

Nicias emerged and set pine-knot torches, kindled
from the bride's family hearth, into stands outside
the house, while accepting congratulations on his

own upcoming marriage. Inside, cakes and wine were consumed, and Irene and Bopis were getting Narcissa ready.

When they came out, Phitias had her arm linked firmly through his and was smiling proudly, unaware that his bride could have been carved out of wood for all the expression she showed. The village lined up behind them in procession, bearing the pine-flares, and, singing, set out for the house which Phitias had borrowed for the night. In the morning they would attend Nicias's wedding to Narcissa's mother, and the four of them would set out for Nicias's village on the other side of the mountain.

The procession halted outside the door, and the maidens of the village clustered around the bridal pair.

"Long life and many babies to Phitias and Narcissa," they sang, their voices blending sweetly in the smoky dusk. "Grow old together, keep each other safe."

Then Phitias opened the door, and they disappeared inside. Echo caught one last glimpse of Narcissa's pale face, her eyes blank.

In the morning they began the ritual all over again for Irene to wed Nicias. Narcissa stayed inside until afternoon, as befitted a bride married only the night before, but Echo paced in the square outside Phitias's door, hoping for a glimpse of her.

"She won't come out this morning," Hermes said, leering. "Got other things to do."

"You don't understand," Echo said, not even bothering to be angry at him.

Clytie giggled. "Narcissa likes girls," she said to Hermes.

"What?" Echo spun around to face her, fists balled.

"I'm not saying she ever *did* anything," Clytie said slyly. "But you know she never wanted to marry."

"Fine talk from you—you've done plenty," Echo said, "and you like *anything*!"

Hermes hooted. "Narcissa wanted to marry little freckled Echo, not Phitias. Phitias is too big and hairy for her!"

Echo turned on him. "If you say one more word about that, I will kill you while you are sleeping," she told him.

"Hold on! It was just a joke!" Hermes held his hands up. "No need to take offense."

"I mean it," Echo said. "Now, you go away from her house now, and don't get near her or her husband or his brother before they leave, do you hear me?" She stood as close to him as she could get, staring up at his surprised face, her jaw set.

After a moment, he backed away. "All right, you cat." He turned on his heel.

Echo turned to Clytie. "You, too."

"I didn't mean any harm," Clytie said.

"No, you're just stupid. Stupid and a slut!" Echo retorted, and stomped off, immediately ashamed of herself for having called Clytie names.

Narcissa emerged from the house in time for her mother's marriage. Her hair was pinned up like a married woman's, and her grave dark face oddly serene, as if she were somewhere quite unreachable behind it. Echo tried to talk to her. "How is it, being married?" she asked, because that was the question girls asked each other.

"He's kind," Narcissa said.

Echo let her breath out. "Then it's all right?"

"No. He's just kind."

"Harmonia says it gets better after a few weeks," Echo offered.

"Harmonia *wanted* Tros," Narcissa said. "That makes all the difference, I expect." She pulled her mantle over her head and went into her mother's house, leaving Echo in the street.

Irene was married to Nicias, in much the same fashion that Narcissa had been wed to Phitias. The torchlit procession sang them to Nicias's quarters, with somewhat less ceremony, and Narcissa disappeared back into Phitias's house. In the morning they all packed up their belongings and left for Nicias's village on the other side of the mountain, driving Irene's goats ahead of them. The house was rented out.

The weather stayed as contrary as a wild goat. At the dark of the moon just past the solstice in Skirophorion, on a day that Aristippus said Zeus had pronounced auspicious, he took Demeter to the Temple of Hestia again to consult the goddess.

The village went with them, trailing through the agora in a murmuring band, shivering in the cold wind that blew from the north. Echo and Doris bundled up and went, escorted by Echo's uncle Phaedon. The limestone and mud brick temple was icy, and the dark smoky walls smelled of old fires and wet ash. A stone statue of the goddess, blackened with smoke, stood at the rear beside her altar. The face, carved by the island's first refugees, was impenetrable. Hestia was both guardian mother of all households and virgin goddess, procreative power held in check and so doubly potent. The fire in the hearth, never allowed to go out, gave off a sullen red glow, the only light in the temple. Aristippus called out to Hesperia, and the old priestess, wrapped in fur rugs, emerged from her lair at the back. Echo, standing on tiptoe to see past Phaedon's shoulder, thought she looked like an insect, waving her thin arms at him.

"We have come to ask the goddess again the question we brought to her a month ago," Aristippus said respectfully, when the sacrifice had been made. Hestia's fire blazed brighter with the oily bones and the aromatic herbs that Bopis, elbowing Aristippus aside, strewed on it.

"Then let a woman ask it," Hesperia said. Her voice was a thin croak. "This is woman's business."

Demeter fell to her knees in front of the altar. She looked nearly as thin as Hesperia, her face stretched taut against her skull, as if the outer part of her was disappearing and soon all that would be left was her bones. "Mother, tell me how I may bring back my child." Her voice was a pleading whisper.

Hesperia sucked in her breath, making a low hum at the back of her throat. Her eyes rolled up. The smoke rose around her and the kneeling form of Demeter. She rocked back and forth on her heels until Echo thought she would fall over. Bopis seemed to think so, too—she stood with arms outstretched as if to catch her if she toppled.

"Hnnnn-nnnnh!" Hesperia opened her eyes wide. "The messenger shall be sent in the spring, to open the earth. Zeus will command it, and send him." Her eyes snapped up again, only the whites showing.

"What messenger, Mother?" Demeter asked her.

"He has already spoken," Hesperia rasped. "He has named his journey and his price." The whites of her eyes glistened, and her mouth opened and closed silently several more times. She crumpled abruptly, and Bopis just managed to catch her as she fell.

"Who has spoken?" Bopis asked her, but she didn't answer. A long snore came from her lips.

Echo slewed her head around, scanning the crowd. She knew who.

Demeter did, too. She rose slowly and pointed a finger at Hermes. He stood beside one of the limestone columns that held the temple roof, looking as if he rather wished he were inside it instead. "You," Demeter said, finger still pointing, "you will go and fetch my daughter."

"Why? Why am I to go?" Alarmed, Hermes swiveled his head around, as if seeking someone more suitable.

*Because you bragged you could, and you caught the gods' eye,* Echo thought. The gods' attention was never something you wanted.

"Because it is your task."

"Down there? With three-headed dogs?"

"You bear a message from Zeus," Aristippus said. "The dog will not hurt the messenger of the gods."

"I would feel better if the dog told me that," Hermes said. "You're the priest of Zeus. Why are you not to take the message?"

"I am old," Aristippus said.

"Aristippus is needed here," Bopis announced. The corollary was plain: *And we can do without you.* She laid Hesperia on a rug and beckoned Echo forward to fan her face.

"And how am I to make him give her back?" Hermes demanded.

"You are to tell him that Zeus commands it. He

will not refuse an order from Zeus when Zeus sends his own son to bring it."

Hermes looked as if he were willing now to argue his mother's version of his origins, but Aristippus held up a hand. "The gods have spoken. Zeus and the Great Mother have laid this on you. It is your fate."

Hermes looked at the new roof thatch, already beginning to darken, as if he might find some escape there, another hole perhaps, blown by Demeter's storm.

"You will be famous," Bopis told him, smiling proudly at her great-grandson. "Zeus will guide you." Maia, who had been silent until now, wailed suddenly and threw her mantle over her head. "Hush," Bopis said.

Hermes had gone white, but no one argued with the gods, and this pronouncement had been less ambiguous than most. He narrowed his eyes angrily at Demeter. "If you hadn't allowed her to run wild like a she-goat this wouldn't have happened. She should have been married two years ago to someone who could control her."

His voice was bitter, and Echo thought about how fine the line was between love and anger. Hermes might be faithless, but he had wanted Persephone since they were children. If he had her, he would still be faithless, but he would still want her. (She thought of Aristippus, who had fought four other men for Bopis in their youth, so it was said.) She knelt on the rug, waving the fan over Hesperia's face, and rubbed her hands. They were almost fleshless, like chicken feet. Behind her she could hear Demeter's angry voice, and Aristippus's soothing one.

"There was a price!" Hermes spat. "You needn't think I'm going to go down there without that."

"She is not going to marry," Demeter said flatly. "Not him, not you."

"Then there is no bargain. You heard the old woman. I named my journey and my price. No price, no journey."

"The gods have spoken, Demeter," Aristippus said.

Bopis nodded. "Indeed, and we must not ignore the gods when they speak, or be begrudging with the things they ask of us. Agamemnon gave his daughter Iphigenia to the gods when they asked it of him."

"That is a *story*!" Demeter spat.

Bopis looked horrified. "You will bring all their anger on us. Best that Hermes fetches her home and marries her. Then we'll have no more trouble with her."

Echo, patting Hesperia's cold hands, thought that unlikely. Persephone was trouble from the start, just like her mother. Some were victims of fate, like Narcissa, she thought. Some were the force that drove fate; that was Persephone. Some, like herself, just trundled along, making things suit them as best they could. Others, like Hermes, poked fate with a stick to see if it would bite them.

"I will make this bargain with you," she heard Demeter say to Hermes. "You shall have my daughter if you can find her and bring her home unscathed."

# VI

❧

# The Bull Dancers

"Something is the matter." Persephone said it again, insistently, as the thought coalesced in her head. Something above them, in the upper air, had gone wrong. They were walking down a corridor into Hades's mountain. Somehow she discovered that she had taken his arm. Cerberus paced beside them, drooling. "Something is the matter."

"What would you like? Anything within my command."

"No, something is wrong up there. On the earth. Where I come from."

Hades patted her hand. "Something is always wrong up there. That's why I find it so pleasant down here."

"No, something bad is the matter, and don't treat me as if I were six. Not if you plan to marry me."

"Then you are considering it?"

"I am not considering it. I am giving you advice on courtship. In case you abduct someone else."

"I doubt I shall try. Lycippus has convinced me that it was ill-advised, so I won't make a habit of it."

"Has Lycippus convinced you to let me go?"

"No."

She was beginning to think that he would, in a while, if she insisted on it. Knowing that made it easier to stay. Now that she was no longer afraid of him, every time she thought about leaving, she thought of all the things here that she hadn't seen, things she might not even know existed, or know about, like the monkey, if she left without seeing them. She ran her fingertips along the hurrying people carved into the walls, moving silently beside them. "Who made these?" she asked him, distracted from her own quest by theirs.

"A stone carver who stayed with me for a while, a very long time ago. His boat was wrecked on the shore here."

"Where did he go?"

"I don't know. He died, and we buried him."

Persephone thought of pursuing that story but she suspected she would get nowhere. Every time she asked Hades directly if he was Death, or ruled the dead, or had power over them somehow, he sidestepped. She didn't know what to make of his refusal to either reassure her or display his true nature. He seemed to be waiting for her to reach some conclusion of her own.

They came to a fork in the corridor, and he stopped. "I promised to show you my kingdom. What would you like to see?" he asked her.

"I want to see the chamber I found when I tried to run away. There were bones in it." She didn't

know why she had asked to see that. The bones were
the first things that had come into her head.

"Very well," he said, as if she had requested a tour
of the kitchen or his storehouses.

They turned down corridor after branching corridor, and the walls grew rough, as they had in her
earlier flight. Cerberus leaned against her thigh as
they went, in what she thought he took to be a reas-
suring gesture. It was like being leaned into by a
cow. She had given up refusing Hades's garments
and had even allowed Lycippus to throw her own
away. (He had bundled them into a neat pile with
just his fingertips and whisked them away, to some
fire, she suspected.) The silk gown rustled around
her feet, over new sandals of deep sea blue leather.
The mantle around her shoulders was wool against
the chill of the caves, but so finely woven that it
could have passed through a finger ring. A pattern
like waves was woven into its borders.

The oil lamps in their niches grew farther apart,
and Hades plucked one out and carried it to give
them more light. The painted octopus on its base
looked in the flicker as if it had coiled about his hand.

"I believe this is the chamber of which you spoke,"
he said quietly, stopping abruptly opposite a door
she hadn't expected. She must have approached it
from the opposite direction in her flight. The chamber was small, low-roofed in rough stone, and the
bones lay on a bier of stones and clay. Persephone
could just see faint traces of red paint on the clay
where age and dampness had not quite rotted it
away. The bones were those of a woman, she thought
from the shape of the hips, and she murmured a
quick prayer to the goddess for her. The head and

foot of the bier were coated with a dusting of powder, and some dark liquid had dripped to the floor below. Among the scattered bones she could see the glint of gold—a twisted collar, a finger ring slipped from separated phalanges.

"Who was she?" she whispered.

"I don't know," Hades answered her, and she thought he was telling the truth. "She has always been here."

"She is older than you?"

"Apparently so. She frightens Lycippus. He brings her offerings of meal and oil."

"Are there more?"

"No, she is alone. There were more chambers, but no one lived in them but her."

*You are Death*, Persephone thought. No one but Death would take up residence in a tomb. Again the feeling that something was wrong seeped through the stone to her from the earth above. A faint breath of air stirred, and she looked at the chamber ceiling and saw a shaft rising through the rock. There was no light, but she could feel the earth breathing through it.

She waited until they were out of the burial chamber before she asked him, "What is wrong up there? I know something is."

Hades took her arm again and tucked it into his, as if they were out for a stroll through the agora. "They are looking for you, I expect."

"Do you think it's Mother?"

"I wouldn't be surprised. Mother and whoever has been touched by her anger."

"What will they do?" Why was she asking him that? Did she *want* him to be prepared for a rescue?

"They will come after you," Hades said. "They will send a hero, I expect. It's traditional."

Persephone hadn't thought of that. She had assumed that Mother would come. If they sent a hero, then they would expect her to marry the hero. Rescued maidens always did. "Mother won't agree to that," she said firmly.

Hades chuckled. "Perhaps you should make your own plans, then."

When had anyone given her a chance to make her own plans? Mother had let her run wild, but forbidden her to marry. How long could you amuse yourself playing with wild animals and stringing daisy chains? But what did she want instead? To yearn like Harmonia over a village lad with rough hands and not much more between his ears than his goats had between theirs? To give herself to the goddess and grow old like Hesperia, alone with no one to talk to but the gods, who didn't speak often and made little conversation? To live like her mother, tending the garden and sleeping alone in a narrow bed, growing everything but children? None of those prospects seemed satisfactory. And in any case, if she chose Harmonia's life, where would she find her Tros? All the boys in her village, with the exception of Hermes, were afraid of her. Hermes really did want to marry her, she suspected darkly, and suspected also that no good would come of it. He was like fire in thatch, as greedy and unpredictable.

The thought flickered through her mind that here there was someone who knew things, who had plainly been across the world before he had settled, for reasons of his own fate, into these caves. Who owned wonders she hadn't even discovered yet.

Would Hades allow her to stay here if she wouldn't marry him? Would he settle for companionship, and leave her free to go to the upper earth and breathe when she felt the need?

He had an uncanny way of catching her thoughts out of the air. Now he said, "I have always felt sorry for her—the woman who lies on that bier—alone like that forever. I hope she didn't lie by herself in life."

"Show me where you live," Persephone said abruptly. A wave of loneliness seemed to wash from the burial chamber into the corridor and lap at her ankles. "Show me what you do all day."

"Really?" Hades smiled. She thought he was pleased.

They retraced their steps, with Cerberus padding beside them, branched at Hades's direction into a new corridor, and came to the central hall through which she had been dragged when she had first come. Braziers burned cheerfully in each corner, sending out gold pools of warmth. Cerberus flopped happily beside one, nearly tumbling it over. Among the bronze and marble statues, Persephone took note now of a desk littered with tablets of wax and clay, a stand in which rested a cithara whose frame was inlaid with bits of ivory, and elaborate silver lamps suspended from chains secured in the stone ceiling. The walls were dressed stone, hung with alternating painted panels and tapestries of the sea creatures of which her captor seemed so enamored—huge squid with beady eyes, bulbous-headed octopi, a school of dolphins. On the other hand, the wooden panels depicted scenes of the upper air—youths and maidens gamboling in the forest, a herd of fauns romping with a nymph, a field of flowers bright with the scarlet heads of poppies. Persephone didn't remember these. She went to them, staring, as if she could breathe in the scent of the flowers.

"I hope you like them," he said. "I had them done so you'd have a taste of home."

Had them done? Did he keep an artist on his staff? Along with the cook, the gardener, and who knew how many maids to clean? "How many people are here?" she asked him.

Hades looked a little embarrassed. "I don't quite know." He brightened. "Lycippus would," he offered.

Was he offering to make her mistress of a kingdom with so many servants he couldn't count them? What on earth would she do with them? Demeter had never kept so much as a maid. No one in the village except Glaucus's daughters did. It was considered the wife's job to do the work.

"Where do you get your food?" she demanded. "You can't live on the sheep people bring you."

"Well, one doesn't want to waste a good sheep."

"Someone fishes."

"True. I am fond of fish. I have always lived by the sea, one place or another."

There was always the faint scent of the sea in his caves, just as there was on her island above them. Hellas was born of the sea. But she had never seen work like the creatures that adorned nearly every piece of clay in his halls, from the lamp in his hand to her bathtub. "Is it one of your servants who paints these?" she asked him.

"No, these are old. They come from that place I told you of where they danced with bulls."

"You lived there?"

"For a little."

"And took much with you."

His lip twitched. "I have ships that sail out to trade with the world. There is a lot of the world, and many people's treasures are for sale in it."

Persephone sat down on a couch, which was spread with a woolen cloth and a fur blanket. "Tell me," she demanded. She pulled the fur over her feet and curled into the cushions.

"Tell you what? Tell you what is for sale?"

"Everything is for sale, I expect," she said. "Tell me about the world."

He sat on the end of her couch. "Is that what you want? Is that the thing that would make you stay? Not jewelry or silk dresses?"

"Maybe." Maybe it was. "Maybe I would just want to go and see these things myself."

"Maybe they are overrated."

"Not to someone who has never seen them. I should like to see those people dance with bulls."

"They are long gone. You can see pictures of them, painted on their walls."

Persephone's eyes roved over the room, looking for something to query him about. "Those." She pointed at the desk. "What are those?"

He rose and came back with a wax tablet and a stylus from the jumble on the desk. "For keeping records. So many jars of oil, so many bushels of wheat. See. . . . This is ten jars . . . and this is four oxen."

She watched while he inscribed a series of marks in the wax with the stylus, and she knew instantly that this was brilliant and important, a turning point, a new pattern in what he had called the dance of the world. At home people put stones in a bag to keep track of things. This would make all the difference. An idea like this could have been what made him rich.

"When you want to use it again," he said, "you melt the wax." He held the tablet over the lamp and smoothed the softened surface with the stylus. His marks disappeared, sinking rippleless into the wax.

"Let me try," Persephone demanded. "How did you think to do this?" This was an idea as magical as what her mother knew about the tree inside the seed.

"It isn't my personal invention," Hades said, handing her the tablet and stylus. "They used it at Knossos where they danced with bulls, and at Mycenae."

"Why do we not know about it?" Persephone made three squiggly scratches in the wax. "What does that mean?"

"Nothing. You have to learn the symbols first. That's why this way works better than just making a mark for each one when you have three thousand thirty-one cows."

"No one has that many cows."

"That was an example. Say you are a king and you do have all those cows. This means 'cow.' " He made a mark. "And this means 'three thousand thirty-one.' "

"And people have forgotten how to do this?" She remembered his saying that those cities had fallen to wars and pirates.

"In Hellas they have forgotten. Not elsewhere. There are many ways to write things down. This is just one of them."

She took the tablet back and copied his marks in the wax.

"If you want to keep a permanent record," he continued, since she seemed so interested, "you write it in soft clay and fire it. Then it will last."

"Teach me to do this." Was this how Mother had gained her knowledge? From a man who wanted to keep her? Was that why she was so determined that Persephone not marry? Had the price been too high? Persephone yearned to learn this anyway. This was power, the kind of power Mother had.

"All right," Hades said. "What do you want to keep track of?"

"I don't know. How many servants you have. And don't say you have to ask Lycippus."

"Very well. Fifty-one."

"Fifty-one servants." She handed him the tablet and stylus.

Hades made the marks, and she copied them.

Cerberus, bored, came away from his brazier and laid his huge head on her knee. "One dog."

"One dog." Hades inscribed him on the tablet.

Persephone copied it. She looked about the room. "Four braziers. Six marble boys with no clothes. One cithara."

Hades dutifully wrote them down. "This means 'none'" he said solemnly, "and this means 'clothes.'"

Persephone copied the marks. "One woman. One . . . What *are* you?" Maybe if she asked him, this time he would tell her.

"One woman," Hades said, incising the wax. "One man."

"Does that mean human man?"

"Are there other kinds?"

"Well, there are gods. My second cousin Hermes says *his* father is Zeus. Although we all think if he was, it must have been dark. Aunt Maia is no beauty."

"Oh, well, Zeus. He'll lie down with anyone. That's no test."

Persephone cocked her head to one side, to indicate that she was thinking that over. "If someone was a god—the god of Death, for instance—why would he need to steal women? Wouldn't there be lots of women just waiting to go off with him and have little godlets?"

"One would think so," Hades said.

"On the other hand, my aunt Maia insisted that Zeus met her in the woods in the form of a black bull and ravished her against her will. That's what Mother says she said."

"And was Mother ravished against her will, too?"

"I am beginning to suspect not," Persephone admitted. "I don't think anyone could manage it."

"I don't imagine so, if she can make it fall off afterward."

"I hadn't thought of that before, really," Persephone said. "It seems more complicated than I had expected." She poked at the wax with the stylus, making little circles with the tip.

"What does?"

"Being ravished. Or not ravished. Or seduced. Or however you want to look at it."

Hades took the tablet and stylus and set them on the floor. He propped himself on the other end of the couch, leaning on one elbow, hand in his dark hair. "Personally I have always found it unnervingly complicated. There is a deeply uncomfortable wisdom to be gained from one's forays into that realm."

"And are you wise?"

"Not yet. Perhaps I should have said knowledge, not wisdom."

She looked at him carefully. His eyes were friendly, the deep startling blue of seawater. She could see the dark shadow on his pale cheeks where he shaped his beard into a fashionable line. Dark hair curled over his forehead, twining around the silver fillet. He put his hand on her foot, fingers curling lightly around the instep. Her skin tingled. She wondered if it was possible to be seduced by your own body, rather than by someone else's; if simple longing for human contact was most of it. He was human, she was absolutely certain of that. Maybe something else, as well, in the same way that Maia's Zeus might have been a god and at the same time merely a red-haired man she felt disinclined to name.

"Come. I want to show you something." He stood and held out his hand, and on impulse she gave him hers. They went out through the door by which they had entered, accompanied by the dog, and took an unfamiliar corridor that sloped downward. At its end were two steps down and the smell of baking bread. There were no travelers carved on these walls, but instead the outlines of people kneading dough, measuring oil, frying fish, and a woman with a cleaver chasing a chicken.

A woman in a bloody apron (perhaps the model for the one on the wall) ducked out of a doorway, and seeing them, snatched the apron off and stuffed it behind her back.

"Good evening, Lord."

"Good evening, Scylla. We are on our way to see the gardens."

"Pomona will just be out watering, Lord."

"Where do you grow gardens?" Persephone demanded.

"You will see." Hades smiled, and seemed pleased with himself. Scylla stood at respectful attention, the bloody apron still bundled behind her back, as he led Persephone through the kitchens.

The other servants ceased their work and bowed their heads respectfully. A whisper followed their footsteps. *Master's young lady. Look at that hair! Will she stay? I heard she threw his necklace in the drain! She did; Lycippus sent Apis to fish it out again.* Persephone saw the dog poke his huge head into a bowl of meal. A girl in a flour-daubed tunic whacked him on the nose with a wooden spoon.

An elderly man with his head halfway into a clay oven popped it out again, bearing a loaf on a wooden paddle. "Would madam like to try a bite? Fresh from the oven." He tore off a piece and dipped it into a bowl of olive oil.

Persephone took it, holding it over her other hand so it wouldn't drip. It was hot and wonderful, the oil fresh and full of the scent of the olive groves her mother had planted. "This is fresh oil. You can't have olive trees down here!" she said to Hades.

"Wait," he said, smiling. He led her through the far end of the kitchen where a boy was cleaning squid, turning their long tubular bodies inside out with a practiced flick of his wrist. He tossed a head to the dog who caught it with a *clomp!* of jaws. Drying herbs hung from racks bolted to the ceiling, and a live chicken fussed on the floor underfoot, pecking at spilled grain.

"Get her back in the henhouse, please," Hades said as they passed.

Beyond the kitchen a door opened onto a court-yard bigger than Hades's great hall. To Persephone's amazement, light rained down on it, the brilliant blue white sun of the upper air, not the flickering yellow of oil lamps. At its center an ancient olive tree lifted limbs to the light, which she now saw came down a shaft in the rock. If she craned her head, she could see sky.

A woman with a watering can bustled around a raised bed of onions with a basket in her other hand. "It's been a mess, Lord," she said to Hades when she saw him. "Very peculiar weather up there, and snow of all things. I've had to tent all the vegetables, even down here."

"I'm afraid we're responsible for that," Hades said. "We are working on the problem."

"The fruit trees don't like it. You know the soil doesn't go very deep here, and they won't stand the stress."

Hades turned to Persephone. "My dear, this is Po-mona. She oversees the garden."

Persephone almost informed him tartly that she wasn't his dear, but it didn't seem civilized. Pomona had a nice face, broad and friendly. Her slightly froggy mouth stretched into a smile at the sight of Persephone. "I know your mother, of course," she said. "Or I know *of* her—she's done some excellent work with beans. We grow most of what we eat right here," she told Persephone. "We buy wheat, of course, and wine, and extra oil. But as you can see,

we have persuaded the apples, and the figs and
pomegranates to bear very nicely."

Persephone gawked about the courtyard, feeling
like the country cousin come to town for the fair to
see her first pig. Autumn vegetables grew in raised
beds—onions and garlic and purpley bronze cabbage
and yellow squash. The pomegranate tree was studded with round scarlet fruit, and two boys were picking apples, piling them into baskets.

"I thought perhaps you might like to come here,"
Hades said to her. "Perhaps it will assuage your
yearning for the upper air. I'll make sure you know
the way."

Persephone breathed in the apple smell, tinted
with garlic and onions from the basket in Pomona's
hand. Hades broke off a ripe pomegranate from the
tree and cracked it with his fingers, spilling a crescent
of ruby seeds, still embedded like jewels in their
membrane, into his palm. He pried a few from it
and ate them, and handed the rest of the piece to
Persephone. She picked six seeds delicately from the
membrane and put them in her mouth, staining fingers and lips. They were tart and sweet, and the tiny
seeds under the ruby flesh crunched between her
teeth.

Pomona, who had been watering cabbage seedlings, took her basket and can into the kitchen, leaving them alone, except for the hen who had escaped
the roost and now flew up into the branches of the
olive tree.

Hades offered the rest of the pomegranate to
Persephone.

"I would give you anything you asked for, if you
would stay with me," he said quietly.

Persephone looked around the garden. She could come here to smell the air and the apples any time she wanted to; he had said so. Why did that seem no less and no more interesting to her now than returning to her village? She took the split pomegranate and studied its chambered interior.

"Would you take me to see those pictures of the people who danced with bulls?" she asked him. "Would you take me there?"

"Away from here?"

"Yes," she said firmly. "Into the upper air, away from here. I won't try to run home. If I did I would never see anyone dance with bulls."

Hades leaned against the rough gray bark of the olive tree, apparently thinking. The tree was old and gnarled, far older than Demeter's grove. Persephone wondered if it was as old as the woman whose bones lay on the bier below them. She watched its leaves stir in the faint wind, the breath of the caves that whispered in the shaft, and waited to see what he would say.

He looked up finally. "The sea is rough this time of year."

"You said you would give me anything I asked for."

"Very well, then."

The boat was dark. It nearly disappeared against the night and the sea. Persephone watched as Lycippus, muttering, and six sailors loaded it with jars of water and boxes of provisions. Cerberus sat beside her on the sand, head against her knee. She was almost used to him now. His warm breath blew against her shins. The tide ran little strings of white foam along the dark rollers that rumbled in from the west.

She wasn't sure where on the island they were, or even if they were still on her island. Hades's caverns might be deep and long enough to reach under the sea to some other island for all she knew. The wind blew chill, in long whining gusts, and she wrapped herself in the heavy woolen mantle he had given her.

"Ready?" He was at her shoulder. "Are you still sure? It's a long voyage."

"I'm ready."

He took her arm and helped her into the boat, and the sailors pushed it out into the tide. Cerberus splashed after them and heaved himself over the bow. The tide was turning, and they set the mast and raised the sail, a dark splotch against the dark sky. The helmsman looked over his shoulder at Hades, and Hades nodded.

There was a shelter in the stern, enclosed on three sides and laid with carpets, hides, and pillows, which Persephone knew must be for her, but she sat on deck as long as she could stay awake, watching the dark water slip past the bow, and the slow wheel of the stars overhead. Just as for her mother, boats and the sea held no terrors for her. Hades stood in the stern, the wind whipping his beard and hair into damp wisps. She thought he was watching the water, but for what she didn't know. Once, as they slid past the last of the breakers rolling inland, he threw a handful of meal onto the water. The moon, a waxing half circle of silver like a cat's eye, slid into the water ahead of them, and the dark sail bellied full of wind.

There was something odd about Hades's boat. It seemed to cut straight through the water no matter which quarter the wind came from. When Persephone woke in the morning, stretching and yawning under the shelter of the deckhouse in the stern, they were out of sight of any coastline, plowing through blue water toward a blank horizon. Her eyes widened, but she didn't say anything. Nearly all the shipping in Hellas hugged the coastlines, clinging to the safety of known landfalls. She saw Charon, the helmsman, drop a lead line and inspect the sand that stuck to the wax embedded in its bottom core, when he had hauled it up again. What it signified, he didn't say, but he seemed satisfied and turned the tiller to angle the boat a bit more to the south.

Hades knelt beside her with a cup in his hand. "You are an admirable sailor," he commented.

"You said the sea would be rough," she said.

"It may yet, but perhaps certain quarters favor us. I've done my best to placate them." He handed her the cup of watered wine, and she drank. Two of the crew were cooking cakes in a pan over a charcoal brazier, and when they were done he brought her one. She ate it, hot and sticky with honey, with her fingers, and licked them clean. Hades presented her with a clay pot, and he and the crew politely turned their backs while she used it and flung the contents overboard. It occurred to her, not for the first time, how usefully men were constructed for such things as sea voyages. With any luck, she thought, counting fingers, she would not begin to bleed on this journey. In the caverns, Lycippus had tactfully presented her with a basket of clean rags and taken the soiled ones away to be washed.

The sun bounced a bright gray white winter light off the water, making her squint her eyes. "How far have we come?"

"With luck we'll make land tomorrow night," Hades said. He stood beside her, watching the horizon to the southwest.

"Storm coming, Lord," Charon said abruptly and they turned.

Lycippus, who was packing the kitchen gear, looked up to the northeast, the way they had come, and swore. There was just the faintest smudge along the horizon, but it darkened as they watched, and the wind picked up.

"Mother?" Persephone whispered.

"Maybe," Hades said. "But it's the time of year for it. We'll try to outrun it."

The sailors scurried to tie down the kitchen gear and everything else, stuffing Persephone's bedding of hides and cushions into boxes and roping them to the deck. (She wondered, watching them, where Hades had slept.) The dark clouds grew nearer, and the chop of the sea increased. She whispered, "Mother, leave us be. I'll come back, I promise," but the wind didn't abate.

"Come belowdecks." Hades took her arm and led her to the stairs that descended three steps to the lower deck. She had to crouch to duck beneath the low ceiling, and he motioned her to a bench where he wrapped her in more warm hides and braced her against the pitching of the ship. Cerberus thumped down the stairs after them and lay at her feet. It was dim, the only light coming from the stairs and the gaps between the planking of the upper deck. Above them she could hear the shouting of the crew and Lycippus cursing. He came belowdecks, too, abruptly, and sat looking furious, on the bench opposite them. Persephone thought Charon had ordered him below.

Hades stood, tucking the hides around her, and said to Lycippus, "Look after the lady." He climbed back up the stairs. Cerberus started to follow him, but he said, "Sit," in a voice that brooked no argument. Cerberus sat. The sky darkened quickly, throwing the chamber belowdecks into a charcoal gloom. Cerberus whined and stuck his head in Persephone's lap. She stroked his ears as the ship heaved from side to side.

They heard more shouting above deck, Hades's voice above the rest. The wind howled, and water spat through the gaps in the decking and sloshed down the stairs.

"Mother, don't!" Persephone said desperately, but she didn't think it was Demeter. There was a crack of thunder and a flash of light, then a downpour of rain. Someone above them slammed the trap down over the stairs, plunging them into near total darkness.

The boat plunged on through the storm, running before it, but it was like trying to flee from an oncoming arrow. They walloped from side to side in the waves while the wind howled around them. She heard Hades shout to the crew to take down the sail before it capsized them. What if he were washed overboard, she thought suddenly, desperately. She would be alone with these men of his who would blame her. She was sure they already thought she was responsible for the storm—she was half afraid herself that she was. She could hear Hades on deck bellowing at someone, or something, promising it something if it called off the storm. She couldn't make out all the words. Lycippus moaned and put his head in his hands.

Persephone tried again to talk to the sea. "Be still. I asked to take this voyage. I can't go back to Mother if you drown me. Or him. Be still."

Nothing outside heard her, or was willing to bargain if it did. The wind roared again, and she felt the ship shudder against its force. The trap slammed open, and Hades blundered down the steps, water streaming from his cloak. He grabbed her hand. "Tell it you come willingly!"

"I tried!" she gasped, staggering as he pulled her to her feet.

"Up here where it can see you. Up where the storm can see us!"

The trap banged shut behind them, and she followed him, slipping in the water that foamed across the deck, bending into the wind. A wave slapped them, and they both staggered. Hades gripped her more tightly. The deck dropped from under their feet, and they fell thrashing on the sloping planks. Hades pulled her upright, and they leaned together as they fought their way through the wind to the stern. Persephone leaned against the stern rail, gripping it tightly as the storm pulled at her and whipped her hair about her face.

"Tell it!" Hades shouted over the wind's roar. "Tell the sea!" His own hair was plastered to his head, and water sheeted from his beard.

"Let us be!" Persephone shouted into the storm. "This was my choice! Let us be! I swear I'll come home again!"

"You heard her!" Hades bellowed into the wind.

The wind seemed to circle them as if it was listening. It roared around the two of them on the deck while the helmsman and crew struggled with the tiller and the boat lurched in the waves. Hades gripped her to him tightly, hands clenched around her waist, feet braced against the heaving deck. She leaned into him, struggling to stay upright.

"She *chose!*" Hades shouted into the wind again.

Imperceptibly at first, the gale lessened. The ship righted slightly. "I *chose!*" Persephone shouted, echoing him.

The wind dropped further, and the black sky paled. The rain fell in a fine mist and then vanished entirely as the sun broke from the black clouds. The clouds retreated, leaving the sun to draw them westward.

For the rest of the voyage the sun shone and the sky was clear as obsidian at night, the stars winking bright against it. Persephone spread her rugs and furs out on the open deck where she could see in all directions and reclined, watching the stars. At the back of her mind was the knowledge that she had made a promise, maybe two contradictory promises, but she would worry about them later. For now the voyage filled her, and the anticipation of seeing what she thought of as "the world" excited her. Hades dragged his own sleeping gear from wherever he had been the night before and lay beside her, but never touched her. He just lay and watched the stars with her and listened to the murmur of the water parting beneath the keel and the creaking of the hemp ropes that stayed the sail. In the morning they sighted land.

"Crete," Hades said, leaning on the rail and pointing to the low hump that rose from the western horizon.

"Is that where they danced with the bulls?"

"Yes."

As they neared the coast, she could see huts along the shore, the antlike figures of people, and the dark curves of beached boats.

"We'll skirt the coast a bit," Hades said, "and make land a bit farther along. We may not be welcome if they know we come over seas."

Persephone hadn't thought of that. She had pictured a ruined palace empty of people, inhabited maybe by the scurryings of mice and rats, the bull dancers solemn and solitary in their paint. "There are people there?"

"They are ghosts of an old civilization," Hades said. "No place ever entirely empties. They live on the edge of what they once were, and camp in its ruins."

He brought the boat to shore around the curve of a headland where the sea washed onto a rocky inlet. The sailors dragged it up on the sand into the scrub that grew above the tideline and covered it over with cut brush. They left two to guard it, and the rest followed Hades and Persephone, with Lycippus in attendance. They were a little cavalcade of retainers escorting a merchant and his lady, so Hades said. Privately, Persephone thought his presence carried an aura that would unnerve any bandit enough to keep them safe. It wasn't anything she could put her finger on, no corpselike tinge of the Underworld seemed to follow him, and yet somehow he was a personage one would think twice about annoying. With that observation came the realization of the privileged place she occupied. After all, she had put his gifts down the drain and thrown an omelette at him.

The landscape was much like that of her island. The sky above them was a bright clear blue now, bouncing off the blue green of the sea and the white foam of the breakers that slid onto the rocky coast and rolled away again endlessly. They took a path up from the beach, which seemed unmarked and of which Hades seemed quite certain. On the headland above they found a road, a rough track rutted by wheels and the hooves of cattle. They followed it for a ways and then turned inland on a narrower, less used track. The way was rocky, and Persephone stumbled on the stones.

"Shall I find you a mount?" Hades asked her. "It isn't very far, but I can buy you something to ride in a village, I expect."

She shook her head. "I asked to come here. I can walk."

"As you wish." He didn't seem inclined to argue with her or to cosset her if she didn't demand it.

They stopped to eat in the shade of a plane tree, where a stream burbled by to provide them with water for the wine. Demeter's anger-fueled weather did not seem to have reached this far, and the hills were the normal verdant green of winter in Hellas. The day was mild and Persephone shed her woolen mantle and stretched her arms to the sun. When they had eaten, the servants packed up the bags and boxes of dried fruit and fish, bread and olives, and flasks of unwatered wine, and strapped them to their backs. They set out once more. At dusk they came to the ruins.

Seen from a distance, Knossos might have been the enchanted land of her nursery tales, Mt. Olympus where the gods had gone to live. What had been a single building covered more ground than her village twice over. Persephone gaped at the stone walls and tumbled stairways, now leading nowhere, that must once have reached the sky. "Men built this," she said, assuring herself that it must have been so.

"And men destroyed it," Hades added. "In the morning I will show you the bull-leapers, but you must stay close by me. It isn't entirely safe."

They camped for the night in a tent which Lycippus produced from somewhere in the baggage and pitched in the shadow of the ruins. Cerberus, Lycippus, and the crew slept outside under the stars, and Persephone didn't protest when Hades lay down beside her. As before, he made no move to touch her, but merely bundled himself in his rugs and began, she thought, to snore. She woke to a bright cool dawn and the sound of birdsong in the plane trees and the tamarisk branches.

"How can you live in caves when there is this to sleep under?" she asked Hades as he woke.

She hadn't really expected him to answer her, but after a long silence he said, "Men."

She raised her eyebrows at him, mocking his habitual gesture, and he laughed. "No one enters *my* domain who hasn't been invited." He stood and stretched. "Come. You wanted to see people dance with bulls."

When they had eaten, he led her toward a crumbled stair. A shadowy figure scuttled out of their way and vanished into a doorway. Persephone turned to follow its flight and noted that Lycippus was just behind them with a large sword in his hand. Cerberus, pacing beside them, bared his teeth.

"All ruins have their rats," Hades said. "You are

not to go gawking and get separated from me. The stones are unstable in places, as well."

The stair led upward to a wide hallway, its roof supported with red pillars. Many had cracks running down their length, and Hades walked carefully. He whistled Cerberus away from his investigation of a fallen cornice. The walls were painted with the sort of sea creatures that she had seen on lamps and pottery in his house. In the room beyond there were scenes of women dancing. The women's dresses left their breasts bare, and their wild black hair curled down their backs in ringlets. Their skirts were made in pleated tiers, one above the other, and even more startling, they carried snakes in their hands.

"They dance for the goddess," Hades said.

Persephone thought that looked considerably more interesting a form of worship than the rituals practiced by Hesperia in Hestia's temple. They went cautiously through a sagging doorway into yet another chamber. The walls here were also cracked, and she could see where ornaments and gilding had been pried from the pillars and the stone benches that lined one wall.

"There is nothing left but the paintings on the walls," Hades said. "No doubt they also would have been stolen if anyone could figure out how to do it."

Persephone raised her eyebrows at him, since that had worked the last time, and he laughed. A great many things in Hades's domain had come from here, she realized. The lord of Death, it seemed, gathered in dead civilizations as well.

"Here," he said. He led her past a row of red pillars, and there they were, leaping on the wall, the people who danced with bulls. Before her a red and white bull bent his head, huge horns pointing forward, and a pale girl caught them in her hands. You could see the way she was going to go, flipping heels over head, up over the horns to land on the bull's back, where a red-skinned boy danced on his hands. Behind the bull, another girl stood waiting to catch him.

What would that be like, Persephone wondered. To fly over the bull's horns, courting death, and land on his broad back. How wonderful a thing to be able to do, but why?

"For the gods," Hades said, as she stood gaping. "Or maybe just for sport. It's hard to say. Sometimes a thing is both."

She spent the rest of the day wandering wide-eyed through the palace of Knossos while Hades told her the legend of King Minos who had kept his court here, and of his miraculous monster, half-man, half-bull. The Minotaur was the child of his wife who had fallen in love with a bull, and he kept it chained in the labyrinthine corridors below them.

"Was it real?" she wanted to know. "Was there really such a thing?" It seemed possible after hearing of elephants and monkeys.

"I have never seen one," Hades said.

There were stories of gods taking animal form to court mortal maidens, but Persephone had always only half believed them, and in any case the resulting children were always human. Still, in a place like this, you never knew. She craned her neck, peering into the shadowy depths of the roof, where birds had begun to nest. As they passed a broken stairway, she saw the glint of water below them in a sunken pool, and a snake slithered past her feet.

"Soon they will own it," Hades said. "When man moves out, the creatures of the wild move in. They reclaim a place. It doesn't take very long."

On one wall a woman in a barebreasted dress stood crowned with a diadem and holding two snakes aloft, as if she offered this place to them. Persephone wouldn't have been surprised to see them slither from her fingers. The shadows lengthened, and she began to hurry, scrambling to see all that there was to be seen before the darkness fell. Hades had warned her that they would spend only a day here; to stay longer would attract undue attention from the watchers she already felt in the shadows. She and Hades had taken nothing away, which so far had given them free passage, but it wouldn't last. "Looters are quite territorial," he said, "and there are tombs beneath this place that have not yet been robbed, I imagine."

When they left, they passed through the chamber of the bull-leapers again. In the dusk the dancers moved on the walls as if alive in the flicker of Lycippus's torch. Persephone held her breath, watching them. She could feel how you would do it. The waiting for just the right moment in the bull's stride, balancing on the balls of the feet. The running start, no going back after that, the horns in your grip, the flip, the broad hot back under your palms, just for an instant, and then the flip down to the waiting catcher on the floor, the turn to catch the dancer coming after you. The sense of it ran through her like the spark off a cat's fur.

"What happened to them if they missed?"

They were sitting on a flat stone in the darkness,

watching as the moon washed the ruined walls. That thought had been in her mind.

"They died," Hades said. "Most likely. I think part of the dance was the risk of death."

Behind them the servants were putting away the kitchen gear, and chasing Cerberus out of the dirty pots. Lycippus busied himself fluffing blankets and pillows in their tent. Their homely bustle made a comforting counterpoint to the great bulk of the ruined castle and the vastness of the sky overhead. Persephone thought of the Minotaur, the wild cursed offspring of King Minos and his love-besotted wife, Pasiphaë, who had lusted after a bull. The arc of love was very wide, she thought, and as often as not it lay down in darkness.

She could feel Hades's warmth at her side, the slow intake and exhale of his breath. Whatever he was, he was alive, and her skin began to yearn toward his as the bull dancers had yearned toward the bull. There was some dark knowledge to be gained from him, and not just the awakening that came with binding your body to another's. It occurred to her that she had a knowledge he wanted, too, something he might have possessed once and lost in his caves after so many years. Might that make a man desperate enough to steal it? She put her hand on his, and she felt him freeze, as if he feared movement would frighten her off.

"Why did you steal me?" she asked him. "Truly?"

He was silent a long time. "I don't know," he said at length. "I thought I did. You were so beautiful; you have no idea. Like a little ball of light. I thought you would light the caverns."

"And did I?"

She thought maybe he smiled. "In your way. But you didn't want anything I could give you, and I didn't know you the way I thought I would. You were just some angry girl I had stolen, and I didn't know what to do with you. You weren't the woman I made up for myself when I watched you up on the headland."

"And now?"

"Now if you go away the caves will be darker than they were before you came."

"You could get a monkey," she suggested, and he laughed. His right hand closed over her fingers where they lay on his left. Her skin felt warm, cheeks flushed so that the cool air stung, and when he stood, she rose with him, hand in hand still, and went with him into the tent.

Hades closed the tent flap and stood waiting, she thought, to see what she would do. Persephone unpinned her gown at one shoulder and let it slide, thinking of the dancers who bared their breasts to dance for the goddess. Whatever it was she was doing, it was a dance of its own sort, a dance with the heart or some more insistent organ, the dance her mother had tried to shield her from. Had the mothers of those leaping figures told them not to dance with bulls? Had Pasiphaë's? She lay down on the blankets and the piled pillows, and when he lay down beside her he was naked, too.

"Are you sure?" he whispered. If she changed her mind, he would stop. She knew that. Hermes wouldn't have, but this man would.

"I'm sure." She hadn't known it until just that moment, but she was. All the mothers' warnings, all the fear of whatever ghosts followed him, even—for now—her yearning for the sun, rolled away on the murmur of the distant waves. The moonlight outside was bright enough to sift through the tent walls, and she could see him, a pale outline in the bed beside her. His skin was always milky, and now the moonlight tinted it with silver so that he looked like one of his statues.

He stroked his fingers down her throat to her breast. She turned to him, and they danced a very old dance, indeed.

# VII

❧

## Poppies and Centaurs

"The change in master is quite astounding." Lycippus beamed at Persephone in a congratulatory manner, and apparently waited for her to blush, which she declined to do. Hades stood whistling in the bow of the boat. The weather seemed to have taken on his mood, and the air was golden and balmy for midwinter. Persephone favored Lycippus with a grin and a snort of amusement.

"Is there anything which I may bring madam?" Lycippus inquired primly. Clearly he wasn't going to make any clearer reference to the goings-on in the tent the night before, and just as clearly he had been in full earshot. Persephone was under the impression that they had not been quiet.

"No, thank you," she said sweetly. *A magical messenger to explain things to my mother*, she thought. Mother hadn't mentioned to her that it was so much fun. Maybe that was why Mother had been so adamant that Persephone never marry, or even lie down with a man—Mother knew how much fun it was, and that had cost her something. Persephone still wondered what the price of her joy had been.

She joined Hades in the bow, and he broke off his whistling in midnote. "Are we going to sail into another storm?" she asked him. She wasn't sure what Mother was aware of by now, but she was fairly certain it was more than Persephone would care for.

"Oddly enough, I don't think so," Hades said. "Your mother will try other things, no doubt, but you made a free choice. She'll have to respect that."

"Why?" Persephone wasn't at all certain of that.

"It's the rules," Hades said, but he didn't elaborate.

The rules for what? For minor deities having congress with mortal girls? Or girls who slipped their mother's leash?

"We will invite your mother to visit us. That may soothe her feelings," Hades said.

Persephone swallowed. She had known this was going to come up. "I didn't say I would marry you," she said carefully.

"You slept with me!" he blurted, startled.

"I chose to. As you pointed out. It happens all the time in the upper air; I'm sure it must be the same everywhere."

He was standing next to her, and she felt his muscles tense, as if he had flinched, or braced himself for something. She thought, frightened, her stomach suddenly queasy, that he might actually love her, that he might have meant everything he had said.

"I will stay awhile," she said carefully, because anything else seemed cruel. It seemed to her that now she had the upper hand.

"I was about to say that I would have a door cut between your quarters and mine," he said. His voice was matter-of-fact; he might have been discussing buying grain with the cook. "The design of the inner chambers is a spiral. They are actually next to each other."

Persephone slipped her arm through his. "I would like that," she told him.

"Then you will stay?" He sounded puzzled.

"I will stay for a while," she told him. "I will yearn for the upper air eventually; you know that. And the kitchen garden won't be enough."

"I see."

"You don't see," she said, suddenly irritated. "I don't see, either. I don't know what I want, but I've never had the chance to decide for myself before." She didn't say that when you married someone, then you were stuck with them no matter what, as Dryope had been. Only death had freed Dryope, and she had had to launch herself on an unfamiliar wind to make her escape even so. Narcissa and Harmonia would doubtless be married by now. Could she go back to the upper air and ask them how it was? If they were sorry; if it had been worth it? How on earth did you know?

"How do *you* know?" she demanded of him. "How do *you* know you want me forever?"

"I am older than you," he said. "By rather a lot, I'm afraid."

That was normal in Persephone's world, and she said so.

"Not the best system, perhaps," he admitted. "Perhaps a couple ought to be wild and young together."

"And then when they discover they hate each

other, they're both unhappy," Persephone said darkly. "For longer, because he's young."

Hades laughed. She could feel his bunched muscles relax like a loosened bowstring. "You're a pessimist," he said, chuckling.

There was no question of locked doors now. Hades gave Cerberus some mysterious command, and the dog appeared at her doorway whenever she opened it, and padded silently at her side wherever she went. If she got lost she told him so, and he led her to familiar territory—usually the kitchens.

"That one has enough appetite for three heads," Scylla said, giving him the shank bone of something, which he retired into a corner to gnaw. They heard crunching sounds as he worried it.

"Do *you* know your way around everywhere down here?" Persephone asked, hoisting herself onto a stool to watch Scylla knead bread. She had got lost again and found herself, abruptly and unappetizingly, where the drains emptied into the sea.

"Mostly," Scylla said, slapping at the dough. "I've been here two years come this next equinox."

"How did you come here?" Surely he didn't have to kidnap his staff, as well. But where did he find them? Did he send a crier around the agora? *Come and work for the lord of the Dead. Excellent wages, quiet neighbors.*

"I was running away from my husband, the old swine," Scylla said. "He used to beat me and one day I couldn't take it anymore. I knocked him on the head with a stone quern and ran. Lycippus met me on the road. I don't know where *he* came from, or why he was on that road. I've never asked."

"Did you come by boat?"

"Oh yes, the strangest thing. We saw storm clouds in the distance, but whatever way the helmsman turned the tiller, the clouds just moved over somewhere else. We had a fair wind and no breath of bad weather the whole way."

No wonder people thought of the weather as a god, Persephone decided. It probably was.

In the next months she explored the whole of Hades's caverns, with Cerberus as her lifeline. He followed her anywhere, as she poked her nose into storerooms full of oil jars and sacks of meal, into chambers of ice where Hades apparently stored meat—the haunch of something huge hung from a hook in the ceiling—and into a little room where a man she had never seen before sat on a high stool before a table, tallying something. His table and the floor about him were stacked with wax tablets and sheets of soft clay in wooden frames. A shelf behind him held clay tablets already fired, their information frozen in them forever. Persephone could see nothing to count in the chamber with him. When she stopped in the doorway he looked at her over his tablet, stylus in hand, but didn't speak. She was afraid to ask him what he counted, for fear it would be souls, and fled.

After a while the corridor before her began to slant downward abruptly, and she could smell the sea. Cerberus woofed happily, following the brine scent. A set of stone steps went farther down, and she followed them. Cerberus was running before her now. At the foot he stopped and waited for her, tail wagging. The stone floor was damp now, and puddled with seawater past the steps. Persephone wondered if it flooded at high tide. There were no lamps, but a faint pale light shimmered on the stone. When the corridor bent abruptly she found its source: a bright flare of daylight and the sound of gulls squawking in the air outside. The opening was low, just high enough for the dog to squeeze through, and Persephone followed him, bending to wriggle through. Outside, the light was so bright she had to close her eyes. Cerberus barked again and darted forward to splash in the tide pool just beyond the cave mouth. Persephone waded into it after him and turned to look at the cliff. This entrance was so small no one would notice it, and it was clearly underwater at high tide. She could see the waterline and the seaweed that had caught on the jagged rocks just above the opening.

She played happily in the tide pool with the dog until the sun began to sink, and they retreated back into the caverns. She was sure Hades knew where she had been—she and the dog both stank of seaweed at dinner—but he didn't question her.

Another day, down a different passage she found a shaft opening to the surface above them. It lit a courtyard where a garden was planted with the same poppies that grew on the headland. The leaves had gone brown and flat, but the seedpods rustled in the air that whispered down the shaft. Hades himself was tending them, and he smiled when he saw her.

"If you like, I will teach you to use these," he said.

"What are they for?" She had always thought them useless except for their ephemeral beauty that withered by dusk when you picked them.

"Something your mother doesn't know. Another lost art, the art of sleep." He cupped the pod left at the stalk's end when the scarlet petals had fallen. The pod had been slit in several places, and he inspected the gummy juice that ran from the cuts. He smelled it and tasted it on the tip of his finger. "Not quite."

Hades knew so many things that Persephone had never heard of that she wondered sometimes if he made them up to keep her there. By day, or at least when the servants, who seemed to know, told her it was day, she explored the caverns. The only path she never tried to find now was the one that led to the beach where she had entered. If she found that, she would have to decide what to do about it. At night, in the chamber that now opened off Hades's own, she lay propped on one elbow in the feather bed and listened to his stories of other worlds where half-human creatures like centaurs roamed and faithful wives were turned into birds.

"Tell me a real story!" she said, annoyed at so many magical beings, and he laughed.

"Very well," he said, "I have seen your friend Narcissa whom you told me of."

"Narcissa! Where?" Persephone put her hand to her mouth. Was Narcissa dead? A horrible vision of Narcissa with a knife to her breast filled her mind, although she didn't know why.

"No. I am sorry if I frightened you. No, she is living with her husband on the north island—she married the younger brother of her mother's new husband." Persephone had told him stories in return for his, of her village. He had seemed as interested in their homely doings as she was in his tales of wonders.

"Why were you there?"

He was silent a moment. "I thought that if you

knew what was happening above, then you might not want so desperately to go there yourself. It is not a lovely place."

"Is she happy?"

"No."

"And you thought that a good tale to tell me?"

"No, I thought it truthful. Would you go back there and be the same?"

"I am not Narcissa."

"True enough. Your mother has promised you to your cousin Hermes if he can rescue you from me." His lip curled as if he didn't expect Hermes to offer him any trouble.

*"What?"*

"Indeed. I was there. The goddess spoke, and your mother acquiesced."

Persephone sat up in bed. "And you were there? They would have speared you on sight."

"As well they didn't get sight of me, then." Hades poured wine from a silver ewer into his cup and added a splash of water. He poured another for Persephone. "Shall we drink confusion to your cousin Hermes?"

Persephone drank indignantly. "I can't believe Mother agreed to that."

"Your mother wants you back. She loves you dearly."

"All mothers love their daughters," Persephone said rebelliously. "Then they marry them off. Mine was different."

"Perhaps your cousin seems the more palatable of two unpleasant choices," Hades said gently.

"And *you* are arguing her case for her?"

Hades chuckled. "No, I am considering the odds."

"Of what?"

"Of sending your cousin Hermes away with a flea in his ear without actually killing him, which would anger certain quarters."

Persephone folded her arms across her chest. "It wouldn't anger me. Mother! How could she agree to that?"

Hades blew out the lamp. "Think about it in the morning."

He was persuasive, or her body was easily persuaded; it amounted to much the same thing. Persephone gave herself over to new-found pleasures and refused to contemplate either Hermes or Demeter until daybreak. Narcissa, however, troubled her dreams when she finally slept.

In the morning she whistled up Cerberus, although she was fairly sure she didn't need him still, and went to sit among the poppies and think. He barked cheerfully as they set out, apparently hoping they would end in the kitchens again; when she came to the poppy garden he lay down to sleep on the cool stone that marked the paths between the rows, disappearing from sight in a rustle of drying poppy heads. Persephone sat on the bench in the middle of the garden, where Hades had laid his cutting knife while he told her what poppy juice could do. It had seemed to Persephone at first to be kin to death and had frightened her, but she had come to see that it gave a shorter sleep and the rest that let bodies heal, and she began to see what had happened to the people who had been brought to him living. She wondered if poppies offered the same balm to a restless mind, and Hades had said they did, but at a price. Now she accorded them a wary respect, but their beds were a place where she could sit and catch a breath of the upper air without the bustle and busyness of the kitchen.

Spring was coming up there. She could feel it by day, a green yearning in her veins, nearly as strong as the one that drew her to Hades by night. She thought she could hear her mother's voice on that current, a whisper of air down the shaft, saying, *You cannot stay. Come away. You cannot stay.* And Narcissa's whispering, *Go back; go back. I am lost; I am lost.* Persephone didn't know what to make of that; it was fainter than her mother's voice, and thin with some sadness Persephone didn't recognize. But her mother's voice grew stronger. If she stayed and Hermes came for her, she would have to marry him, which would be worse than marrying Hades. If she went back of her own will, she wouldn't have to have Hermes. It mattered when you chose something instead of letting it come for you. Hades had said so. Why should she have thought that she could keep this man and her freedom, too? Was that the lesson her mother had learned?

Persephone watched Hades as he slept that night, sleepless herself. Narcissa's voice had faded into a faint sad whisper, as her mother's grew louder and more insistent. *You cannot keep him,* her mother said. *You can never keep them. I know. Come away. Come away before Hermes finds you. I had to promise him.*

"Why did you have to promise him?" Persephone whispered urgently to the empty air.

*Promise him,* the whisper said. *Had to.*

"Mother!" Persephone crept from the bed and wrapped herself in her mantle. She wasn't sure whether she was actually talking to Demeter or to some ghost that moved through her chambers on the breath of the caverns. Nothing answered her. She paced the chamber while Hades slept, apparently oblivious for once. Her bare feet made no sound on the rugs, and she could hear Cerberus snoring in the next room. Lately she had had to whistle him up if she wanted his escort. If she slipped out now, she thought he wouldn't wake and come with her. She shed her mantle and pulled her gown over her head, pinning it with the old bronze pins she had worn when she came here. If she was leaving she would not take with her any of Hades's gifts besides the clothing she wore.

Persephone slid from the chamber into Hades's rooms next door. He had easily opened the wall between them, and she thought that doorway must always have been there, waiting for her to come through it. His chambers were dimly lit by a single oil lamp, as hers were, and she took this light, lest the absence of hers wake him. The walls in his chamber were painted black, and on one poppies grew, some in full bloom, some gone to seed, their crowned pods waving on slender stalks. Above them stars pricked the blackness so that the poppies seemed to have opened in the moonlight. On the opposite wall a silver river flowed through a dark valley, dark trees bending over it. A boat lay on the near shore as if it waited for a passenger.

Persephone padded silently past the poppies and the boat, her sandals in her hand, until she was in the corridor outside. She closed the door in a silent whisper, almost as faint as her mother's voice, and set out along it, pausing only to buckle her sandals. She knew the way now, she was nearly sure, and she became certain when she reached the journeyers on the walls. They hurried along in the opposite direction, set faces fixed on something Persephone couldn't see. One of them bore Echemus's face, Narcissa's father, or a visage very like his. Had he been there before? She began to hurry, half-afraid she would see someone else she knew, someone who should have been alive.

As she got closer to the cave mouth she became surer that she was going in the right direction. The scent of the sea came to her as it had in the corridor near the tide pool entrance. When she had first come she had smelled the sea everywhere in the caverns, but she had grown used to it over the months. Now only the sharp scent near the cave's entrances was noticeable. It was cold here, too, colder than it had been deeper inside where Hades kept braziers burning. A high thin wail, like a keening child, came to her ears, and a little cold wind stirred around her ankles. She began to wish she had brought her woolen mantle with her after all, but it was a long climb up to the headland, and easier without its enveloping folds.

The keening grew louder, and she knew it was the wind outside. A storm was brewing. She hurried along before she changed her mind, racing for the faint spill of daylight she could now see coming from the entrance. It must be just after dawn. The passage was wet at its lowest point, the water nearly to her ankles as she splashed through the opening, and the wind was wild even in the shelter of the overhang. It whistled and howled between the great boulders that littered the cave mouth, stirring the incoming tide to a froth.

"Mother! Stop it!" she hissed, but the wind paid no heed. Maybe it wasn't Mother this time. The water was cold around her ankles, and she pulled the hem of her gown up and tucked it in her sash. A little later, she thought, and she would have had to swim. She squeezed through the gap between the sentinel stones that guarded the caverns' true entrance and splashed into the oncoming tide, buffeted by the wind that threw her against the boulders. Spray rose from the breakers and blew in her face, stinging her eyes and half blinding her. She slipped, turning her ankle on a stone. The wind abated for a moment and she saw, crouching on hands and knees in the surf, the low rolling clouds that hid the sky and a wild white light between them.

Persephone staggered to her feet, wondering if she could climb the cliff in this wind. She couldn't go back. If she went back, she would not leave again. She wasn't sure why she knew this, but she was certain of it. Hermes would come for her, and he would be killed for his effort; the chain of blood debt his death would forge would link them all forever. She knew that, too. It had something to do with choices freely made or surrender forced. Whatever she did now would have repercussions, echoes that bounced back and forth through the caverns, and ripples that ran out across the surface of the sea forever.

She struggled through the rising surf, limping on her bad ankle. There was a crack of lightning over the sea and an answering boom of thunder. The rain sheeted down. She struggled clear of the cave mouth and turned to see the stunted trees on the headland above her bent nearly double in the wind. She could barely make out the path up the cliff. She ran for it, and another crack of lightning spun her around in her tracks. Beyond the wall of surf the sea roared, tossing something in its hand. Persephone halted, shading her eyes with her palm, shielding them from the stinging rain. A ship heaved on the water just beyond the inlet that guarded the cave mouth. It had no business here—there was no safe harbor to be found outside Hades's caverns. The bay where the fishing boats anchored was to the east, around the rocky shoulder of the island. This one was a stranger, or one of their own blown off course, but no fisherman of her village would have ventured out in a squall that must have been blowing up since before dawn. It had to be a stranger, come to trade with the village, making for shore to take on water, or lost, driven before the storm from some other place. Persephone struggled through the surf, pulling off her wet gown. She waved it over her head like a flag and shouted, trying to turn them back. The ship came on, driven before the wind. It would founder on the rocks in another moment if it had not already. This inlet was treacherous, fanged at high tide with sharp stones just below the waterline. While she watched, the ship shuddered on the rocks, and she saw the mast tilt as it snapped in two. She abandoned the sodden gown and dove into the surf.

# VIII

## The Men from the Sea

The water was cold and wild, but Persephone had grown up swimming in the waters off her island, in rough seas and calm. Demeter had taught her, saying only that one day she might need to know the way to speak to the waves. Persephone had never swum in seas as rough as this, but she knew the currents off this coast, and the sailors on that boat clearly did not. Sailors, oddly, often were not good swimmers because they had too much respect for the sea, as Echemus had said before he drowned, to meddle with it so intimately.

Persephone shivered as the wild water slapped her face and filled her mouth, but she kept swimming. All she could think was that those were her people, people of the upper air, and what good was her escape from the halls of the dead if she watched them go down into those icy caverns under the sea? She did stop to wonder if Poseidon, the sea god, who was held to be kin to Hades, had sent this storm.

Storms like this were thought to be his doing, when he felt inclined to exact tribute from the mortals who sailed on top of his waters. If so, there might be no saving them—what Poseidon wanted, he took. A wave rolled her under and spat her out again, coughing and gagging. She drew in enough air to shout "Stop it!" into the waves, in case it was Poseidon, his anger stirred by Hades's loss. There was no slackening of the wind or the current. She fought the water, keeping her eyes on the boat, half-hidden behind the sheeting rain and the tumbling breakers.

The wind blew something past her head, skimming the water, and she saw that it was a bird, a gull caught in the wind's fist, tumbling beak over tail. She could hear voices now, faint in the roar of the storm, shouting from the ship. She tried to call back to them, but the wind blew her own voice away and the sea filled her mouth with water.

The waves fought her as she swam, and the wind pulled and tossed her, driving her westward from the ship. She angled back through the roaring water and saw the ship's mast fall away entirely and the bow disappear in the storm. Only the stern, snagged on the fanged rocks, was visible now. Faintly she saw heads bobbing in the water, appearing and disappearing in the curtain of rain and blowing spray. She struggled toward them, her lungs burning. She could feel her feet beginning to numb in the icy sea. The waves caught her like a huge hand, shoving her down into the depths. She broke free and struggled upward again.

"Let me go!" she told it fiercely, gasping. Before her voyage with Hades it would never have occurred to her to speak to the storm or that it might listen;

but lately she had begun to think that it might all be one, weather and people and sea and earth, all breathing with one slow deep breath like the air that stirred in the caverns. "Let me have them!" she said to it, aloud, and a wave smacked her in the face and rolled her under again. She surfaced, spitting and furious. "They aren't yours!"

She had fought her way nearly to the ship. A face and arm broke from a wave before her, choking and flailing, eyes wide with terror. Persephone grabbed the arm around the wrist and hung on. The man thrashed in the water, fighting her or the storm, or both.

"Be still!" she screamed at him over the wind. "Lie still!" She caught him around the throat and began to take him with her, back through the waves. He flailed and thrashed in her grip and then when she shouted again in his ear, went still.

It was easier going back to the shore, even with the current pulling her westward, but she was gasping for breath when she felt sand under her feet. She tried to set the sailor upright, but his knees buckled and he began to slide away in the surf. She grabbed him by both arms and pulled him farther in, to where the water splashed around her calves. He was too heavy to lift, and so she dragged him by both arms to a ' rock, itself by now a third submerged, and pushed him up onto it. She turned him facedown so that the water in him would run out, and looked back at the surf. Another body struggled in the gray water just where the inlet's bottom dropped off into deeper seas. She glanced at the man on the rock. She thought he was breathing, barely. She set her shoulders and turned to the surf again.

*Too far*, a voice said in her head. *Too far, too cold. Too cold.* She ignored it, wading deeper into the surf and then diving through the waves that battered the shore. Even the stern of the ship was gone now. She scanned the sea for the face she had seen and found him again. The waves tossed him up and drew him under; she dove for the place she had seen him.

They surfaced together, face-to-face. He shrieked when she reached for him, as the other one had, as if she were a creature of the storm, come to pull him downward. She shouted at him, grabbed him by the hair, and tried to get her arm around his neck. He fought her and the waves thrust her downward. When she clawed her way to the surface her lungs burned and she struggled to draw breath. She couldn't see him. Another wave pushed her down, and she collided with something cold as a fish: a foot. She reached for it and pulled them both to the surface.

This time she got a grip on him and began to tow him to shore. She knew she was almost done. Her arms and legs felt like lead; her lungs hurt with every breath, and her feet and hands were numb. The shore seemed to recede as she swam toward it.

"You've taken the rest," she gasped. "Give me these!"

The storm seemed to slacken as if thinking about that. Then it redoubled its anger, slamming her down into the freezing water, pulling at her captive, trying to wrest him from her. The sailor began to fight her again, too, disoriented, certain that some creature of the depths had him in its toils.

"Stop!" she shouted at him. "Stop it! I'm trying to get you to shore!"

He wailed something that she thought might be a prayer. It was hard to say to whom. His accent was strange, but she thought the words were her own language.

Her right arm felt as if bone rubbed on bone when she lifted it, and her legs would barely kick. The shore and the entrance to the caverns looked ever more distant. She knew she was too numb to feel the cold when she thought that it would be so easy to stop now and to let the sea take them both. So easy just to float on the storm, light as a bird's feather. . . .

She saw herself in the surf with her mother. Demeter held Persephone under the arms, letting her find her place on the sea's breast. The water rolled under her, easy as a cow's gait. *Speak to the sea with respect,* Demeter said. *Don't fight it, and it will take you where you want to go.*

The shore was even farther away, she thought, sliding away from them as she swam. Speak to it. How did you speak to the sea except with your body? She swam on, pulling the drowned sailor with her. The shore was a high cliff of white stone with red flowers blooming at its top. It was a dark tumble of boulders where the octopus hid and reached out his long tentacles for wayfarers. It was a silver beach where a black river ran into the ground and a boat waited for them on its shore. The arm that stroked through the surf was all bones; she could see the separate finger bones like the bones of the woman on the bier. They were too thin to catch the water. She stroked again and kicked, and her face ran aground on the sand.

She lay with her head in the water, chin on the sand and the sea wrack buried and unearthed by the

storm, until she took a breath and choked on seawater. She lifted herself and saw the headland before
her veiled in rain, and the sailor facedown on his
rock. The water lapped at his feet, higher now. The
one she had brought in with her floated on the waves
beside her, her fingers tangled in his hair. She struggled to her feet, swaying as the wind buffeted her
and the current battered her legs. She lifted the second man from the water, heaving him up under his
arms, and pulled him to the rock. The cave mouth
was filling fast with the tide, and she knew this rock
to be underwater when the full tide was in. There
might be time to get the man she held through the
rising water and into the caverns, before the other
drowned. There probably wasn't, though. Neverthe-
less, she pulled the man to her again and began to
half drag, half float him through the swirling current.
He was inert now, and cold as ice. She wasn't even
sure he was alive.

Getting him through the narrow gap was hard. The
current tried to pull him from her grip, and his
shredded clothing snagged on the stones. Her
numbed fingers refused to close tightly, and he kept
slipping from their grasp. She tugged at him furi-
ously, unwilling to lose her prize at this juncture,
while the storm wind howling in the cave mouth
whipped her wet hair into her eyes and battered her
bare skin with blowing sand.

"Persephone!"

She heard her name shouted above the wind and
looked up to see Hades wading toward her from the
cavern. A wave buffeted her, trying to drag her out
into the sea, and he gripped her by the arms. "You've

gone mad! Come inside. You can run away from me some other time!"

"Help me with him!"

"Leave him! The water will fill the entrance in a few minutes!"

"No! And there is another on the rocks out there. Their ship went down in the inlet."

"And you went out to get them?" He took stock of her, naked and shivering, the drowned sailor still in her grasp, and his eyes widened with respect.

"Help me get them inside."

"They are the sea's," he shouted at her over the wind. "It won't let you have them. And I won't lose you in trying."

"They are mine," Persephone said flatly.

"And you are mine." He glared at her, the blowing spray soaking his hair and beard. "Even if you won't stay with me." He was still wearing the tunic he had slept in. It was soaked and plastered to his body. "I'm not going to lose you. Leave them!"

"No!" Persephone wrested the man free of the rocks and struggled to carry him past Hades's bulk, which guarded the narrow passage. The water was up to her waist now, and only Hades's grip kept them both from being pulled under by the current. A spar from the drowned ship tumbled by them, borne on the roaring current.

"Leave them before you drown!"

"I won't!"

"Leave them. This is the land of the dead, isn't it?"

She stopped struggling with the sailor and looked him in the eye. "Not if I am going to live here."

He paused. They eyed each other for a long moment, considering, and then he nodded. Persephone still clutched the inert sailor with frozen hands. Hades took him from her grip. "Lift his feet."

Persephone grabbed the man's feet as Hades's servants had once carried her, and they struggled through the rising water with him. It was waist high going through the wide entrance, and the lower passage was flooded, as well. The stone journeyers rose from the lapping water as if they were swimming. The two fought their way through and up the first sloping corridor until the floor was visible. The drowned man weighed more with every step.

"Here! Stop here!" Hades gasped. "The water never comes past here even in a storm."

They set the man down on the stone floor and Hades turned him on his face and began to press on his back. Water ran from the open mouth, but he didn't move. "Go and fetch Lycippus," Hades said. "Send him to me and get yourself dry and warm."

"There is another out there!" Persephone said urgently. "We have to get him."

Hades sighed. "The water will have taken him by now."

"No, it won't," she said stubbornly.

"Then this man may die if I leave him now. It is always a trade, and there is always a price. You decide."

"I'm going back for the one outside." She turned and started back through the lapping water in the corridor and he leaped up and followed her.

"I will get him. Go back."

"No. It will take both of us."

"You are the most aggravating woman I ever met. Who are these sailors to you?"

She shivered, wrapping bare arms against wet skin. "People from my world. And if I'm so aggravating what do you want with me?"

"I ask myself that." He turned and plunged through the water, which was rising rapidly.

She followed him. By the time they got to the entrance, they were swimming. The water was nearly to the roof. He looked at her, shaking the water from his eyes, held out his hand, and she took it. They dived through the opening and slipped underwater between the stones that narrowed the passage. Persephone followed Hades blindly. He seemed to know where he was going and she wondered, with the half of her mind at leisure to contemplate stray thoughts, if he had gone in and out this way at high tide before. Outside the cavern mouth they surfaced sputtering and saw the sailor miraculously still on his rock. The water licked his face, and the cold spray blew over him.

"If he isn't drowned now, he will be by the time we take him back through that," Hades said, pointing an arm above the water to the swells that rose and fell inside the cavern mouth. "And so will we."

"I want him," Persephone said stubbornly.

"Consider him a wedding present," Hades said, floating beside her. A strand of seaweed clung to his head. He heaved the man off his rock and into the water, keeping the head aloft as well as he could. "You take one arm," he said to Persephone. "We'll have to separate to get him past the rocks. When we get there, I'll go first, then turn and pull him through. You follow. Keep your hand on the rock so you remember which way you're going, and which way is up. I'll catch you as soon as you come through."

She nodded, and said to the silent sailor, "We're going under the water," unsure whether he could hear her at all. She had seen his chest rise and fall faintly when Hades had picked him up. "Hold your breath," she told him in case he could.

They each took an arm and dove, Persephone following Hades's lead through the boulders that guarded the entrance, mysterious and distorted under the water. The salt stung her eyes, and her bones felt like ice. At the narrow gap, she clung to the rocks while Hades went ahead. The man stuck between them, and she shoved at him desperately. His knees were bunched under his chin, pinned by the rocks. Her lungs started to burn. Hades motioned for her to go back and surface outside the cave, but she shook her head. He yanked violently at the man, putting his foot against the folded knees. They buckled and he floated through. Persephone felt her way after him and felt Hades's hand close around her wrist. He put the man's other hand in hers, and they swam for the entrance.

The water was all the way to the cavern roof now and had completely flooded the lower passage. It was as black as night inside the water-filled corridor. She tried to surface and bumped her head on the stone. The memory of Glaucus's grave passage filled her mind. She felt Hades's hand close over hers and pry loose her grip on the sailor's wrist. He had the sailor in one hand and her in the other, she thought, or at least she hoped he did, and she followed blindly. The freezing black water surrounded them and she knew she would be lost, drowned before she could feel her way to the surface, if she let go of

Hades's hand. The dark flooded passage was more terrifying than the open ocean had been.

She began to see things again in the darkness, white shimmery lights that she knew didn't exist, the headland oddly rising in the distance, a cow floating in the water ahead of them. Hades yanked hard on her wrist and she surfaced into the dim glow of the lamplit passage. She gasped, sucking in air.

The stone figures swam beside her, gradually rising from the black water. The sailor floated at the end of Hades's other arm, hair drifting like weeds around his face, gray as the stone people's. She paddled until she could stand on the floor of the corridor, and together they pulled the sailor from the water.

"Madam!" Lycippus bustled down the corridor from above and wrapped her in a blanket. He must have heard the commotion, or Cerberus had. The dog sniffed suspiciously at the inert forms on the corridor floor. "Madam will take her death from cold." Lycippus added another blanket, this one wrapped about her head so that she could barely see out. More servants pattered after him down the corridor. "Madam needs a hot bath," he said firmly. She was sure that the unspoken comment just beneath was that Madam needed to get her clothes on. She shivered violently, teeth chattering, thinking longingly of the bath, but she knelt to look at the sailors first. She wasn't sure either was breathing.

"Go away and get warm," Hades said, bending over them. "I'll throw them back in the water unless you do."

"Master knows what to do for them," Lycippus

said, tugging at her arm. She saw Scylla from the
kitchen standing amid the crowd, a flour-streaked
apron wrapped around her middle, and turned
toward a known face. Scylla held out her arms, and
Persephone went to her.

"Oh, you poor thing, you're cold as ice." Scylla
put a floury hand on Persephone's and looked
shocked. "We must get you warm right away.
Come along."

Persephone let Scylla lead her up the corridor to
her chamber, with a detour at the kitchen where
Scylla shouted for help. Four or five people came—
Persephone lost count—carrying buckets from the
hot pool to pour into her tub. When it was filled,
Scylla shooed them all out again, unwound Persephone from her blankets, and ordered her into it.
Scylla dumped a basket of some kind of herbs in
after her. The hot water felt blissful against her
clammy skin, but her teeth kept chattering.

"Whatever were you doing out in that storm?"
Scylla demanded. She wrapped a towel around her
hand and dragged a bronze brazier across the floor
from the bedchamber so that Persephone could feel
the heat from its coals.

"I was leaving," Persephone said.

"Leaving the master?"

"I thought I'd better." Persephone sighed. "They
are sending a hero after me."

"Oh dear, that's always bad," Scylla said.

"I know," Persephone said miserably. "Hades will
kill him, and then dreadful things will happen."

"Who is this hero?"

"My cousin Hermes."

"Oh dear," Scylla said again.

Persephone sank down in the tub so that only her eyes and nose showed, like a frog. The hot water made her sleepy. She would think about the hero later. Scylla sat with her until the water cooled and Persephone began to shiver again. Scylla held out a towel, and Persephone hauled herself from the tub into its folds. Scylla put a hand to her forehead. "You feel warm enough now. I'll make you some hot broth, though, to clear your lungs."

"I want to see them," Persephone said.

"Who, dear?"

"The men we brought back. Their ship broke up in the storm. On the rocks in the inlet."

"And you and the master went out after them?"

"I saw them when I was leaving."

"*You* went out after them? Alone?" Scylla's eyes widened.

"I only got two of them," Persephone said. "There were more, but the storm was bad." Her eyes closed. She was sleepy.

"Mercy!" Scylla eyed her shrewdly. "No wonder. . . . Well, then, you go and see them, they'll be in the infirmary. I'll have some broth sent along up there for you. Then I'll just get on with my baking." She bustled off, muttering, and Persephone thought regretfully that now the story would be all over the caverns by nightfall, no doubt embellished with fanciful detail.

By the time she got to the infirmary it was clear that the tale had made its rounds without waiting. The servants stepped aside for her as if she had been Hades.

Lamps lit the walls of the dim chamber where the sick of Hades's kingdom were treated, and where, she had learned, he took those left at his gates. The shreds of the drowned men's wet clothing had been stripped off and they lay wrapped in blankets, their beds circled by braziers for warmth. She could hear a faint rattling breath from one, the younger of the two, an olive-skinned, dark-haired boy who looked not much older than she was. She could see that the other one, older, had pale hair, nearly colorless now that it was dry, and his skin looked as though it should have been pink. Just now it was ashen. They were foreign, she thought, from the way their beards were trimmed, but oddly matched as ships' crews often were.

"Where are they from?" she whispered to Hades, who sat on a stool between the beds.

"North of here, I think. Neither of them is right in the head." He looked at her. "Are you warm? Does your chest hurt? Are you still shaking?"

"No, and no, and no," she said. She yawned.

He looked relieved. "If you begin to cough, you must tell me."

She drew up another stool and sat beside him.

"You won't make them better by watching them," he told her.

"Tell me what you have done with them." She felt proprietary about them somehow. They were hers.

"Very well. We have held them upside down and beat them on the back and drained as much water from them as we could. We have put them to bed in warm sheets. We have boiled mullein and propped them up to inhale the vapors. We have given them both a dose of poppy syrup to bring sleep and ease their pain."

"Will they live?"

"That I do not know. You can pray for them if you think it makes a difference."

Persephone wasn't certain who might answer her prayer. Hestia had apparently ordered her brought home, and Great-Grandfather Aristippus was a priest of Zeus, and so must certainly have that god's ear. And what would the sun god Apollo care for pleas from someone living beneath the earth where his light never came?

"They will heal themselves or they will not," Hades said. "That has been my experience." He looked weary. He too was bundled in dry clothes, an extra cloak about his shoulders.

"But you help them heal somehow. Isn't that why people bring their desperate ones to you?"

"I only offer them sleep and what little knowledge of healing we possess. We are ignorant, my dear."

If Hades considered himself ignorant, she wondered if anything could be known for certain. Maybe that didn't matter. Maybe things could be believed into being. She looked at the younger man, whose breath rattled in his chest. His lips were blistered from the salt water and he had sores around his mouth. "We don't know their names," she said. "How can I pray for them if they have no names?"

"Name them, then," Hades said. "They are yours."

She hadn't thought of that. Maybe naming them would bind them to her, keep them living. "Then I will call him Ceyx," she said, for the drowned husband of Hades's tale, who with his wife had become a bird nesting on the open sea.

"And the other?" Hades looked indulgent, as if she were naming puppies.

"Oceanus," she said.

"Excellent choice. And what will you do with them if they live?"

"Set them free, I suppose. My village will take them in."

Hades raised an eyebrow. "All that trouble and you don't plan to keep them?"

"You have no slaves here. You said so."

"True. And I should be grateful to them, since they brought you to me again."

Lycippus and the other servants moved a tactful distance away. Persephone looked at her hands, folded in her lap, the fingers twisting at her gown. "I have lost the silk gown you gave me," she said.

"There are more."

"And the blue sandals."

"The sea nymphs will like them." He smiled and took her hand. "We will go out in a boat someday and see them combing their hair in the waves, wearing your clothes."

"I didn't really want to leave you," she whispered, "but if they've sent Hermes for me, he will make dreadful trouble."

"Heroes always do," he said.

"Hermes is worse. I don't know how to explain it. Things happen when he's around. Balls fly into hornets' nests. Soup boils over and scalds someone. If you kill him—"

"I have no intention of killing him. Inconveniencing him, perhaps."

"I'm not sure that will be enough," she said sleepily. "People like Hermes seem to need . . ."

"Forceful measures?"

She nodded, yawning. Suddenly she was as sleepy now as if he had fed her poppy syrup, as well.

Hades snapped his fingers for Lycippus. "Escort madam to her chamber," he said. He helped her to her feet. "Go, my dear. You are worn out and you will take sick if you don't sleep."

"What about Hermes?"

"Hermes is nowhere about at the moment, unless he has been washed out to sea, a development earnestly to be wished."

Persephone nodded sleepily. The water would keep him out for a while. Long enough to sleep. She was so sleepy. She let Lycippus take her elbow and guide her down the corridors to her chamber. She yawned again and fell into the bed she had left that morning. The blankets were in a heap on the floor as if Hades had put them off all at once when he saw she was gone. Lycippus drew them up over her and blew out all but one lamp, in a high niche where its flame made a little pool of gold on the wall, its light blowing through painted anemones. Persephone wasn't certain where those had come from. They had just appeared one day, after their return from Knossos, the colors still wet. Hades had a way of thinking of things she might like and providing them. She had considered asking him for bull dancers on her wall, but had thought better of it. The bull dance had been some kind of offering, and it still held power. It wasn't just something to decorate your house. She would be content with anemones, and with his other small gifts from the outer world— sailors for instance.

She slept deeply and when she woke, there was a tray of fruit and cold fish beside the bed, with a pitcher of sweet wine. Persephone sat up, rubbing her eyes. They stung and her hair was sticky with salt. She stood, yawning, rotating her arms to ease the stiffness from them. At her first step, a small maidservant popped in from the outer chamber and a moment later another parade passed her, bound for the bathchamber with more buckets.

"Scylla said madam would want to wash her hair," the maidservant said. "Shall I help?"

"No," Persephone yawned. "No, I will be all right by myself, but tell Scylla thank you."

*I could have a lady's maid*, she thought as she bent over the tub, drowning her hair in warm water. *Someone to dress my hair and buckle my sandals and bring me things. I could be utterly useless. I mustn't let him do that.* She worked soap into the stiff strands, and thought, *And if I stay here, what will I do instead? Besides be his wife?* She couldn't imagine. Hades's wife had no work to do. The distaff and the loom had been only for her amusement, to play at work, should she wish to. She poured a pitcher of clean water over her hair. *And if I went home, what would I do?* She saw herself there—endlessly a child, frolicking on the headland, braiding anemones into garlands to wear in her graying hair—and shivered.

She toweled her hair dry and pinned it into a knot at the back of her neck with the silver pins that had just appeared one morning on her dressing table. *I will ask him for something practical now*, she thought firmly. *Before he brings me a troop of jugglers or a dancing sheep.*

He was still in the infirmary, brewing some kind of potion in a clay beaker that sat on bronze legs over one of the braziers. He tasted it carefully with the tip of the stick he had used to stir it.

"Ah!" He put the stick back in the beaker when

he saw her and came to meet her. "Are you better, my dear?"

She smiled at him. "I am awake at all events. Have you been here this whole time? Are they better?"

"Yes, and no," he said, turning to the beds. "Your Oceanus is breathing somewhat more easily, but Ceyx is feverish."

"And is there nothing to be done for that?"

"Willow, which I have tried."

She looked down at them dubiously. "I have never tried to heal anything but sick goats. Will you teach me?"

"It's much the same in some ways. Except that goats rarely fall in the water." He sat down on the stool beside Ceyx and motioned her forward.

She dragged another up beside his and sat. "I am beginning to think I shouldn't have called him for a drowned man," she whispered. "Maybe he wouldn't like being a bird. I don't suppose he will turn to one, either, if he dies."

"If he dies, it won't be because of his name."

"Names are powerful." They both knew that. When you named a thing you called it, in one way or another. Bound it, perhaps to some fate that you didn't know about, but the name did.

Ceyx's breath came harshly from his throat with a thin whine behind it that was the air trying to get out through too narrow a passage. Persephone took one of his hands in hers, while Hades watched her gravely.

"He's young," he said. "Have you fallen in love?"

Persephone shook her head. "No." She turned to Hades. "Not with him."

"Then why do you weep for him?" Her cheeks were wet with tears.

"Because I can't make him stay with me. I felt the same about the jackal pup."

Hades nodded. "I will teach you about the poppies. They don't always work, but when they don't, they ease the passing. This one"—he gestured at Ceyx—"will reach the crisis soon. Do you want to stay?"

"I will stay." If she was going to live in Death's kingdom, best she become acquainted with it.

Ceyx died on the breath of the morning tide—so said Lycippus; Persephone had no way to see outside—so perhaps he was well named after all. She imagined his spirit as a small feathered bird, borne aloft on the coast wind. Was there a mate waiting for him somewhere, by the hearth on some other island? And what would she think when the brown bird landed on her sill?

They wrapped his body in the sheet, and Lycippus and another took him away to the realm of the woman on the red bier. Persephone saw that Lycippus carried oil and a bag of meal.

In the other bed, Oceanus lay quietly, his breath a whisper, but his color was better; he looked less as if he had been sculpted of white marble. He had a deep wound in one thigh, ripped into his flesh by his dying ship, no doubt. Awake, it would have pained him greatly, but he slept on under his blanket of poppies. Hades and Lycippus had dressed the wound with honey, and she could see that it was less inflamed than before.

Hades stood, stretching. "After sickroom air, it is a good thing to breathe fresh. Come and I will show you how to use the poppies."

He took her first to the garden. Before they had

reached the courtyard where the poppies grew she could smell the clean air that whistled down the shaft, and the faint scent of salt hanging in it. Daylight spilled through the arched door that opened on the poppy beds, white and clean as sea foam. She took a deep breath and heard Hades do the same.

Even this far down the shaft, the new leaves were wet with dew. There were no flowers yet, only the bristly young green of the new season, and the occasional dry stalk of last year's stems. The poppy heads of last year had all been gathered. Hades knelt and brushed his fingers against soft, hairy leaves beginning to push from the soil. "These will bloom in a month," he said, "just like the ones that grow wild above. That's where I dug the ancestors of these."

She nodded, kneeling beside him.

"When the petals fall, the seedpods form, and they are what make the poppy juice. You saw me in the winter tending them. You make small slits in the pods and the juice runs from them and thickens. That is what makes the drug. I'll show you how that's done." He took her arm, and they wound their way back through the corridors to the infirmary.

Hades had his apothecary in a room adjoining the sickbeds. One wall was lined with shelves laden with clay pots and beakers, and spoons for measuring. On the opposite one, another field of poppies bloomed. They bent their heads seductively in an invisible breeze. A large brazier heated the room, and a smaller one sat on a table for heating potions. Persephone stood gazing about the chamber, wondering what was in each jar and pot. There were too many to count.

"The tricky part," Hades was saying, "is that each

year's crop is different. One must guess at the strength, and too much is dangerous. If you give them too much they never wake at all."

Persephone left off contemplating the pots as a new thought occurred to her. "Have you ever done that?"

"Done what?"

She thought he was deliberately misunderstanding her. "Given someone too much?"

He was silent for a moment. "A hopeless case, you mean?"

"Yes."

He was silent again. Finally, he said, "No."

So he had done that. Mercy on the wings of sleep.

Hades turned toward the sickroom. "Let us look at your remaining jackal pup."

Oceanus's eyes opened at their footsteps. He saw Hades first and breathed through parched lips, "Water." His accent was odd but understandable.

Persephone fetched a cup and poured it full from the ewer on the table against the wall. She bent over him and he screamed. The cup flew from her hands as she retreated.

"The Nereid!"

Persephone picked up the shards of the broken cup. "I am not a nereid," she said to him shortly.

"Don't let her take me!" he implored Hades. His eyes were wild with fear.

"I will protect you," Hades said solemnly, and Persephone glared at him as she filled another cup. Nereids were sea nymphs, who lived in the depths and rode the waves on dolphins. They were often kind to sailors, but took the drowned ones to their underwater kingdom to live. Apparently this one went in fear of such a briny courtship.

"She came for me, in the storm," he whispered. "I felt her take me by the hair."

"Then how do you know you aren't underwater already?" Persephone asked him crossly as she held the cup to his trembling lips.

Oceanus wailed and tried to bat the cup away.

"Be still! You aren't underwater, and I am not a Nereid. Look—no fins!" She held her sandaled foot out for him to inspect.

"Look for seaweed in her hair," Hades suggested solemnly. "It's a sure sign."

Persephone caught his eye and burst into laughter. Oceanus looked dubiously from one to the other.

"We found you in the storm, sailor," Hades said. "My wife braved the waves to rescue you."

"Am I the only one?" he whispered.

"The only one who lived."

He closed his eyes. "This island was always cursed."

Persephone studied him curiously. "Where are you from?"

"Eleusis." When he opened his eyes, they were a bright pale blue. They fixed on her with apprehension. "The other one came from here," he said.

"What other one?"

"The witch."

Persephone carefully set down the cup, from which he had finally been persuaded to drink. "The witch?" she asked him.

"I found a witch on these shores once. I was mending my boat and she came up out of the surf and threw an enchantment over me so that I took her away with me."

"Oh?" There was a quiet, thoughtful silence as Persephone busied herself with straightening his blanket and fluffing the pillow behind his head. "Sit up a bit for me—just so—there, that's better. What happened then, when you took her home with you?"

"She set an ill spell on my brother with her wiles, and he burned to death. Then she bore me a child, a useless girl. I was going to expose it, but she fled in the night and took the child with her. She stole my best boat," he added, aggrieved.

*Mother!* Persephone thought. It must be. "Men like that," Mother had always said dismissively. Men with a practiced explanation for everything that befell them, none of it their own fault. How often had a man like that found a woman somewhere and molded her in his head to his own liking, only to find that she was nothing like that in reality? Persephone slipped a glance at Hades. Hades had done that and seen the folly in it. That might be rare. More to the point now, how often had a woman done the same, and found herself trapped? Persephone could tell that this one had been handsome in his youth. His pale hair looked as if it has once been bright as hers. She could still see glints of gold among the white strands. Had Demeter yearned, as Persephone had, for knowledge beyond her own shores, and had the misfortune to look for it in this sailor? Persephone was conscious of Hades watching her astutely. She patted Oceanus benevolently on his forehead. "There, you'll need to rest now. I'll send someone with broth for you to drink."

"You know something your jackal cub does not," Hades said when they had left the sickroom.

"Maybe." Persephone was reluctant to say it aloud.

"I could hazard a guess," Hades offered.

Of course he would have heard the old gossip. He seemed uncannily able to come and go about the village unseen. "I am not certain of it," she said, but she was.

"What will you do with him now?" he asked.

"Give him to Mother." Persephone had just decided that. She had heard in Oceanus's bitterness the bones of a tale told often, over and over to himself, to explain why things had happened as they had. It held the echo of her mother's explanations. She supposed that always happened; you had to have some story to tell yourself about why you had done what you had done. "I'll send him up to the village when he's well."

Hades chuckled. "It may have been pointless to rescue him in that case. I doubt she'll be glad to see him."

"Or he her. But they have business that is not finished. When it is, things may be easier for us here." And maybe neither of them would have to spend their lives in endless bitter justification, explaining to themselves again why they had left a man they loved.

Hades looked mournful. "If he doesn't want a bride price."

Persephone gave a hoot of laughter. "You can give him those aquamarines."

# IX

## Demeter's Garden

But it wouldn't be that simple to stay here, Persephone knew that. Nothing to do with the heart was ever that simple. Her childhood had been filled with Demeter's warnings—veiled allusions to "men like that," admonitions to be wary of strangers, not to be seduced by promises lightly spoken. Not to marry, to leave men alone. Now that she had done all that she had been warned not to, she could feel her mother's fingers on her wrist, tugging her toward the upper air, Demeter's voice whispering that "men like that" were never reliable, would bring you to grief, that it was much better to stay mateless and safe.

And on her other side stood not Hades, but her grown-up self, the self that knew what it wanted, the self that had seen the bull dancers and felt the leap in her blood, and the joy and terror of the dance. Had her mother felt that with Triptolemus? Persephone had learned from him his true name, and had asked him the witch's name; now she knew for certain that names held power. She had not told him what she knew, but she studied him so intently as he grew well that he became suspicious and pleaded with Lycippus not to allow her to carry him off to the sea.

"No one is going to take you under the sea, you crazy man," Lycippus said briskly, shaving him. He had propped Triptolemus up against a pillow.

"I don't like the way she looks at me. There's something about her eyes."

"The mistress has very nice eyes," Lycippus said primly.

"They glow," Triptolemus said fretfully.

"Nonsense." Hades had failed to confide in Lycippus that this sailor might be the mistress's father, but attentive servants had ways of knowing these things. The man was very nearly well now, well enough to be sent on up the stairs to the village where he had been assured that the local folk would take him in. If that didn't cause a change in the weather, Lycippus would be very much surprised.

They sent Triptolemus on his way on a balmy spring day when little patches of cloud drifted over the island like tufts of wool and the poppies on the headland bloomed. Hades gave him a woolen tunic and cloak and new sandals, and bade him tell the village folk that the lord and lady of the lower caverns had fished him from the sea and healed him.

Persephone hoped that news of her contentment might sway Demeter to her side. On the other hand, it was entirely possible that Demeter would take one look at Triptolemus and allow him no chance to say anything at all. *That is my father,* Persephone thought, watching him climb the cliff. It was an odd sensation. Persephone and Hades stood side by side at the cave mouth, just visible beneath the overhanging lip of the cavern, and waved jauntily. Hades's arm was about her waist, as if they were gracious hosts and he a guest setting out along his road home. That seemed to worry Triptolemus, too. She thought regretfully that he wasn't very astute. When he had realized that Hades's domain was under the ground, they had had to convince him all over again that not only was he not drowned, but he was not dead on land, either. Now he looked back at them every so often, his brow furrowed with worry. The sea breeze blew his new cloak clumsily about him.

Triptolemus climbed the last step and pulled himself up onto the headland to stand for a moment among the blooming poppies. The wind stiffened; he wrapped the cloak about himself and headed toward the village, following the path through the meadow until he could see the lime-washed walls of the island's houses and the Temple of Zeus and Apollo gleaming in the white sun. The air was dusty with pollen and the smell of goats.

A boy with red hair and a traveler's hat and staff was loading a pack under the olive tree in the agora when Triptolemus reached it, but there was no one else to be seen.

The boy put his pack down. "Who are you?"

"A stranger seeking shelter. I was wrecked off your coast." He was aware that his clothes were new, and that that looked odd.

"Wrecked? There hasn't been a storm in weeks."

"Someone took me in—in the caverns below the headland." It was difficult to explain because Triptolemus wasn't exactly sure where he had been.

The boy's red brows rose under his hat. "Someone took you in," he said carefully, but his voice was friendly. "What sort of a someone?"

"A lady. I thought she was a Nereid . . . I still do . . . she swam out and took me by the hair, and they bore me away into a cavern where a man with a dark beard gave me a potion. He must have been Poseidon. It's all very strange now. . . ." Triptolemus's voice trailed off. He wasn't sure he remembered it very well.

More people began to appear in the agora, drawn by the voices.

A woman with thin dark hair pinned to the top of her head like a bird's nest said to the boy, "Hermes! You were to have set out by now!"

"Mother! This sailor—"

The boy was interrupted by an old man with a long white beard and an authoritative look. "We welcome the stranger at our shores," he told Triptolemus, "but you come at an ill time."

"Well, we are always glad to welcome a traveler. We are famous here on the island for our hospitality, and no doubt he'll be happy to repay us in some fashion, so . . ." That was an old woman with a water jug. She looked nearly as authoritative as the old man and went on talking while the rest talked over her.

"Mother! Great-Grandfather! He says he's been in the caverns!"

"What of your boat, fellow? Anything left of it?"

"Why have you not set out to rescue my daughter?"

Triptolemus turned to see who it was who had spoken last.

"What is your name, man?" the white-bearded ancient asked, and Triptolemus told him.

That was when the sky exploded. A thunderbolt came out of a dark cloud that hadn't been there two minutes before. The bolt cracked across the agora and sizzled on the ground where the stranger stood. It tossed him into the air, where it hung him in the olive tree. The rest of the village fled indoors, cowering while Demeter stood beneath the tree, her eyes blazing like the lightning. Rain poured down in sheets, and the wind blew up until Triptolemus thought he was at sea again and wailed despairingly, clinging to his branch.

By the time Hermes and young Tros had retrieved him, under Aristippus's direction, Triptolemus knew whose village he had come to.

They carried him to Demeter's house, through the storm and her desolate garden. "I think he's fainted," Tros said. He sloshed through a mud puddle, gripping Triptolemus under the arms.

"Wouldn't you?" Hermes said. He shifted his hands for a better grip on Triptolemus's feet.

Demeter walked beside them, appearing not to notice the sheeting rain. Hermes thought maybe she didn't feel it, since it was her rain.

They put Triptolemus in Demeter's bed, at her direction. He opened his eyes once, saw Demeter's face looming above him, and closed them again with a whimper.

Tros left in a hurry, but Hermes stood shivering by the fire. "I'll stay a moment if I may," he said to

Demeter. "He says he's been in the caverns, so maybe he can . . . and after all, if he's really . . ." The latter was territory he was reluctant to tread on.

*"Go and fetch my daughter!"* Demeter spun around, eyes blazing, and pointed her finger at him. Hermes swore he could see lightning coming from it.

"Of course." He backed up a bit. "I'll just have to repack my things. The storm has ruined all of it," he added pointedly.

Demeter narrowed her eyes at him. He could see the lightning dance in the pupils. "You don't need anything but a spear. You are to rescue my daughter, not recite a poem." A muscle ticked just under her eye, as if something were working its way out. Hermes left without seeing what.

Triptolemus woke in Demeter's bed. Rain was still pouring down outside, and the sky was nearly black. Inside, the house was warm and smelled of broth. Triptolemus buried his head in the pillow. He should have let the Nereid keep him. It might not be so bad at the bottom of the sea. Sea nymphs were said to be ethereally beautiful and amorous, besides. It had just been that he was so afraid of the water. He heard footsteps and groaned.

"So my daughter has sent you back to me, from the realm of the Dead. Does she know who you are?" Demeter stood over him with a bowl in her hands.

Triptolemus shook his head. "I don't know." He sat up. "Is that my daughter? She is beautiful," he said hopefully, as if Demeter might give him credit for his part in that.

"The one you were going to expose? That daughter?"

"That was my mother," Triptolemus said sulkily.

"Don't lie to me. You are too stupid to get away with it."

Triptolemus sighed. "I know. Demophon was the smart one. He could always figure things out."

"Was that why your mother was going to kill my child? Because hers had died?"

"Demophon was her favorite."

"You're like me then," Demeter said with a snort of anger. "You've never been anyone's favorite."

"No." That was the way it had been; she was right.

"Drink this." She handed him the bowl. He regarded it suspiciously. "If I was going to kill you I would have just cut off your head while you slept. Poison is too much trouble. Drink it."

Triptolemus drank. It was warm and faintly sweet as if it had honey in it, but it didn't have the aftertaste of the potions they had given him in the caverns, so he went on drinking. He didn't want to fall asleep in Demeter's bed again with Demeter awake.

"Is it true my daughter has married that man?"

Triptolemus put the bowl down. "I don't know. He called her his wife."

"He may call her a sea snail and it won't make her so."

"How did our daughter come to that place? And why are you angry about it? She seems very well-off."

"I never said she was *your* daughter." Demeter glared at him.

Triptolemus sighed. "She is, though, isn't she? She's the right age. And she has a look of me, now that I think about it. She looked familiar."

"She looked familiar because she looks like *me*," Demeter said, exasperated.

"I don't know." Triptolemus tried to figure it out. "Maybe she looks like us both?" he suggested.

"Maybe *you* should go and fetch her back to me then."

"She sent me up here. I don't think she wants to come back."

"She must come back." Demeter looked out the window at the sheeting rain. Lightning cracked again in the storm's heart. "It won't stop until she does."

"Did you do that?" Triptolemus looked even more unnerved.

"I think so," Demeter said. "It just happens when I want it to. It doesn't matter if I try not to want it. It happens anyway."

Triptolemus eyed her uneasily, wondering what else she might want. "And what will you do with me?"

"I don't know," Demeter said.

Triptolemus shuddered. He could think of several unpleasant possibilities.

"You can start by digging the garden while I think about it."

Triptolemus didn't object. He had been half-afraid she would want to feed it with his blood. She disappeared and left him in her bed, and it was a long time before he fell asleep.

In the morning the two of them went out to look at the sodden ruin that was Demeter's garden. She had planted nothing this spring, and all that grew was weeds and what had come up from plants left to rot in the fall: stray rambling squashes and pea vines, leeks and overwintered parsley. The rain had stopped, but the sky was sullen, matching Demeter's mood.

Triptolemus tried to think what had come over her. He had never been afraid of her when she had lived with him at Eleusis. His mother and sisters had bullied her, he remembered, and she had spent all her time in the garden with old Faunus, his mother's slave, who was older than the stones in the earth. She seemed to have acquired some dangerous abilities since then. She didn't look any older, either, although if you saw her next to Persephone you would know which was the mother and which the daughter. Persephone was lithe and oddly regal, while Demeter's body was generous, sensual, like the fruit of her apple trees. He watched her round hips shift as she bent to pull a thistle from the mud beside her doorway, where crocuses were blooming white and purple in the muck, and felt himself hardening in spite of himself.

"You can start by cleaning up the mess," Demeter told him, interrupting this meditation, and the urge vanished, to his relief.

He found Demeter's plow in a shed, half-broken and dull, and set it to rights, whistling between his teeth. This, at least, he knew how to do, having served an apprenticeship of his own with old Faunus in his youth, before he began to sail on the sea, before Demeter, before Demophon. He had been the favorite then, the only son.

When the plow was mended, Demeter sent him to Aristippus to fetch the village's ox, used to till the wheatfields in the spring.

"Staying awhile, are you?" Aristippus asked him.

The plow bit into the mud and turned the sodden weeds over. Demeter watched him from her house, pausing in the window as she cleaned the muddy floors and shook out the bedclothes. She took a basket of laundry to the stream, and came back with a garland of red poppies about her head.

The village watched this development with uncertainty.

"Do you think she's going to *keep* him?" Harmonia asked Tros over a breakfast of figs and cheese. She patted her rounded belly and smiled when she felt the child kick back at her hand.

"Ill luck to speculate about that, I expect," Tros grunted. "I'd as soon put it in a beehive, if you were to ask me."

"I remember when we were girls," Doris said to Echo as they milked the goats. "She was never happy with any of the village boys. She wanted I don't know what, but it wasn't here. And *that* is what she found? The gods help us all; you might as well stay at home." The doe turned her head to mouth a strand of Doris's hair, soft nose rubbing her cheek. "Stop that!"

"Who knows *where* he's come from?" Glaucus's daughters said. "He could be anybody, and I don't believe he's that girl's father. How could you know after all this time? We all think so. She ought to send him about his business before he robs somebody or worse." They nodded their heads firmly, like a row of crows.

"You have a responsibility to see that he marries her," Bopis told Aristippus. "Living with that man without any proper ceremony, it doesn't set the girls a good example."

"A misalignment of the humors," Phaedon said to the vintner, whose boil he was lancing. "Too much black bile makes a man melancholic. He should come to me."

"Do you suppose he'll stay here?" the vintner asked. "Ow! With her? Ow, you ham-fisted ox!"

"Now, your problem is yellow bile that causes eruptions of the skin. It is to be hoped he stays. She needs a man. It's not natural the way she's lived. Sexual intercourse opens the entrance to the womb, and allows blood to flow out so it doesn't back up into the heart and lungs, causing licentiousness and dangerous hallucinations." Phaedon applied the needle again to the other side of the boil. "The womb may close up again when a woman is widowed; I've seen it happen. Then it begins to wander, moves about the body, and causes all manner of trouble. She'll do well to take him."

The vintner nodded. "Just goes to show. Look at all this weather. Ow! Didn't even have the decency to dedicate herself to the goddess if she didn't want a man. Nobody worries about priestesses; they're all crazy anyway."

Hesperia pottered among the bones and ashes behind the altar in the Temple of Hestia. They would mate and bring forth children; she had seen it in the smoke. Or maybe they already had. But whether they would be monsters or blessed ones, she couldn't tell, or even which couple she was watching. Sometimes she thought they were the same people.

"What am I to you?" Persephone asked Hades. She sat in a chair, playing for her own amusement with the distaff and wool, while he stretched on a couch like a comfortable cat and watched her.

"My queen, my heart." He smiled in the firelight.

"How flattering. Oh, I've snarled it again, bother!" She struggled with the recalcitrant threads. "It's a mercy I won't have to wear this. No, I meant something else. Mother wants me back; I can still feel it. Every time I go near any of the entrances, or into the gardens, the hair stands up on my arms and the back of my neck prickles. I want to get married."

"And you think that will keep your mother away? I had considered that we *were* married."

"You didn't grow up in my village."

"No. Regrettably."

Persephone snorted. "My dear, I am not even yet entirely sure you're human, and my village most certainly isn't. If you don't want Mother to take me back, you will have to marry me properly, in the human fashion."

Hades chuckled. "You put my bride price down the drains."

"Will you be serious?"

His face darkened. "I am. I came here to live because I saw little good in the affairs of people like those of your village."

"That doesn't matter," Persephone said with certainty. "It's the choice that matters. You said that yourself. It's making the free choice. If you don't want Mother to take me back, you will have to make *your* choice, before witnesses."

"If it's a free choice, why before witnesses?" he inquired.

Persephone set the distaff spinning again, and the

thread lengthened from her fingers. "Because what you won't say before witnesses, you don't mean. Then I am no more than poor Cousin Maia who claims she slept with Zeus and got my cousin Hermes."

Hades looked thoughtful.

"Now it's your choice," Persephone said.

She stood fidgeting on a stool while Scylla and Pomona tugged and fiddled with her gown. How many brides had stood thus, Persephone mused, wondering what the man they were going to wed would be like. Some would not have seen him at all, or very rarely, just a face glimpsed by lamplight, in conversation with her father, with talk of oxen and goats and jars of oil, flowing over watered wine and sweetmeats that weren't offered to her. Some, the ones who weren't wealthy, whose marriage and bedding made no difference to anyone, might have picked him out themselves, tested him out, too, in the hayfield on a warm midsummer night, and be already swelling with the first child. But they wouldn't know him, either. Not really. Did anyone ever?

"You're lovely," Pomona said. "It's lighter in these caverns already for your presence. The master's a different man."

"Who is he?" Persephone whispered.

"He'll make you a fine, faithful husband, not like some." Pomona stood back to admire her veil, crowned with scarlet pomegranate blossoms.

"That's not what I asked you," Persephone said, pursuing it.

"Well, we don't know," Scylla said, "but no one

who comes here wants to leave, so that's a good sign."

Triptolemus had, Persephone thought, but he had had unfinished business elsewhere. Maybe no one knew more of her prospective husband than the fates had revealed to her. Scylla held up the silver mirror that had been Hades's gift to her, and she looked at her reflection in its watery surface. Her wheat-colored hair fell down her back in waves, and the veil, sheer as gossamer, floated out over it, anchored by the wreath of pomegranate.

"Lovely," Scylla sighed. She gave Persephone her hand to help her down from the stool, and, Pomona carrying the ends of the veil to keep them from the floor, they set out solemnly for the great hall where Hades was waiting for her.

He was there, beside the hearth, with Lycippus in attendance. Odd, Persephone thought fleetingly, to be taken to your marriage by servants; no friends, no family, unless you counted Cerberus, stretched beside the hearth, panting. His fangs glinted milky white in his mouth, but it was a cheerful expression, a wolfy smile of goodwill.

Hades wore a black tunic stitched with white and scarlet poppies, and Persephone thought as she walked across the hall to him, how alike the poppies and the pomegranates were when they had made their fruit. Each bore on its head the little crown that had been the pod of the blossom. *I will be queen here,* she thought. *Queen over the flowers of sleep and the fruit with the seed at its heart, and the shades of those who have eaten both.*

Hades took her hand and with his other, strewed meal on the stones of the floor for whatever gods he prayed to. If he did. Sometimes she thought he spoke directly to them. He filled a cup of wine and dipped his fingers in, flicking a spatter onto the floor. The ruby drops shone against the meal like pomegranate seeds; then he held the cup to her. She took it and drank, the silver of the bowl cool in her fingers. She could see their faces in it, wavy and distorted like looking into a pond with ripples. His face, dark and smiling, shimmered beside hers, and she thought she saw people behind him, faces she didn't know, but when she turned there was no one there.

The wine was thick and sweet, almost unwatered, and it made her head spin. He took the cup and drank after her; then he bent his head to kiss her. "You are chosen," he said. "I am chosen. We are each freely chosen of the other."

It seemed an odd wedding ceremony. Usually you asked the gods for prosperity and children, and the grace to get along with each other. But their needs were different, and these seemed the right words. "Chosen," she repeated after him.

There was something in the air over the island just then. It hung below the clouds like a face, curious, watching, transparent yet visible. It saw the handfasting between Hades and his bride, and it saw the two in the garden, pulling weeds—turning the earth, upending the warm soil, slipping in the seed. It saw the two below again, standing among the vegetable beds now where the bright air drifted down through rock to touch their hair. Hades had ordered wine and sesame cake for all his servants, and they crowded the gardens, drinking to the lord's and lady's health.

Whatever was in the air drank, too. Its breath was sweet with the scent of wine and cake when it drifted over Demeter's garden. Demeter stopped pulling thistles and lifted her head. She stretched her neck like a cat's, following the air. Triptolemus eyed her warily.

In Hades's garden the servants were getting drunk. Lycippus leaned against an apple tree, clay cup cradled in both hands. His bushy brows looked to Scylla like hairy caterpillars, and she giggled as they went up and down while he spoke to her. The kitchen boys and the girls from the laundry were dancing in a line, spiraling hand in hand around the raised beds, while the baker played the flute and an old woman who swept the floors kept time, beating a saucepan on her knee with a spoon. A man Persephone recognized as Charon, the helmsman of Hades's boat, played the lyre, and the dancers danced faster and faster around them. Cerberus ran behind, barking joyfully, tongue flapping, and upended a small maidservant.

When all the wine had been drunk, and Hades was reasonably certain that no one was sober enough to find more, they took their leave, and slipped away to bed to seal the marriage in the usual way. They could still hear Scylla and Lycippus, of all people, singing behind them, and Charon bellowing a sea chantey over it all.

"They'll all have a bad head in the morning," Persephone said.

Hades chuckled. "No one feels that they have properly celebrated a wedding without a bad head."

Persephone slipped a hand into his. At the end of

the corridor, he pushed open the door of his chamber and drew her inside, "Come in with me—wife." His eyes gleamed, and he bent to kiss her.

She smiled, and the longing for him ran clear down her body when his beard brushed her chin. His hands fiddled with the pins at her shoulders and tangled themselves in the billowing veil. "This is a dreadful thing," he muttered, half laughing. "Take it off."

"I don't think I can. Scylla pinned it in my hair with wire, I think. Or glue."

"Come into the light." He led her to the glow of a pottery lamp, its surface painted with one of the sinuous, bug-eyed octopi he was so fond of. It appeared to be smiling at her, or maybe that was just the wine. She tugged at the veil and its pomegranate crown. It didn't budge.

"Hold still while I untangle you." She could feel his fingers in her hair, fishing for hairpins. "Aha!" A pin like a bronze fishhook skittered across the floor. "That woman is wasted in the kitchen. She could build military defenses."

Persephone stood obediently while he dismantled her headdress, turning around when he told her to, and giggling when he swore at it. Finally he lifted it from her head and set it on a table. She shook her head, and the last tresses fell loose.

"Oh, my dear, you are so beautiful." His voice was low and soft.

"More beautiful than yesterday?"

"Infinitely." The gown, too, slid from her shoulders. He put the pins on the table with the crown and veil, all her finery now just a little pile of cloth, and the real bride in his arms. He ran his hands through the cascade of her hair. She leaned against him for a moment, listening to the steady thud of his heart, before he lifted her in his arms and took her to the bed.

The plowed earth in the garden was thick with worms, wriggling indignantly as the blade turned them over to the light. Triptolemus held a clod of earth in his hand and watched the worms, pink squirming ribbons seeking blindly. What did worms look for? he wondered. Refuge, he supposed. He scratched his head. Triptolemus was not given to pondering matters. Thinking things over was foreign to him, and he had never thought of himself as a man whose ideas were clever. The worms were a good sign, though. This dirt had been well tended. He put his hand to the plow again and hee-yup'd at the ox, who switched its ropey tail and began to lumber reluctantly down the row. The feel of the plow came back to him, familiar as the pull of a tiller in his hand. Why had he quit working the earth and gone to sea? He couldn't remember now. It had had something to do with Demophon, who had somehow claimed his mother's land as his, without anyone ever saying so, even though he was the younger. So Triptolemus had gone to sea, and sold the grain and olive oil that Demophon raised, and brought back wondrous things from far away, and still his mother preferred Demophon.

Triptolemus turned the ox at the end of the row, coming around behind it, holding the blade's path smooth, its feel satisfying in his hand. Demeter followed behind him, sowing seed from a fold of her apron. Triptolemus was conscious of her there, like being stalked by some large beast. She had seemed better tempered this morning and had even cooked him a breakfast of cheese and eggs from the hens that scratched in the turned earth for bugs. He had slept in her bed again last night, and she had slept he did not know where, but he had lain awake for most of it, half wishing and half fearing that she would get in beside him.

Hermes saw them as he made his way out of the village toward the headland and the path down the cliff. He had put the journey off as long as he could, hoping that Persephone might come home on her own or Demeter might change her mind and the weather improve, now that she had a man in her bed. Hermes assumed the old sailor was in her bed. What on earth would she want with him otherwise? The earth felt unsteady under his boots, as if it were getting ready to buckle. Hellas was a jumpy country; they were used to having the dishes rattled suddenly off their shelves and the wine jars overturned. But something in the air felt different. Something in the world was realigning itself, settling into some new pattern. He had wanted Persephone for years, he thought grumpily. Since they were fourteen, at least. If he had had her then, they wouldn't have all this trouble now. He would probably be tired of her by now, and glad enough to let another man have her. It was her mother's fault, that was what came of living without a man. Old Phaedon was right—the womb closed up and mysterious forces built up inside. Although if that were the case, Hermes wondered uneasily what would happen if Demeter set hers loose again.

He began to cross the meadow, thumping his staff on the ground to scare snakes. There had been more of them than usual this year, driven from their burrows by the rain and found hiding in cookpots and empty jars, or hanging coiled like a rope from the rafters under the thatch. His footsteps seemed to fall into rhythm with whatever was happening in the earth as behind him Demeter and Triptolemus finished plowing the garden and went into her house. Below, Hades and Persephone slipped away from the revelry among the fruit trees. The ground shuddered slightly. The skies opened, and a warm, soft, drenching rain began to fall, slicking the steps that zigzagged down the cliff face and soaking his hat so that the brim turned downward and he might as well have had his head in a kettle. Hermes swore, and pulled his traveling cloak about him, his pack bumping against his back. His plan was to come to the caverns as if he were a traveler who had lost his way, and insinuate himself inside. That shouldn't be hard to do. Triptolemus had spoken of servants. No doubt they would answer the door, so to speak, not the master himself . . . *him* . . . Hades. Hermes allowed his name into his head with some trepidation. Best not to use a name like that too often. If you spoke their name, they heard you, and knew you were coming.

The rain was coming harder now; he stumbled on a loose stone and bumped down three steps on his backside until he could grab a sapling that clung to the cliffside beside the stairs. It rubbed his hand raw along the palm, but he got his footing back. He went more cautiously after that, clinging to whatever grew beside the steps while the rain poured off his hat.

Out to sea he could see blue sky and the gold glint
of sun dancing on the water. Apparently it was only
raining on this island. He slithered to the bottom of
the stairs and saw what the rain had blinded him
to—the tide was coming in. He hadn't thought of
that, and neither had anyone else, he thought. They
were all so anxious to send him on his errand. His
foot slipped on the last stair, and he landed with a
splash in water a hand's span deep. He righted himself, wrung the water from his hat, and rolled the
brim back up, rather unsuccessfully. It slowly unrolled again as he splashed his way toward the cavern mouth.

The tide licked his ankles, and suddenly it was
deeper than it had been, deeper than it had any right
to be, as if it had begun to hurry. The wind picked
up, knocking him sideways, so that he struggled to
keep his footing. Something knew he was here, he
thought. He bent low into the wind and forced his
way through the rising water. The tide was foaming
about his waist now, and he could feel the current
as it ran out again, sucking at his knees, trying to
pull him under, take him out to sea with it.

Ahead he could see the cavern mouth, nearly filled
with seawater. The tide lapped against the stones,
colder than the rain. There was an entrance here, he
knew. Hermes had hidden on the headland and
watched when Echemus and two others had been
left. He had seen the old servants with the long faces
come out and carry them into the darkness under the
overhanging lip of rock, and not appear again. Lately
he had seen the dog, too, the one that Arachne saw
come out and play in the surf. It was huge, he re-
called uneasily, although he thought she had been

anciful about the number of heads. With a dog that
ig, it didn't matter. One head was plenty. So there
vas an entrance here, hidden at high tide. Like all
he island's children, Hermes could swim, and had
explored other caverns that ate into the shoreline
around its edge. He was angry at Persephone for
outting him to this trouble, and at Hades for thinking
e could have what Hermes wanted. He shed his
oack with some reluctance, and his hat and staff, set-
ing them on the top of a half-submerged boulder, in
he hope that the tide might not rise that high. He
loundered deeper into the cavern mouth, seeking the
vay in that he knew was there. He was swimming
now, his head nearly bumping the stone roof above.
A wave came in, and rolled him under the surf. It
smacked him against a submerged rock, and the
rough stone scraped his face raw. He surfaced, sput-
ering and cursing, and hit his head on the cavern
roof.

Hermes took a gulp of air before there was no air
o be had, then dived, feeling his way between the
ooulders, trying to keep his orientation. It would be
so easy to turn back or even upside down without
knowing it. The waves tried to roll him head over
neels, and he floundered, feeling only a wall of stone
oefore him. Finally his fingers found the gap between
he two pillars that guarded Hades's kingdom, and
e pulled himself through. The lord of the caverns
was no match for him, he thought with satisfaction,
swimming. But he was getting very short of air. He
ried to surface, and hit his head again.

This was someone's fault, and it wasn't his.
Hermes plowed ahead through the dark water. The
swell of the tide buffeted him, and the salt stung his

eyes. It was dark as a hole in the water here. He blundered on, lungs burning, thrashing with growing anxiety in the darkness. Something seized him by the throat, and he expelled the last of his air in an involuntary scream. Seawater ran into his mouth. He fought desperately with whatever it was: something huge with powerful jaws that gripped the back of his neck. It pulled him down into the depths, and his lungs filled with seawater.

Hermes awoke on a stone floor, facedown. His chest burned with each breath. He lifted his head, and a monstrous wet dog looked back at him, a hand's span from his nose. It lay on the floor, drooling, paws crossed one over the other. Hermes lowered his head again, groaning.

"The master doesn't care for unexpected visitors," a voice above him said. "That was most ill advised. And at high tide, too." The voice tutted and sucked at a tooth disapprovingly. "You are lucky Cerberus went to get you."

Hermes raised his head again, and this time propped himself on his elbows. His head ached nearly as badly as his lungs. "That's a fine way to keep your front door," he said testily. "Full of water."

"Allow me to help you up," the voice said, and a pair of hands gripped him under his arms.

Hermes staggered to his feet and turned to find himself with one of the old servants he had watched take Echemus in. "It started to rain," he said. "It never rains this time of year. And the tide doesn't come in that fast, either."

"The weather has been odd lately," the old servant

said. "I am Lycippus. Permit me to take you to my master. He'll be the one you're wanting to see, I expect."

Hermes wasn't at all sure of that. "I am a traveler," he said, recalling his story. "Lost in the storm."

"Odd," Lycippus said. "We don't get many of those here."

"I imagine not," Hermes said. "Perhaps I might beg a warm corner from your mistress. No need to trouble the master."

"I shall inform them both of your presence," Lycippus said. He beckoned Hermes down the corridor.

Hermes followed him, shivering, keeping one eye on the dog and the other on the carved journeyers on the wall. It might not be a good idea, he decided, to stay here any longer than necessary.

Lycippus led him through a series of passages until Hermes began to worry that he would not be able to find his way out again if he wanted to. Escorted to a large room filled with marble and bronze statues, he was left dripping by the hearth. The dog sat down next to him and began to give off the warm odor of wet dog in the heat from the fire.

Hermes pulled a chair to the hearth and sat next to the dog. "Thank you," he said to it, in case it could talk, because it paid to ingratiate oneself with the servants of those one wished to put something over on.

The dog didn't answer, but a furious voice from the door said, "What are you doing here?"

# X

*The Hero*

It was Persephone, dressed in a purple gown that made Hermes's eyes bulge at the thought of its probable cost. Her golden hair was crowned with a fillet of gold set with gold poppies, and she wore a necklace of deep green stones. He blinked again. The maid who had run wild in the woods was gone. This girl was regal, and he could tell by her expression that she knew things she hadn't known when she left.

"I came to fetch you home," he said, hoping she was in a receptive mood. By the look of her clothing she might not be. "Zeus commands it," he added for good measure.

"Bah!" she said. "You are dripping on a good carpet."

"You might have offered me dry clothes," Hermes said.

"I might have."

"I nearly drowned getting here," he said. "There was a storm and the tide was coming in, and I was attacked by the dog."

"The dog has good instincts."

"That is an ungrateful way to treat the one who has come to rescue you," Hermes said, aggrieved. He was surprised by how much he wanted her now. Wet and cold as he was, it made him stiffen just to look at her.

"I don't need to be rescued."

"Of course you do. You're in the toils of a monster. He'll likely kill you soon."

"You're an idiot. I don't want a hero. Heroes only make trouble."

"Well, if you had married me when you should have, you wouldn't need a hero," Hermes retorted.

"You didn't want to marry me. You wanted to lie in the hayfield with me. Me and a dozen other girls!" She glared at him. "Faithless goat."

"What if I had wanted to marry you?" Hermes asked her. "What then?"

She thought about that for a minute. If he hadn't been faithless . . . but faithlessness was his essence, his core. Hermes would always look for something new. "You're like Great-Grandfather. You'll lie with anyone. Your wife will run herself ragged trying to keep you out of other girls' beds."

"That didn't mean I didn't want to marry you," Hermes protested.

Persephone chuckled. She sat down in a chair. "You would have been sorry, the first time you did it with another girl. Go marry someone who won't cut it off with a carving knife some night while you're asleep."

"I can't," Hermes said gloomily. The prospect sounded all too likely. "I have to rescue you, and if I rescue you, your mother will give you to me."

"Nobody can give me to anybody now."

"You have to marry the hero who saves you," Hermes said. "It's the rules." He turned with his back to the hearth, trying to dry his other side. It was dank in the caverns, and his nose felt blue. Persephone, he noted, had an elegant woolen mantle about her shoulders. "I'm cold," he told her.

"Maybe you'll die," she said without much sympathy, but she clapped her hands and a servant who must have been lurking in the corridor appeared immediately. "Bring our guest something dry to wear, please. And something to eat."

"Oh, no," Hermes said, "oh, no. You won't trick me that way."

Persephone ignored him. She rose from her chair and took her wool and spindle from its basket. She began to draw out a line of thread, considering him silently as she twisted it between her fingers.

Hermes edged away, eyeing the twirling spindle at the end of the strand. She looked a bit too much like the Fates who spun the thread of life and clipped it off at its other end. Perhaps it had not been the best idea to demand her for a wife, but that wasn't the sort of thing you could go back on. And he had enjoyed thinking of himself in the hero's role. The hero always married the maiden when he had saved her. Otherwise, what was the point in saving her? One might as well let the sea monster have her. "I did want to marry you," he said crossly. "You're the only one I could ever be faithful to."

Persephone snorted.

Lycippus appeared with an armful of dry clothes and a tray bearing a bowl of fruit and savory pies.

The other servant came behind him with a jug of wine and two goblets.

"With the master's compliments," Lycippus said as he handed the clothes to Hermes. Hermes looked about him uneasily. "The master is occupied at the moment," Lycippus said blandly. "But he bids you welcome." He set the tray on a table and looked firmly at Cerberus, who pretended he wasn't interested in it.

Persephone gathered up her wool and spindle. "I'll just leave you for a moment while you change into something dry." She left him with the two servants.

"You've caught a nasty cold," Lycippus remarked as he pulled Hermes's wet tunic over his head. "I've seen cases like this before, very dangerous."

Hermes sneezed.

"Reckless to stand around in wet clothes all this time."

"You didn't bring me any dry ones!" Hermes said.

"Ah! An oversight." He removed Hermes's loincloth and toweled the visitor off briskly, ignoring Hermes's protests that he could dry himself. "Perhaps a cup of wine to warm the blood." Lycippus whipped the towel away and helped Hermes into a loincloth that appeared to have been made for a horse, and a tunic that was three sizes too large and came halfway down his shins. "The master's best," he said. "He wishes you to feel welcome." He scooped Hermes's wet clothes up in his arm.

Persephone reappeared as Lycippus and the other servant left. She snorted again when she saw the tunic, and Hermes glared at her.

"You need a cup of wine," she said, laying aside her wool. "Let me pour you some."

Hermes watched her suspiciously. She handed him the cup and began to peel a pomegranate from the fruit bowl, her nails biting into the smooth shiny skin just under the crown.

"Don't eat that!" He lunged to take it away from her.

"Don't be silly." She held her hand away from his reach. "They keep very well down here, in the cold cellar. They remind me of Mother's garden."

"That's the last you'll see of your mother's garden if you eat that," Hermes said urgently. "If you eat in a place, you bind yourself to it. We mustn't eat here."

Persephone put the pomegranate down carefully in the bowl—the juice stained anything it touched a bright red purple—and stared at him, as if a fish had begun to talk to her.

"Hermes, I have been here since last summer. I've been eating since I got here. How do you think I survived?"

"The dead don't need food." He tried to move the fruit bowl out of her reach.

"Well, I'm not dead!"

"How do you know? We must be careful taking you home again. I'm not allowed to look back, I think." He frowned. "Or maybe that's for fighting gorgons. I don't remember." He rubbed his head as if it hurt.

Persephone put down the wine cup as well as the fruit. "Hermes, who sent you here?" she asked him gently.

"Your mother. I said I could save you if she would give you to me. Maybe I bragged a little. Then Hestia's priestess said to get you back because your mother was making it snow—it's been dreadful weather ever since you were taken: snow and rain and windstorms. It's a wonder we.didn't have a volcano explode somewhere. And she said to send me because I said I could save you, and she told your mother to give you to me if I did."

"And you thought I would go with you?"

"When you save a maiden, she doesn't have to help you," Hermes said with dignity. "Most of them faint with fear, I believe."

"And how are you planning to save me?" Persephone inquired. "Just for the sake of argument."

Hermes rubbed his head again. It ached with a dull throbbing roar that he could almost hear. "I believe if we just wait for low tide, then we walk out together—I'm almost sure it's gorgons you aren't supposed to look at—then if you really are still alive you probably won't fall into a pile of bones at the entrance."

She looked at him suspiciously and decided he was only half joking. He really thought she might. It would serve him right if she did. She wondered if she could manage it. She suspected that imagination could conjure whatever image it expected and toyed with the idea of a basket of bones over a doorway before discarding it as ignoble. It would amuse Hades, though.

Hermes was sitting still now, his slightly slanted gray green eyes alert, waiting to see what she would do. And on the other hand, Hermes had done something quite dangerous for her sake.

"It's not your world down here," he said quietly. "You belong to the upper air. You're what makes the trees grow." He sounded serious.

Persephone contemplated him thoughtfully, distracted by the clear memory of his lips nuzzling her neck and the shiver that had run through her when he did it. He was like a goat, playful and charming, alarmingly sexual, with a knowing eye and with a goat's morals. Fine for a fling in the vineyard under a solstice moon, if you could be sure you wouldn't fall in love and pine for him while he was off on the next chase. Persephone had always been pretty sure she wouldn't, but not sure enough.

And why was she thinking of that? She glared at him. He smelled of the upper air, she realized suddenly. Even in Hades's tunic, his hair drenched with seawater and the dank tinge of the caverns that never quite went away, he smelled like sunlight and grapevines and olives on the tree. He would talk her into going with him if she wasn't careful.

"It's dark here," Hermes said. "Don't you long for the light?"

"It's light enough. There is a garden I go sit in. There are shafts that open to the sky."

"It will call to you. If you don't come home, it will call to you all your life."

That might be true. "Hermes, listen to me." She leaned forward and put her hand on his, because he had been willing to come for her. Great-Grandfather might have ordered it, but Hermes could have lied and said there was no way in, that the door was sealed. He hadn't, though. "The world is full of wonders. Every place I have been will call to me afterward. But I will live here."

"Always? In the dark? With your only light from a shaft in the rock?"

"I have been places, outside these caverns. I am not a prisoner. I have seen the people dance with bulls on the palace walls at Knossos. He took me there because I asked him to. I have seen things you can't imagine. Go and see them for yourself, but don't try to take me with you. I have seen what I need to."

He turned his hand palm up and gripped hers. "Not everything. I could show you things you haven't seen."

She tried to pull her hand back, but he wouldn't let her. "Those I don't need to see."

Green eyes, the color of the shallows around the island, held hers. "Let me show them to you before you decide."

Goat eyes, and something dancing goat-footed in the grass. Flute song. It was the same dance he proposed that the bull dancers danced. *I have danced that with someone else. Not with you. Too late for you.* "All you can offer me is the attraction of your body," she said, knowing that that was substantial. He breathed the scent of the upper air through his skin; she could taste it. "Hades is more complicated. I'll take the complication. I'll keep my bargain."

"With him?"

"No, with myself." She didn't think he understood, but when she twisted her hand gently in his, his fingers loosened.

"Ah!" said Hades from the doorway. "I see you have welcomed our guest."

Persephone snatched her hand away from Hermes's. Hermes stood, tucking the monstrous tunic into its sash to shorten it. She thought he was annoyed by the joke, but except for a twitch of his mouth, he gave no sign of it.

Hades wore a tunic of black silk stitched with

green leaves, which fit him perfectly. He took the pomegranate from the bowl and broke it the rest of the way open. "Just come in on the tide?" he inquired pleasantly.

"In a manner of speaking," Hermes said.

"I see you've met my wife."

"We are old acquaintances." Hermes stood his ground. He was a good head shorter than Hades.

"Cousins," Persephone said firmly. *Not old lovers. We could have been, but we weren't.*

"All my wife's relatives are welcome here," Hades said. He picked a few blood-colored seeds from the pomegranate and ate them. Persephone wasn't sure whether she imagined it or not, but she thought there was a touch of something sinister in his voice. Maybe it was just the way he put it.

"Kind of you," Hermes said.

Hades smiled. He had very white teeth, and Persephone thought suddenly that teeth were the only part of people's bones that showed outside their skin. Hades had a way of making people think of things like that when he was so inclined. "I have asked the kitchen to send us some dinner," he said.

"I don't want to put you to any trouble." Hermes edged closer to Persephone. He eyed the doorway suggestively, and she shook her head at him.

"He thinks if he eats here, he won't be able to leave," Persephone said.

"We'll make sure he can leave," Hades said. He looked closely at Hermes, whose russet hair was beginning to dry but whose nose and eyes were red. "A sustaining broth first, perhaps." He set the pieces of the pomegranate back in the bowl, where they gleamed like living rubies. Lycippus and two others entered, bearing trays, and he motioned them to the small tables that populated the room. The servants drew three couches up to the hearth beneath the gaze of a marble boy with shepherd's pipes, and arranged the tables handily with plates of dried, spiced fish; a dish of lentils and mutton, olives, figs and onion; and an omelette of eggs and oysters.

Hermes saw Persephone stretch herself along one of the couches to dine as a man would do. She saw him watching her and said very quietly, "I am queen here. You don't understand that."

"And is being queen better than being free?" he asked her softly.

Hades smiled at him with a little more tooth than was really necessary. Persephone thought he looked like Cerberus. "There are many definitions of free, my friend. The dead are free. The stupid are free of knowledge. How free would you hope to be?"

"Free to wander the upper air," Hermes said. He glanced at the painted panels on the wall. "To breathe that in without the smell of paint to tell me it is false. To live a true life, not one of visions conjured from smoke."

"There are no visions here!" Persephone said angrily.

"How do you know?" Hermes demanded. "How do you know all you have seen here has not been visions in your head, born of sorcery?"

Persephone thought of the ghosts she had seen when she first came. She looked uneasily at Lycippus. He looked more like a sheep than ever.

Hades speared a fish from the platter with his knife. The marble boy looked over his shoulder, motionless in his music. "For all you know," he said, "your own world might be illusion. How will you prove differently?"

Hermes looked hungrily at the fish but he didn't eat.

"If that's an illusory fish, it shouldn't hurt you to eat it," Hades commented.

Hermes sat on the edge of his couch as if he thought it might swallow him if he reclined. "Zeus commands that you return her to the upper air. I am sent to fetch her."

"That is her choice," Hades said. "Tell that to Zeus when you see him."

Persephone looked at Hades. She thought he meant that, despite her promise to stay with him if he would save two lost sailors from their own sea. The air stirred in the chamber, drifting down the series of shafts and connecting tunnels that Hades—or whoever had come before him—had devised. It carried the scent of apples, or maybe that was Hermes, sitting beside her. *Mother?* She let the thought float out onto the air current, but nothing answered her. If she just knew that things were well with Mother, she could be easy. "What of the upper air?" she asked Hermes. "What of my world? What happens in it now?"

"The weather is bad," Hermes said. "It is likely we will starve."

"What of Mother and the sailor?"

"Your estimable father? He is living with her and goes in terror of her, I think. That and some other urge."

Persephone smiled.

"Don't think she has forgotten you, though," Hermes said. He sneezed. "I wish everyone's emotions didn't come out in the weather. I suppose you know you spoiled the vintage," he added. "It's a dire state of affairs when the town can't drink its sorrows away."

The vision of her village, white and dusty against the gray green hills, came into her head. She wondered if this was what always happened when the gods gave you what you wanted. You had to give up something in exchange, and that was the price. "Tell me more. What else is happening?"

"Narcissa and her mother are both married. I wouldn't ask more about *that* if I were you. Tros and Harmonia have a son. Bopis caught Great-Grandfather with Clytie in a goat shed."

Persephone clapped her hand over her mouth to stifle a snort of laughter. "Oh, no!"

"We all knew they were in there. It was like watching a rock overbalance from a cliff. You couldn't do anything to stop it; you just watched it fall."

"But what did she do?"

"She chased Clytie out with a threshing flail. Clytie climbed a tree and Bopis danced around under it, shrieking imprecations and waving the flail while Great-Grandfather took refuge in the Temple of Zeus and Apollo. Bopis was afraid to go in there after him, so she waited outside, sitting on a bucket, for most of the day until he came out; then they went home together."

"Oh, I wish I had seen that!" A wave of longing for village doings washed over her until she caught Hades watching her and sobered. "What about Echo?"

"She misses you. If you came home you could see her. You could see Narcissa. It might save her."

"It won't," Hades said. "I have seen Narcissa. Unless you want to kill her husband and promise she will never have to wed again, you can't save her. It's very often like that, in your world."

Hermes looked at him a moment, considering. "And yours is better."

"It's another choice. That's all."

Persephone turned to him. "Could I really not save Narcissa? If I went there and then came back?"

"Even if you did not come back, my darling. No."

"Why should she have a dreadful life? It isn't fair. That was her father they brought to you last year, the one who died."

"I never promised he wouldn't," Hades said.

"That's just it," Hermes said. "You hold out false hope. Take him to the lord of Death and he may give him back. Bah!"

"Life holds out false hope."

"Better to be dead?" Hermes leaned forward, green eyes intent. "To forgo the smell of new grass in spring? The feel of water on your skin, the taste of wine, of ripe figs in your mouth?"

"All of that you may have here."

"What about the new kids in the spring, the lambs kicking in the field? What about the linnet's song or the sweep of the shearwater's wings over the sea? What about the moon? Let alone the sun and the gold warmth that lies like a blanket on the earth? The smell of new wheat, and the scent of the threshing floor? Have you seen the way the moon shines on limestone walls when it rises? Have you watched the sun go down in the water like a puddle of fire, with your arm around a girl?" Hermes's voice was impassioned. "Have you danced knee-deep in the grapes at the vintage? Have you done any of those things? Will you let *her*?"

Persephone yearned toward him in spite of herself. He made it all sound so real.

"I have done all those things," Hades said quietly, "and found them wanting. And have *you* watched one army roll toward another, spears flashing, banners waving, determined to kill, to bloody their path, and slaughter the widows and orphans afterward? Have you seen a city topple and all its wonders lost from sheer blind spite and ignorance? What about pestilence? Have you watched that black cloud sweep over a land because its inhabitants were too stupid to keep themselves clean?"

"That's just life," Hermes said sulkily. "You take the good with the bad."

"Precisely. All part of the dance. Even us down here. We are the other side of the wheel, my friend. There is no difference."

"There must be," Hermes said.

"No."

Hermes glared angrily about the room, at the fish and sinuous octopi, whose style Persephone now recognized from the walls of Knossos, and the painted panels of the Upperworld where the sun shone unendingly on ever-blowing poppies. His eyes fell on the statues, the bronze and marble youths and the lovely maidens resting white arms eternally on empty air. Their cold beauty made him wonder, as Persephone had once, if they might be all that was left of someone. Someone with nothing but beauty to leave behind. The warmth in the chamber came not so much from the hearth, he thought, as from Persephone on her couch, blond hair spilling over one

shoulder where it had loosened from its pins, pale
hands playing with a fig. Her skin had been golden
once; now it was white as milk. It didn't matter. She
exuded an aureole of light, just visible to the eye.
No wonder Hades had wanted her. She brought the
Upperworld into this one, kept the wheel from stopping in the darkness.

Hades stood up. He looked at Persephone thoughtfully. "I believe I will leave you to show your cousin
our domain here, if he is interested. I shall be in our
chambers, my dear." He bent, kissed her cheek, and
departed, whistling Cerberus after him.

Hermes stared. "It's a trick," he said quietly.

"No." No, he was giving her the chance to go with
Hermes if she wanted to. Persephone sat up. "He
wants you to see his kingdom. You may find something to tell Mother that will ease her mind."

"He is attempting to lure me into his lair." Hermes
folded his arms.

"Well, you might as well come, because you'll
never find your way out without me to show you."
He hesitated and she said, "Come *on*. You should be
glad I'm willing to talk to you after the way you've
behaved." Maybe he would tell her some more about
the village and Mother before he left. There was no
harm in asking him that.

Hermes rose and followed her into the corridor,
looking uneasily over his shoulder for whatever
ghosts or monsters might be lurking. She led him
with no apparent uncertainty through a maze of passageways, some of which displayed the journeyers
he had seen earlier carved into their walls, some
plain, some ancient and roughly hewn like the chambers of a tomb.

"This is what makes the people who are left with him here live or die," she said, showing him the garden of poppies, now bright again with scarlet blooms. "They are the secret of sleep. Take that back to Mother as my gift to her. Tell her to slit the pods and let the juice that runs out thicken."

"Poppies are poison."

"Too much, yes. Like too much wine. It's all a circle that comes back again, Hermes. You know that. You knew it before I did." He had, too. It was what made girls go lie with him when they knew he was unfaithful.

He thought that she knew an uncomfortable amount now. It would not make her easy to be married to.

She drew him down the corridor into the oldest caves. "This is the storeroom. I think we could live a long time on just what is put by here."

He peered into the dusty recesses at row after row of clay jars, the farthest ones thick with dust and cobwebs, their necks incised with strange markings.

"He has ships that sail places you have never heard of."

"So he says."

She thought of taking him to see the woman on the bier, but it seemed disrespectful, and Persephone felt protective of her. Hermes would act as if he were seeing a dancing bear. She took him to see the pool instead, assuming, rightly, that it would impress him.

Hermes did his best not to let that show. She had led him in through the door from her sitting room, avoiding the suggestion that might be implied by taking him through the bedchamber. The marble servant with the towels hung over one arm was just visible in the bathchamber doorway, and Hermes jumped when he saw it. He glared at the pool and the painted squid on the bottom as he had glared at everything else in Hades's domain.

"Put your toe in," Persephone suggested.

"Very likely something will pull me under."

"Bah! Don't be a baby," she said scornfully, as if they were ten again and she was daring him, or he her, to try to ride a wild ram. She knew he wanted to. He was like a ferret; he would investigate anything.

He bent and stuck a cautious finger in the water. "It's hot!"

"It comes from a spring below the island," she said, knowledgeable now. "Where the earth is hot. And look at this!" She pulled aside the hanging from the doorway beyond to display the stone seat.

As she had expected, the seat and its drains caught his attention. He left the pool and peered down the hole, not even wrinkling his nose, trying to see where it went. "Even old Glaucus didn't have anything like this," he said, marveling.

"Dryope!" Persephone said, tugging at his arm. "That's what I wanted to ask you. Get your head out of that; it isn't sanitary. Has anyone heard of Dryope?"

"No," Hermes said, emerging reluctantly.

"She can't have just vanished."

"Of course she can. People just vanish all the time. Probably taken down here," he added ominously.

"Don't be ridiculous." If Dryope were dead, would she have seen her? Would her face appear suddenly among the journeyers on the wall?

"I did hear," Hermes said, "that a man from the north island was paid in gold to take a woman nobody knew to somewhere he was forbidden to mention. It was all so mysterious that even the gossips couldn't get a grip on it. There are four versions circulating now. One of them holds her to have been Athena in disguise. A rival faction has decided she was a queen from the East, fulfilling a vow. Nobody seems to think she was just a happy widow who looted her husband's treasury."

"That wouldn't make such a good story," Persephone said, relieved. "Do you think it was Dryope?"

"I could think it was a sea turtle or Apollo in a dress and it wouldn't make any difference. It was or it wasn't."

"You are the most exasperating person! It makes a difference to *me*. You know things. I don't know how you do, but you do, and you're usually right."

"All right then, I think it was Dryope."

"Good."

"That doesn't mean it was, though."

"Stop that! Come along, and I'll show you the garden and the kitchens."

"Who needs food here?" Hermes asked suspiciously. "The dead don't eat."

"There are fifty-one servants who aren't dead, and they eat. I eat. My husband eats. You watched us."

"Illusion," Hermes retorted.

"You are maddening. Come along."

"And then will you come away with me like a sensible girl before that monster gets you?"

"If you are referring to my husband," she said haughtily, "you had better be more respectful." If she told him she absolutely wasn't coming with him, he would probably leave, and she was enjoying the novelty of a visitor, even if it was Hermes. "Come on." She motioned him through the outer chamber and into the corridor. She was almost certain that Hades was in his own chamber, well within earshot. As he had told her, the rooms in their quarters spiraled around each other like a nautilus.

In the corridor they found several servants, just passing by with arms full of linen, or trimming lamp wicks. Hades was not as careless as he had seemed. Hermes took note of them, too. "We are being watched," he hissed to Persephone. "Be on your guard."

Persephone didn't respond. She was certain now that Hades would let her go if she wanted to leave, and also that he would know about it instantly.

They found Scylla bustling in the kitchen, chopping cabbage. "Ah! It's the hero!" she said when she saw Hermes. "We heard one was coming. It must have been wet getting in; you look half-drowned. I'll fix you some hot wine."

Hermes eyed her suspiciously.

"Baker has just made some lovely bread, too."

"Oh, I want some." Persephone looked for it. "Hot bread is the best thing."

"Well, sit yourselves down, and I'll fetch you something nice." Scylla shooed them toward stools in the corner of the kitchen, as if they were children.

Hermes looked annoyed. This was not how heroes were supposed to be greeted. He was either supposed to fight his way through armies of supernatural soldiers, or be greeted by a grateful populace, joyful at their liberation. Possibly both. He was definitely not supposed to be sat down in the kitchen and fed bread as if he were a playmate come to visit.

He looked grumpy, and Persephone noticed it.

"There's no point in giving yourself airs with Scylla," she said.

"Here we are." Scylla trotted back with a basket of small hot loaves and a clay pitcher of heated wine. The smell was wondrous. Persephone inhaled a deep breath. "I just ate, and I'm starving already. This is so good."

"Now, I've watered the wine a bit more than usual because you can't be too careful." Scylla held out the pitcher, and Persephone, puzzled, rose to take it. Did Scylla think she was going to get tipsy and be kidnapped again by her hero? As she stood, Hermes saw her outlined against the light that spilled through the door from the garden. His brows rose.

Persephone tore off a piece of bread and dipped it in the little bowl of olive oil that Scylla had brought. "This is wonderful. Hermes, don't be such a fool. Nobody *wants* you to stay here forever, believe me, so you might as well eat. I've been eating since I got here."

"Apparently," Hermes said slowly. He thought. This changed things. Maybe. He wasn't sure. Maybe it didn't. They had sent him to fetch her. And this development might give him some advantages. "I'll take you home anyway," he said, appearing to come to a decision. His expression was magnanimous. "Not every man would, but I'm an understanding fellow. Things can happen."

Persephone looked perplexed.

"Nonsense!" Scylla said briskly. "You can't take the mistress anywhere in her condition. This hero business is all very well, but now she has other matters to think of."

# XI

❧

# Love Is Dangerous

Persephone stared at them both, and very quietly a new piece of knowledge clicked into place with complete certainty. This was a development she had not anticipated. She put her hands to her waist. Scylla had known. Did Hades know? Maybe everyone had known but herself. She counted backward in her head and then on her fingers. It was so hard to tell what time of day it was down here, much less what month, and her flow had been odd since she had come. Scylla said they all were, that it was because they never saw the moon. Persephone saw Scylla beaming at her now.

"Your mother will be greatly distressed," Hermes said sternly.

Persephone burst into laughter. That was an understatement, she felt sure, and certainly an excellent reason not to see Mother for a while yet. "Hermes, I can't go anywhere with you. If you think I'm going home to Mother in this condition—"

"Well, it would just upset the good lady, I'm sure," Scylla said. "She'll come round when she sees the babe; they always do. The same thing happened to my sister, but it was all for the best. She married the boy—he had no prospects; that was why our mother didn't like him—and they were happy, you know. Not like me. My man had prospects, but he was an old beast."

Persephone, thinking, listened to her with half an ear. It appeared that life existed very happily in the land of the Dead, and that there were always more choices than two. Hades had said that, she thought, but she hadn't known what he meant. Now she did. She would have bargaining power with him, too, once this child was born, because half of it would belong to the upper air.

"Hermes," she said, noticing him standing with arms folded, scowling, "go home."

Echo watched Demeter in her garden from a distance. No one liked to get too close to Demeter these days. The weather swerved like a runaway cart, brightening to sun when she smiled, boiling into storm when she grew annoyed. When she looked at Triptolemus, the earth burst with new shoots, indiscriminately growing vegetables and weeds, a hand's span's growth in a night. Sometimes when the two of them went into Demeter's house the sun blazed with a sudden heat as if it were falling to earth, or the warm rain started, soaking everything, only to dry off in a hot mist in an hour.

If the loss of Persephone had set the weather to swinging, then the reappearance of Triptolemus had made it more giddy yet, if somewhat more moderate.

There was no more snow, and the rain kept the hot
sun from cooking the land as it had the year before,
but it was a nervous, unsteady life with weather
like this.

"How can anyone make any plans when it's just
as likely to pour as to bake?" Doris complained, taking her laundry off the line for the third time in a
day.

It didn't seem to be that way on the north island,
as if Demeter's reach was narrowing, using itself up
in a burst of wild energy. Echo had pestered Doris
unrelentingly until she had said they might go visit
Narcissa and Irene, and see how they were getting
on, pointing out that at least there they wouldn't
need a rain hat and a fan in the same day. Echo was
afraid of how Narcissa was getting on, but she had
to see. All her friends were disappearing. She suspected that Doris had some such idea in mind for
her, too. Doris had consulted Bopis before they left,
in a low-voiced conversation that reviewed the merits
of several candidates, as well as their disadvantages,
ranging from baldness and a goiter to a possibly insane grandmother. The only one Echo found promising was the last, a pleasant-faced boy named
Salmoneus, an orphan with a herd of goats to tend
on his own. The possibly insane grandmother was
long dead, and she thought she was willing to take
her chances in preference to the aged miller with the
goiter, Bopis's candidate of choice. Matchmaking was
Bopis's main occupation. She was related to half the
people on the island and could be counted on to
know when someone was in need of a wife, or could
be persuaded that he was. She arranged passage for
Doris and Echo with a potter driving an oxcart of

jugs to the north island to sell, and sent them off with a lunch of dried fish and bread, and encouraging last-minute advice.

"Now, be sure to talk seriously with Irene. She's made a very good match, and she'll be in a position to help you present Echo to some suitable men."

Echo was doubtful as to the benefits of suitability. No one could have called *him*—Hades, she said firmly, naming him in her head—no one could have thought him suitable, but from what Triptolemus had said, Persephone was happy down there. Echo would like to visit her, she thought wistfully, wondering if she had the courage, if the prospect wasn't so frightening. The prospect of seeing Narcissa was almost worse, but at least no more mortal danger than the jolting of the oxcart accompanied it. Maybe, Echo thought hopefully, Narcissa would be happier in her marriage now. Bopis had assured her that nice girls were always frightened when they married, but they got over it. Nice girls being girls who hadn't already tried things out in a hayfield, Echo gathered. Maybe she would try out Salmoneus before she made up her mind.

The weather turned from sun to rain to high wind and back to cloudless sun by the time the cart had crossed the first ridge. On the other side of the ridge it settled down. Clearly Demeter's reach had grown shorter. Echo and Doris, sitting on the seat beside the driver, took off their traveling cloaks and hats and tucked them into a marginally clean corner of the cart. The clay jars rattled gently in their straw beds, and the ox snorted and switched his tail at the swarm of flies that accompanied them. Behind them, on the southern side of the ridge, a dark cloud blew over the place where the village stood, rained like a maid pouring out a bucket, and then vanished like mist.

Doris tutted. "She doesn't know what she wants; that's the trouble. If she doesn't settle down and figure it out, we'll never get anything planted."

"Strangest thing I ever saw," the potter said, flicking the reins. "Hee-yup. I don't hold with messing around with the supernatural, myself. No good ever comes of it. We ought to give the gods their sacrifice every so often, keep 'em happy, and leave 'em alone otherwise. It started with sending that fellow down the cliff. Stands to reason if you've got somebody like *that* living below you, you don't want to call yourself to his attention, if you know what I mean."

"Sometimes he heals them," Doris said.

"Yes, but at what cost? That's what I want to know. Carrying off maidens and all. I don't hold with it."

Doris abandoned the conversation, and Echo thought about the potter's words as they jolted along. The supernatural was all around you. How could you not have doings with it? Some people just had a more direct connection to it than others. For Demeter it was like a fabric that she could fold any way she wanted. For the potter, Echo suspected it was a pitch-black pit that he preferred not to look into. She didn't voice this train of thought, though. The only person she knew who liked talking about things like that was Hermes.

They spent the night under a pine tree, wrapped in their cloaks, listening to the potter snore. In the morning they woke, smelling of pine needles, and washed and watered the ox in the stream that trickled past the cart track. By midday they were in the north island village where Phitias and Nicias had taken their brides.

Irene heard the rumble of the cart in the square and rushed out to see who it was. The north island village did not appear to be much more interesting than the southern one, and anyone in a cart was a diversion. She gave a shriek of recognition as they tumbled off the seat, and embraced Doris.

"It's Echo," Doris said. "She would see Narcissa, and she plagued me until I agreed to bring her."

"Well, of course, and such a nice surprise." Irene hustled the two of them into her house, a much larger one than her old one, and right in the center of the village. "Nicias will be pleased, and it will do Narcissa good."

"How is she?" Doris asked. "Not pregnant already?"

"No, though I know Phitias is hoping. No, she just seems to be in the doldrums. She tells me she is fine, but . . . Well! I know Phitias is a kind husband; it's not that. . . ." Irene trailed off. "I don't know quite what it is. But she'll be glad to see Echo."

"Where is she?" Echo asked.

"Phitias has built her the loveliest house," Irene said. "Just around the corner, next to the Temple of Hestia. I was hoping that might, but it doesn't seem . . ." She trailed off again. Echo thought Irene wasn't really sure what it was she was trying to say. Narcissa seemed to be a thought that eluded her.

What Echo saw immediately was that Narcissa was thin. Not just slender as she had always been, but skeletal. Her eyes were huge and her wrists like sticks where they protruded from her mantle. She kept its folds wrapped about her, the end bundled over her head as if she wanted to hide.

"Narcissa!" Echo stood in her doorway gaping.

Narcissa peered at her.

"It's Echo, you silly girl," Irene said, bustling them all into Narcissa's house. "Come all the way up from the South to see you. Now isn't that nice?"

Narcissa followed them into her house, where Irene bustled more in the pantry, saying, "Well, aren't you going to offer us something to eat, dear? And have something yourself; it will do you good."

Narcissa let her mother fix them a bowl of dried figs and a dish of cold eels and set it all out on a table, but she didn't eat.

"We're going to take a walk," Echo said when she saw that. She scooped the figs into a fold of her mantle. "We'll just take these with us. I want to explore. Narcissa, have you a wineskin?"

Narcissa nodded, but she didn't move.

"Ha!" Echo said. "There it is. We'll steal a bit of this nice wine, too." She upended the pitcher Irene had brought, and poured half of it into the skin. Irene and Doris watched them indulgently, but Echo could tell Doris was shocked by Narcissa, too.

"What have you been doing to yourself?" she demanded as soon as they left the house.

Narcissa was silent.

Echo looked around her at the town, as if it were at fault, and swallowed newcomers. It was bigger than her own, but the air had the same bright, dusty sheen. The sun bounced off the limestone walls in a blue-white flare. People passed them in the streets, bound on the usual errands, carrying jugs or baskets or driving goats. An old woman passed them, clutching by its feet a chicken that clucked in apparent contentment. On the hill Echo could see vineyards. The north island had learned from the south. "Come on." She led Narcissa that way, up a goat track that wound through scraggly grass and a burst of purple anemones. At the top of the hill she sat her down under a grapevine and uncorked the wineskin. She tipped a few drops on the grass for whatever deities might be lurking. "*What* is the matter with you?"

Narcissa was still, hands folded in her lap, lost in her voluminous mantle. Finally she spoke. "I told you I couldn't do it," she whispered.

"Eat this." Echo handed her a fig. "How bad is it?"

Narcissa looked at the fig with revulsion. "I can't. It will make me ill."

"You're ill because you haven't been eating. You're thin as a stick."

"No, it makes me feel like I want to throw up. I'm all right, I just can't eat."

"And that is 'all right'?" Echo demanded. "What is your husband thinking of? Has he had the doctor to see you?"

"He wanted to. I couldn't bear him to touch me."

"The doctor? Or your husband?"

"Both," she whispered.

"Well, you can come home with us," Echo announced.

Narcissa shook her head. "You know I can't."

Echo did know. It was all very well to make wild talk, sitting under a grapevine drinking wine, but no one was going to let Narcissa leave a nice man who had built her such a nice house.

"Are you pregnant? Maybe that's why you feel sick."

"No!" Narcissa shook her head vehemently.

"When was your last flow?"

"I don't remember. But I am *not* pregnant!"

Echo didn't think she was either. Girls who were pregnant had a kind of bloom on them, even if they got thin at first from being sick. That was how the village busybodies always knew. Narcissa looked like someone who was starving.

"Tell me about Persephone," Narcissa whispered. "Has she come back?"

"Not exactly, but the strangest thing—her father is here, living with Demeter! She hit him with a lightning bolt and knocked him into the olive tree in the agora. Then she took him *home* with her!"

"Persephone's *father*?"

"You know, we were never really sure she *had* one. Well, he appeared in the agora last week as if he had just fallen out of the sky like a bird's egg, and said that he'd been shipwrecked and the lord and lady who lived in the caverns had saved him. He said the lady swam out to fetch him in a raging storm, stark naked. He thought she was a Nereid."

"That sounds like Persephone," Narcissa said with a small smile.

"It was, and as far as I'm concerned it's clear no one is holding her against her will; but Demeter still wants her back, and they've sent Hermes off to fetch her! And the weather is stranger than ever since her father moved in with Demeter. It's just like living in a ballad."

"What about you?" Narcissa looked at her wistfully.

Echo surveyed the vineyard. At the far end a boy was pruning the vines. She could hear a faint hum of bees in the air. "It would be nice to be somewhere the weather isn't so chancy. But Bopis has found Mother some prospects for me, and I think I'm going to take young Salmoneus. Do you remember him? His parents both died last winter, and he has all those goats to manage alone—and I'm good with goats."

Narcissa was silent. Echo chattered on, her voice soothing in the warm sun. After a while Narcissa reached for the figs in Echo's lap and ate one. Echo handed her the wine. "He's not so much older than I am. He doesn't talk much, but he doesn't seem to mind when I do—not like Father who's always shushing me. I don't think men like to talk; I don't know why. The only one I know who'll talk about anything but how the plowing's coming or whose goat is sick is Hermes. Demeter says he can marry Persephone if he can fetch her back, but I don't think he can."

"Marry her or fetch her back?" Narcissa asked. She tipped the wineskin up and drank.

"There you go; that'll do you good. Both, I should think. It doesn't sound to me as if Persephone wants to leave—Triptolemus, that's her father, says it's a palace down there, like a whole city underground. And if she did want to leave, you know she wouldn't marry Hermes."

"I always thought she secretly liked him," Narcissa said pensively.

"Love's an odd thing," Echo said. "I always did, too, but he's so flighty, and you could never make him be faithful. Persephone wouldn't put up with that. And personally, I think he might be sorry if he got her. Look at her mother—that old man looks as if someone's put a spell on him. I saw him plowing her garden, and he looked as tired as the ox. Love is dangerous."

"I know that," Narcissa said. She tipped up the wineskin again. She looked fragile to Echo, as if she might crumble into bones at any moment under the folds of her mantle, but her eyes were bright. They glittered like water, and she began to laugh.

"Don't you think you could learn to care for him?" Echo asked her hesitantly. "He doesn't mistreat you, does he?"

"No." Narcissa let out a long breath. "I don't want to talk about it. Just for this afternoon, let's not talk about it."

"All right," Echo said. "We'll be pirates instead. We'll go and salvage the wreckage of Triptolemus's ship and be rich and the terror of the seas. Here." She reached out her hand for the wineskin and lifted it, tipping back her chin.

Narcissa laughed shakily. "That sounds better. We'll kidnap Bopis and sell her for ransom."

"He might not buy her back," Echo said, "and nobody else would! Then we'd have to keep her."

"Horrors. But we could make her do the washing."

Echo snorted. "What we really ought to do is kidnap Aristippus and keep him till he promises not to chase girls. Bopis wouldn't be nearly so bad if she wasn't mad at him all the time."

"That's the thing," Narcissa said, taking back the wineskin. "Like you said, love is dangerous." She upended it and drank the last. "Dangerous."

*     *     *

When they came back to Narcissa's house they were just a little unsteady, and Doris and Irene eyed them suspiciously. "Well! Did you girls have a good time?" Irene asked.

"Yes, Mother." Narcissa kissed the top of her head. "I am going to go and lie down now. I feel a little faint. Echo thinks I might be pregnant."

Irene's eyes lit up. "Oh, yes, do lie down. Take a nice nap, and we'll look in on you later before Phitias comes home. Won't he be excited!"

She swept Doris and Echo up with her and bustled them out again, back down the street to her house. "There is such a lovely courtyard in the back," Irene said to Doris and Echo. "We can sit out there and talk. Oh my, I am so glad you came, such good news. Echo, did she eat?"

"She ate a fig," Echo said dubiously.

"Wonderful. She'll be on the mend soon, I'm sure, I was always taken that way myself in the first few months." Irene took them through her house and proudly showed them the walled courtyard, which Nicias had built for his first wife.

They settled in chairs there, and Echo tilted her head to the sun and closed her eyes, drowsy with the wine, listening to them talk, like the high distant chatter of birds in the trees. The names of the suitors Bopis had proposed for her circled her head like flies, and she batted them away. Irene knew a "nice young man" no more than thirty, with a little vineyard of his own. Nicias had a second cousin. The next-door neighbor was a recent widower with seven children. *I will marry Salmoneus,* Echo thought drowsily. *I would rather have goats.* He would let her come north and visit Narcissa, she thought. Maybe Persephone

would come, too, and the three of them could sit in
the vineyard the way she and Narcissa had today,
and it would be like old times. Echo decided that if
Hermes came back in one piece, she would ask him
to take her to see Persephone. Maybe everything
would be fine. She drowsed in the sun, warmed by
the wine they had drunk, listening to the bees and
her heartbeat in her head. She didn't wake until she
began to snore and her mother pinched her.

Echo fumbled with her mantle, which had fallen
on her feet.

"Disgraceful!" Doris said, laughing.

"I'll just go see if Narcissa is awake yet," Echo said
with dignity.

"That's fine, dear," Irene said. "You go along, and
we'll come in just a bit. Nicias and Phitias will be
here soon, and we'll all have a meal together."

Echo yawned and straightened her gown. She
noted that she had spilled wine on the front and
arranged the mantle to cover it.

Doris shook her head, still laughing.

Echo knew they were pleased because she had
got Narcissa to eat. She kissed her mother and
bobbed her head respectfully at Irene and let herself
back into Irene's house, which was very splendid,
with bronze braziers in all the corners and lamps
hanging from the heavy roof beams under fresh
thatch. Echo trailed her hand along the fine weavings that covered the walls and the painted plaster
leaves that encircled the outer door. She slipped
into the agora and made her way along the street
to Narcissa's house.

No one answered when she tapped her fist on the
door. Echo peered through the crack between the

door and the wall and could see no light. Narcissa must be still asleep. She pushed at the latch and poked her head inside. The house was dark, with only the low afternoon sun falling in a broad band from the window. She didn't see Narcissa at first in the dim light and then as her eyes grew accustomed, she saw her clearly.

Narcissa hung from the rafters just above the cold hearth, on which she had piled a stool on top of a chair. The stool lay on its side among the ashes, and Narcissa's body swayed just barely in the breath of air from the open door.

Echo screamed and righted the stool. She teetered on it and wrenched at the knotted rope, but it wouldn't give. She ran to the kitchen, spilling the stool in the ashes again, and found a knife. She sawed desperately with it at the rope, not looking at Narcissa's horrible face. When the rope gave, she fell, with Narcissa, into the ashes. Echo tore the noose from her neck and began to sob.

*Love is dangerous.* The words came back to her. She stood up slowly and went to the door, to meet Irene and Doris, with Nicias and Narcissa's husband, on the threshold.


"Hermes, I don't love you." Persephone shivered even though she sat next to the cook fire.

"Yes, you do," Hermes said dubiously. "You used to." He looked uncertain.

"No, I didn't. And something awful is wrong. I can't talk about this with you now."

"What? What's wrong?" Hermes looked argumentative. But he felt it too, some slow cold wind down the back of his neck.

"I don't know. Something has happened in the upper air."

"Probably your mother cooking up a hailstorm."

"No. It isn't Mother." She stood up. "Scylla, what is it?"

"Someone coming, maybe," Scylla said. "I don't know. Sometimes we feel them, down here."

"Feel whom?"

"Travelers. The restless ones. The ones who don't know where they belong." She busied herself with the cabbage.

Persephone pulled her mantle about her. "Hermes, I'm going to show you the way out."

"Take some of that nice bread before you go," Scylla said. "It's a cold climb up that cliff."

"I'm not going," Hermes said.

"Well, then eat something and don't be tiresome!" Persephone snapped at him. "I can hear your stomach growling."

"Maybe that's just your ghost coming," Hermes said sulkily.

Persephone slapped him, and he gaped at her. "Be careful I don't keep you here," she hissed. "I could, you know."

Hermes stared. "All right. Show me the way out."

She led him through the maze of corridors, stalking along in front of him, not waiting to see if he followed her. At the entrance, he thought, he would grab her and they would go. When she was in the upper air, whatever spell the caverns had laid on her would dissipate. Probably. "You don't know what's good for you," he said cajolingly. "If you stay here any longer you'll never get out. You'll be like them."

He waved his hand at the journeyers on the passage wall.

She didn't answer, and she didn't look back at him.

Beside him, they almost seemed to be moving. Out of the corner of his eye he saw the flutter of a cloak and caught the faint tap of a staff on the edge of his hearing. They shifted, their pattern realigned, as if they made room for another.

Demeter felt it in the wind that blew over the island, some breath of warning and danger. "Do you long for Eleusis?" she asked Triptolemus abruptly. She had moved back into her bed and kept him in it with her. Now she sat with the sheet wrapped around her waist and studied him as if he were a new sort of plant among her beans.

"I don't know." He was breathing hard, his chest slick with sweat. Whether he did or not, his body responded to hers. "Does it matter?"

She hesitated. What did the body know of what the heart wanted? "I begin to think it is dangerous to keep you caged like this."

"No doubt as dangerous as when I kept you."

She blinked at him, surprised.

"I have thought about it since I came here." He ran his fingers through his pale hair. There were still faint glints of gold in it, but he was no longer beautiful. He was growing old, and his bones ached. "I am not a fool. The winds do not blow a man into the same waves twice in a lifetime without some meaning. I was very young that first time. I didn't know who you were."

Demeter thought of the two of them on his boat,

after he had mended it, asleep on the deck wrapped in the same cloak. The stars had looked like spangles of ice in a warm black sky, puddles reflected in a black sea. They flickered as she watched, and the flicker had bubbled in their blood while the sea rolled under them. "I was just a girl then. It was the baby. And Faunus's garden. That was where the knowledge came from. After that things began to grow when I told them to."

"And now our daughter has married the lord of Death, to whom she would have gone too young to marry if you had stayed. You were right. Mother would have made me expose her."

"And you would have listened."

He nodded. "I owed it to her. I owed her everything, because we killed Demophon."

Demeter laid a hand on his arm for a moment. Gestures of affection from her were rare. Mostly she made love to him silently, savagely, consumingly. "Take that grief and throw it on the sea, Triptolemus." Her voice was low and vehement. "Demophon had an ill nature and a grasping heart. Your mother was a fool."

"The world is mysterious that way," he said. "I never understand half of it."

"Do you want to go back, then?"

"To Eleusis?"

"Yes, to Eleusis."

"Alone?"

"Are your mother and sisters still there?"

"Yes."

"Then alone."

"My mother is still there mourning Demophon. If

I go back I will have to be Demophon for her again. It's hard to do, and painful."

*Love is dangerous.* Something whispered that in her ear. "Am I like that?" she asked him abruptly.

He smiled at her now, rueful. "A little."

"Go back if you will, then," she said quietly, "or stay here if you will." She spread her fingers out. She would open her hand and wait for the rush of wings.

"If I stay of my own will," he said, propping himself on one elbow, "I will not be Demeter's pet." He might not understand things, but he could understand that.

"No." She looked at her open hand. "Nor I Triptolemus's doxy."

"And do you think we may both be easy in that bargain?" He looked hopeful.

"No." Demeter lay down again beside him. "Love is uneasy. Look what my love for my daughter has done to the world, but life is very plain without it." He reached for her, and she knew with a wistful certainty that if you didn't allow the danger in, there was no hope of joy. She knew also that not everybody won.

"This is Chickpea," Salmoneus said. He stroked the goat's pale brown head while it watched him with yellow eyes and black barred pupils. "And this is Pomegranate, and Ivy, and Violet."

Echo brushed her hand down Ivy's back. Ivy swayed a little and closed her eyes. The two bleating kids that had been following her stuck their heads under her belly and began to suck.

"That's Hawthorn." He pointed to the buck who

stood guarding his little flock, beard wagging. "He's a little cranky, but just with other buck goats. He likes me. He'll like you, too."

Echo considered that. Salmoneus had a pleasant face and sandy hair somewhere between tan and brown, like his goats. He smelled a little like them, too. But he was sweet-natured, and she wouldn't have a mother-in-law. That seemed promising. She knelt and scratched the nursing kids behind their ears and they waggled their tails.

"Those two are Acanthus and Anemone." Salmoneus looked doubtful. "I don't have anything for a bride price but goats."

"I like goats," Echo said. Violet butted her knees gently. She sat in the meadow grass and let Violet put her head on her lap.

Salmoneus sat down beside her. "Bopis says your father turned down two other suitors," he said.

"Because I wouldn't have them," Echo said. Technically, he could have made her have one of them, but Doris had convinced him that it would be cruel, after Narcissa. As Narcissa's gift, Echo was to be given her choice.

Salmoneus looked admiringly at this display of will. "Would you have me?" he whispered.

His breath was warm on her neck. Echo thought she could hear the thin sound of pipes. Something just out of sight danced on goats' hooves through the grass, and her blood hummed after it.

Aristippus felt it, too, like the rustle of autumn leaves outside the one high window of the goat shed. These days amorous dalliance was a chancy thing, but Clytie didn't seem to mind whether anything

much came of it. She was content to cuddle with him
and wait to see if something was going to happen,
feed him with her fingers, and play with his hair. He
had given up pursuing young girls years ago, settling
for the more sedate company of lonely widows, but
Clytie had danced across his horizon and winked at
him, and Aristippus had found himself younger than
he had thought. He wasn't so vain as to think Clytie
loved him. He gave her presents, and Clytie liked
presents. But she was a happy girl despite the whole
village thinking she was a slut. Sluthood suited Clytie just fine.

"I wouldn't be married," she confided to him,
"and have some man own me and order me about."
She tapped him on the nose. "And like as not be after
other women all the time as soon as I lost my looks."

"A man needs cheerful company," Aristippus said.
"It wears a man down, all that glowering and
nagging."

"Well, why did you marry her, then?" Clytie had
been trying to figure that out. All the couples of her
acquaintance seemed to grate on each other's nerves,
to have developed little ruts that their wagon wheels
ran through endlessly, digging them ever deeper.

"She was beautiful," Aristippus said fondly.

"See, that's all it is. Just beauty. Me, I'm putting
things by, so that when I'm old and funny looking
I won't need faithless old men. Hah!" She tickled
his beard.

"It wasn't just beauty," he said. "Every man on
the island wanted her. That is always stimulative."

"Every man on the island wants me," Clytie said
cheerfully.

"They don't want to marry you, you wicked girl.

Bopis was standoffish. She made herself look like a challenge." Aristippus smiled reminiscently.

"Bopis is respectable." Clytie stuck her nose in the air and pursed her lips together. "Respectability is overrated. When *I* am old and ugly, I will still have my sheep and a nice house, and I *won't* have an old ugly husband telling me to make his supper and wash his smelly tunic."

Aristippus laughed. "If you married, you would be just as bad as Bopis."

"That's why I won't." Clytie tossed her head of dark curls. "I saw how my mother lived. When she died, I said I wouldn't be like her." Clytie's father had worked her mother to death while Clytie stayed out of the house and slept in the hayfield half the nights. By the time he died, her mother was so tired she had just lain down and died, too. "In fact, I told the goddess so," Clytie said, "and she didn't strike me dead."

"It's not always like that," Aristippus said.

"It's like that often enough. Harmonia *would* have that Tros, and I heard her just yesterday at the well complaining that he never comes home at night now."

"Watch out or she'll be blaming you."

"Tros is dull as a ditch full of water. He's just hiding because Harmonia is too tired to dance attendance on him." Clytie had stood where Harmonia couldn't see her, just in case, though. Respectable women were quick to blame Clytie for their husbands' failings.

"He'll be wanting some loving," Aristippus said. "Women with babies give it all to the baby."

"At least the baby appreciates them." Clytie snuggled closer to Aristippus and played with his beard. "That's another thing I shall remember not to do," Clytie informed him. "No babies."

"Well, you can't predict that." Aristippus slapped her on the bottom.

Clytie snorted. Men were ignorant. Much better not to have babies than let some man who couldn't be bothered with girls expose them on a hillside. The four daughters born after Clytie had been silent, half-blue things, even before her father had ordered them exposed. Her mother was so tired all the time she couldn't make a boy baby, or even a healthy girl. Clytie remembered Bopis now, coming to see her mother after the last one, and driving her father out of the house for the afternoon. Bopis had spoken in whispers, holding her mother's thin hand and stroking her bruised arms. She had left a pouch of something beside the bed, and her mother had got up and hidden it in the clothes chest when Bopis left. After that there had been no more babies, and her mother had shown Clytie where to pick the herbs that had been in Bopis's pouch.

"Bopis knows," Clytie said. "Bopis knows more than you think."

Bopis knew where Aristippus was. He hadn't dared take the little trollop into their own shed again, and so he had gone to ground in someone else's. Bopis had come to speak with young Salmoneus about the betrothal arrangements. Echo was determined to have him, and her parents (so ill-advised, but there was no talking to some people) were going to let her make her own choice. Bopis was clicking her tongue over the folly of that when she saw the scrap of green wool caught on a thorn bush. It had a brown border, and she knew that scrap. It was the one that she had seen dangling from Aristippus's hem this morning. She had told him to take the tunic off and let her mend it, but he had pushed her away and said he had important matters to attend to, more important than darning a tunic.

Bopis narrowed her eyes. Someone had crossed through the tall grass beside the goat track here not long ago. She turned off the path to Salmoneus's cottage and headed for his goat shed, cutting through the meadow to come around by the back. She pricked her ears for incriminating sounds as she went. The low bleating of a goat and the tinkle of a bell came from the hillside as she slunk cautiously through the dry grass, the incriminating scrap of wool clutched in her fist. Aristippus was going to be sorry he hadn't let her mend it.

The goat bleated again as Bopis swiveled her head, trying to see if Salmoneus was about. A faint giggle danced along the air, and she froze, trying to pin-point the sound. There were just the goats' low-voiced conversation and a bee humming past her ear, bent on its own errands. Bopis's mouth tightened. She had been beautiful once, and he had sat at her feet and recited poetry to her. That had been before she married him. She heard the giggle again, some female who would frolic like a trollop in goat sheds, and Bopis knew who it was. She marched purposefully toward the shed now, her mantle flapping behind her like a sail. "I know you are in there!" She thumped her walking staff on the ground as she went, vengeance in her eyes.

She heard a faint shriek, and it seemed now not to be in the shed. Bopis veered toward the oak trees.

There was a rustle among the long grass and last year's leaves. "Aha!" She ducked under a low-hanging branch and came face-to-face with Salmoneus. Behind him Echo was pulling her dress over her head.

"You!" Bopis and Salmoneus stared at each other, red-faced. Echo yanked her dress down and stood, brushing thistles from the hem.

"Oh. I. Er . . ." Salmoneus cast about for the proper thing to say while Echo hid her face in her hands. When it became clear that he wasn't going to think of anything, she lowered them.

"We're very sorry," Echo said. "And we won't do it again."

"Don't be ridiculous!" Bopis snapped. "Of course you'll do it again. Men have no restraint."

"I'm sorry," Salmoneus managed. "It—it was the goats, I think . . . and the grass . . . and . . ."

"Be quiet! Echo, your mother is going to be severely disappointed."

"Do you have to tell her?" Echo twisted one bare toe in the dirt. Her sandals, Bopis noted, were in the tree. "We *are* going to get married."

"Out in the woods in front of anyone who comes along! You could at least have had the decency to go inside."

"Oh. I suppose we could have." Salmoneus lived alone.

"I'm surprised you didn't use the goat shed!" Bopis said, suddenly narrowing her eyes. "Since it's so handy."

"Isn't very clean in there," Salmoneus said hastily.

"Spiders," Echo said. "Big ones."

Bopis slid another suspicious glance at the goat shed, its roof just visible through the oak leaves.

"Please don't tell Mother." Echo sidled up to her, making shooing motions at Salmoneus. "It was just that I was so lonely, and I do like Salmoneus. He'll be a good husband, and I wanted to please him, and . . ."

"There will be plenty of time for that," Bopis said severely. "You will have a duty to do after your marriage."

"I was frightened," Echo said, seizing inspiration. "I thought at least I would know what it was like, you know." She moved farther into the trees, where there was a rotten stump, and sat down on it, making room for Bopis, and looked hopeful. "If I just had someone older to talk to. Mother is so busy, with the wedding and everything. . . ."

"Poor child." Bopis appeared to weaken. She sat next to Echo and patted her hand. "This isn't the way to go about things. You'll get a reputation, you know."

"I know," Echo said sorrowfully. She saw that Salmoneus had disappeared.

"That's important. Men have latitude that we women are not allowed. And wouldn't want," she added firmly. "Whatever a man may do, it is of the utmost importance that his wife be known for her virtue."

Echo thought that sounded unfair, but she didn't say so. You didn't argue about things like that with Bopis. But she did wonder, too, whether Bopis had ever found that rule unfair, considering everything.

She cocked her head cautiously, but no sound came from the distant goat shed.

"How did you come to forget yourself so?" Bopis demanded sternly. "And don't blather at me about grass and goats like that young scoundrel."

It had been the goats, though, Echo thought. There was something old and knowing about goats. You looked in their yellow eyes and things looked back at you, old things, things that had to do with the dark of the moon and new grass in the stubble of a mowed field and some song you couldn't quite hear. She didn't think she could explain that to Bopis. "It just . . . it just seemed to happen," she said helplessly. "Even if I was afraid."

"A girl who will let herself be overcome by her physical sensations is headed on the road to ruin," Bopis informed her. "Women do not have the same sensations that men do, and if a girl gets to imagining that she does, no good ever comes of it. Our function is to make babies, to give birth to the next generation, that is what the Mother wants."

"Uncle Phaedon says intercourse opens the entrance to the womb, and lets the blood flow out so it doesn't back up and cause licentiousness and hallucinations," Echo said.

Bopis said, "Tchah!"

"He says it will travel about in your body if you aren't careful to do it often enough," Echo said.

"How did you come to hear such an unsuitable conversation?" Bopis demanded. "That is talk for a girl on her wedding night, not before."

"Uncle Phaedon explained it to Mother when Father complained that she wouldn't let him in her bed but once a month."

"Men always think they know more than women,"
Bopis said darkly, "particularly when it comes to
knowing things about women."

"Well, how are *we* supposed to know anything,"
Echo said, "if no one ever tells us?"

"There is a time to be told things," Bopis said severely, "and experimentation on your own is a bad
idea. What would you do now if young Salmoneus
decided not to go through with the betrothal? Suppose he didn't like you?"

Echo hadn't thought of that, not with the goat song
running in her blood. "I think he did, though."

"Well, that is doubly disgraceful," Bopis said severely. "It is not nice at all to enjoy yourself the
first time."

"If nobody had a good time, they wouldn't do it,"
Echo said rebelliously. She had thought about that,
and thought about Clytie, just moments ago lying in
Salmoneus's goat shed with Bopis's husband. At least
Echo hoped they weren't still there. She was sure
Salmoneus had gone to warn them. He knew they
were in there; he and Echo had heard them, and
fallen to giggling so helplessly that they had rolled
around in the grass, and then one thing had led to
another. She couldn't tell Bopis that, either.

"A lady has standards to maintain," Bopis said.
"You must understand that. Even if you are so
thoughtless of your own future as to marry this
young man, and I do not think he was the best
choice, but what's done is done, we all make our bed
and then must lie in it, just look at what I have suf-
fered at that man's hands, all for being young and
foolish, but that is another story and the Mother
knows I do not complain of it." She stopped to un-

wind the thread of the conversation and pounced again on the beginning of it. "You must never make it easy for them. Men think what is easy is not valuable; nor is it."

Echo kicked her foot against the base of the stump. "I'll remember that, Aunt Bopis." "Aunt" was a courtesy title for any village busybody to whom you were not related.

"If you do, my child, you'll be better off." Bopis stood, shaking leaves off the hem of her mantle. The goats bleated somewhere deeper in the woods, and they heard the crunch of brush underfoot. Through the branches Bopis caught a glimpse of a green tunic. She swung her head around to Echo with sudden suspicion. "Who was that?"

"Who, Aunt?"

"Someone else in the woods, you wicked child. Have you been keeping me here while he got away?"

"Oh, no. Absolutely not." There was no need to ask who. Bopis spent most of her time vengefully tracking her errant husband. Echo considered that it would serve Clytie right if they were caught, but she didn't want to think about what Bopis would do to Salmoneus for having them in his goat shed. Not that they had asked. No one would tell Aristippus, the priest of Zeus, no to anything. Echo didn't think she could bear it if Bopis changed her father's mind about letting her marry Salmoneus. "I saw him going toward Uncle Phaedon's house just an hour ago," she offered. Uncle Phaedon lived in the opposite direction, and fortuitously, near the cottage where Clytie lived.

Bopis looked at the scrap of wool, still clutched in her hand. "How odd," she said icily. Echo did her best to look innocent. "You talk entirely too much, my girl," Bopis told her. "One of these days that tongue of yours will get you in trouble."

She stalked off, betrothal negotiations forgotten, the wool balled in her fist. Salmoneus emerged from the trees. "The old harpy," he said. "I'm scared to death of her."

"That makes two of us," Echo said. "Do you suppose we could make our marriage not be like theirs?"

"I'm counting on it."

Or like Narcissa's, or like Persephone's, either, for that matter. Echo looked up at Salmoneus's friendly face. He had a smattering of freckles like hers across his nose. "Love is dangerous," she told him.

"Then we'll face it together," he said. "Just us and the goats."

Ivy and Hawthorn appeared, picking their way daintily through the little clearing. They butted their heads against Echo's legs, and she scratched them between their horns.

# XII

❧

## *Pomegranate Seed*

Persephone saw the travelers realign themselves on the corridor wall. She had seen it before, and never mentioned it to Hades. They never did it if you looked right at them, but when you turned your head half away, out of the corner of your eye you saw the movement. When you looked back, you were almost certain there was someone new among them. There were so many it was hard to be sure, but she knew she had seen Echemus, Narcissa's father. He wasn't there now, where she had first seen him, and she had thought yesterday she had seen him near the great hall. She thought they moved, walked on along the corridor wall until they came to wherever they were going. Where the carvings ended, there was a boat carved on the wall, waiting to sail into the stone.

Now she stopped in her march to the cavern entrance, her fingers to her mouth. Narcissa was there on the wall, her mantle drawn over her head, her face as emaciated as if she were bones already. The carver had caught her in midstride, one foot with its toes to the floor, heel lifted, hurrying on. Her feet and the hands clutching her mantle were skeletal, too.

"We had better hurry," Hermes said. "He'll be after us soon."

Persephone looked at Narcissa's face on the passage wall and began to weep.

Hermes took her by the arm. "He has enchanted you. The outside air will break the spell."

Persephone pointed a finger at the wall.

Hermes peered at it. The flicker of the lamps in their niches made the figure seem to move. "That's Narcissa! Do you see what he is now? How can you stay with a monster like that?"

"They come to him," Persephone said, weeping. "He doesn't take them."

"Of course he takes them. He's Death! Can't you understand that?"

"Death isn't a person." Persephone traced Narcissa's gaunt face with her fingertip. "Death is . . . circumstance, maybe. Marriage was her death," she said, knowing that suddenly. Why hadn't her mother and Bopis and all the rest seen that, and not sent her off to this?

"Don't be stupid," Hermes said. "Am I going to have to carry you off over my shoulder? I can do it." He eyed her consideringly.

"You can't." Persephone pushed him away, but he didn't move far. She could feel the wall against her back. "Hermes, you don't want to marry me anyway."

"Well, I have to. That's what being a hero is about. You marry the girl. You save her, and then you marry her."

Persephone laughed, and he looked hurt. "You don't want to be a hero, either. They made you. They burnt some offering and made a lot of smoke, and old Hesperia went into a trance and said the first thing that came into her head. And it was you, because you'd been braggy. I know you."

"You do," he conceded. "That's why I have to marry you. Someone who didn't know me would never put up with me."

"And you think that's an enticement? Nobody will marry you if that's the way you propose."

"I am not proposing," he said. He moved a step closer, pressing her against the wall. "You have been given to me, which is the proper way to do it. Girls don't get to pick their husbands. They are chosen for them, and your mother chose me."

"Well, I chose someone else!" She pushed him, hard, and he staggered back a bit. He lunged at her, gripping her arm, and she sank her teeth into his shoulder.

"Ow! You she-cat!" His hand closed tighter on her arm. She struggled, and her fist connected with his nose. It felt satisfactory, the way she remembered feeling when she had rolled him in the mud for stealing eggs from Demeter's hens when they were seven, and blaming it on her.

Hermes stumbled away from her. "You had better come with me," he said, panting, "and have that baby born in the upper air. If you don't it's likely to be a monster." His nose was bloody, and he put a hand to it. "It may be a monster anyway. You're lucky I'm still willing to have you."

"You've wanted me since we were eight and you got me to let you look under my dress," Persephone said. "You just didn't want to marry me."

"Well, I do now. And anyway I can't go home without you. Your mother will make it rain forever."

"Mother will be fine now." Persephone knew that, too, in some mysterious way. Her mother's garden was growing again and things were coming out of it, and that would be all right. Persephone was surprised by the things that she knew now. How very odd to have learned about the people of the upper air by living underground. Hermes looked at her doggedly. She didn't think he had learned anything and probably wouldn't because he already knew too much. "Oh, Hermes, stop and think about it," she said. "You know you don't want to get married. You'll make an awful husband, and your wife will be just like Bopis, scurrying around after you, trying to keep you home."

"And that monster will make you a better one?" Hermes's pride was stung.

"Don't be an idiot. He isn't a monster." But she thought of the Minotaur for a moment, the monster of King Minos's caverns. His wife had mated with a bull and borne that. No. Her hand brushed against her belly protectively.

Hermes saw it. "See? You *are* afraid. Come out of here with me now. If it's a monster we'll expose it, and no one will have to know."

*My child? If it's a monster I will nurse it at my breast as Pasiphaë did.* "No," she said. "I will stay, and what will happen will happen. Now, go away."

Hermes was silent a moment, thinking. "All right. Show me the door."

"It's just ahead."

"I can't see it. I'm afraid of this place, and I don't

trust *him*. Guide me to the entrance if you want me to leave."

"Very well," she said stiffly. "Come this way."

He walked silently behind her down the sloping corridor, while the stone travelers flowed in the other direction. For a moment he thought they made room for him on the wall. Beckoning hands invited him in. He turned his head from them quickly lest he fall into the stone.

"There," Persephone said. She halted at the wide mouth of the cavern entrance.

"It will still be high tide," Hermes said.

"Look." Persephone stepped a few paces through the entrance. The light outside was clear and golden, and the floor was dry, littered with shrunken patches of seaweed and half-buried shells. His lost hat lay upside down on the sand.

"It must be illusion," Hermes said stubbornly. "He is trying to drown us. It was high tide an hour ago."

"It isn't now," Persephone said. "Time is odd here. Now, go."

He hesitated a moment, shifting from foot to foot, apparently watching the light outside. A gull squawked in the air above the cavern mouth. Persephone moved to stand beside him.

"Go," she said. "Go and tell Mother I am content here."

His hand shot out, grasping her wrist, and his other arm came about her waist. He lifted her half off her feet.

"Let me go!"

"You'll feel differently when you are out of this place," he panted, struggling with her.

"Hades *will* kill you!" she gasped. "Let me go!"

"I am sent by Zeus," Hermes said stubbornly. "Zeus commands even him. Be still!"

She bit his ear, tasting blood.

"Stop that!" His hand covered her face as he tried to get her over his shoulder, and she writhed in his grip as she had writhed in Hades's. Hermes wasn't as big. She pounded his back with her fists and swung her knee into his groin. She sank her teeth in his shoulder again. He howled, but he didn't drop her.

She flailed at him, cursing him and shrieking. Someone would hear her. She wasn't going to go with him. Where was Cerberus?

"I will curse you!" she shouted into his bloody ear. His nose was bleeding badly, too. "I will make it wither and fall off. Mother could do it, and I can do it, too, and I will!"

Hermes didn't say anything, just staggered on toward the open air while she writhed and beat at him with her fists. The two sentinel stones stopped him. He couldn't pass between them with her hanging on his back. He set her down and began dragging her through by her wrists.

She fought him, but he was stronger than she had thought. "You'll never carry me up that cliff!" she gasped at him.

"We'll see." Hermes jerked her between the stones, and their momentum flung them out under the overhanging roof of rock. He pulled her from under it into the sunlight before she could dig her heels in.

Demeter sat up in the bed, her wild hair tangled about her head. Before Triptolemus could ask where she was going, she had flung on her gown and pulled her mantle about her shoulders.

He followed her to the door.

"I heard her!"

"Heard who?"

She didn't answer him. She just ran barefoot through the garden, her feet making urgent prints in the soft earth of the cabbage bed. She splashed across the brook and set out at a run across the headland, toward the cliff.

Triptolemus stood scratching his head in the doorway. He ought, he supposed, to follow her. He doubted it would change whatever was going to happen, but it seemed like a gesture that had to be made. He reached for his tunic.

The sunlight struck Persephone's face in a shower of light, like warm luminescent water. She turned toward it, gasping, breathing in the scent of salt and flowers and hay.

"See?" Hermes said. He was shaking, as if he had run for miles. "It calls to you."

Why hadn't it called to her when she had explored the beach? When she had sailed across the sea? Why now and not then?

Something huge and silent surged past her, nearly bowling her over, and leaped on Hermes.

"Call him off!" Hermes shouted, staring into Cerberus's enormous mouth. The dog's lips were drawn back and he growled, a deep rumble that Hermes could feel clear through the paws pinning him to the sand.

"Cerberus! Come!" The dog backed away reluctantly. "Leave him be." Hermes had grown paler, his face drawn.

"Guard!" a voice said. It was not Persephone's voice; it was Hades's, and Hermes saw him standing on the sand behind Persephone as if he had materialized out of the stone. Cerberus froze. "He will kill you if I tell him to," Hades said amiably.

Hermes sat up, his white face smeared with blood. "Zeus commands you to release her," he said. His tongue felt thick in his mouth.

"He commands nothing of the sort. And if he did, I have no reason to obey."

Hermes stood with an effort, straightening his blood-smeared tunic. He eyed Cerberus nervously. Cerberus gave him a fanged smile. Persephone watched them. This was not over. Something more would happen. She knew both of them well enough to know that. And something was wrong with Hermes. His arms looked like bones. The smell of the air overwhelmed her, thick with grapes and rosemary and the dusty scent of daisies.

There was a flash of light, and she saw the knife in Hermes's hand. He had had it hidden in his tunic. He lunged at Hades, and Hades's arm shot out to close around his wrist. They grappled with each other on the sand. Hermes was smaller, but he was strong and wiry and he had the knife. Cerberus, growling, followed the men with his dark gaze.

They broke apart and circled each other, seeking the advantage. Hermes's red hair was plastered to his head with sweat and blood, and his green eyes were sunken and sullen. He had started this; he would not back down now and be made a fool of. The sun that blazed off the water and the sand flashed on the knife again. Hermes leaped at Hades, and a line of red opened along Hades's left arm.

The knowledge that one was bound to kill the other over her made her desperate. Persephone flung herself at them, and the knife flashed by her ear. "Enough!"

Hermes froze, staring at the knife in terror. Hades didn't back away until she faced him and said between her teeth, "This was about choice. You are not the one with the choice to make." She spun and pointed a finger at Hermes. "And nor are you!" Then she turned slowly, staring at the path down the cliff face. "And nor are you, Mother," she said and set out toward the steps. Demeter was nearly at the bottom by the time she reached them.

"Oh my girl!" Demeter held out her arms, and Persephone went into them.

"Mother!" She clung to Demeter. Her mother smelled of the garden, a scent compounded of beans and figs and green wheat. She breathed it in, like drinking wine too fast, and staggered against Demeter.

"I've come to take you home."

That was why. Because now was the time to choose, not on Hades's ship or in the storm that Triptolemus had come out of. Now, when her mother stood in her arms, and it was all so achingly clear how much she loved her, and the smells of the earth. She turned to look at Hades, standing stock-still on the sand. He wasn't even watching Hermes anymore. He was watching her.

"No." It was barely a whisper, but she could feel the word growing louder. "No."

Demeter couldn't hear it. "He has put some enchantment over you," she said. She marched toward Hades, and a wind whipped up around her feet, thrashing her skirts in its fingers. "Thief!" she spat the word at him.

He bowed his head in a wary gesture of respect. "What I stole is free to go." His voice was sad.

"Set her free."

"I do." He looked gravely at Persephone. He had seen her growing drunk on the air that shone around her like a veil.

Hermes, ignored, glanced from Persephone to the cliff face and back. He sidled toward her, reaching for her arm.

"No." Hades hadn't appeared to see him, but now he bent and plucked a piece of wood from the sand. It might once have been a traveler's staff. Persephone could have sworn it had not been there before. He balanced it in both hands. "I believe this may be yours. You must have lost it on the way in. That happens. People come here burdened with too many things, and they lose them. There's your hat, too."

Hermes looked as if he were going to lunge at Hades again.

"I am very tired of you," Hades said. His eyes flashed with anger, and he pushed Hermes hard with the staff until Hermes staggered. Then he bent over him and said something Persephone couldn't hear. When he was through, he turned back to Demeter, paying Hermes no more attention.

A hand fell on Hermes's shoulder. "You should come back with me now," Triptolemus told him. "You don't know how long you've been gone."

Hermes felt his stomach cramping. His vision

smeared oddly across the sky and water. "What do you mean?"

"Time is odd here. I was underground a few weeks, and a whole season had come and gone when I came out."

"I didn't eat," Hermes said. That seemed now as if it might have been bad advice. He held his hands out in front of him. They were clawlike, the skin stretched on bones.

"That would be it then," Triptolemus said. "You've been gone a month, lad." Hermes was weaving on his feet now. Triptolemus picked him up and slung him over his shoulder. "It's a long way up the cliff, lad. Best to set out now before they start in. It'll spoil the weather for sure."

"What did you do to him?" Demeter demanded of Hades.

"Nothing he didn't do to himself. People are like that, I find."

"Give me back my child." Her expression alternated between pleading and anger, and the wind swirled around her head, making her hair fly with sparks.

"I have. I saw her with you. She longs for you."

"You are wise," Demeter said grimly.

"No." Persephone's voice was barely a whisper, but they both heard it this time. It grew out of the earth under her feet and the cold salt air. It was almost visible, and it had a scent like roses. It stilled Demeter's wind. "No. Mother, forgive me. I love you, but I don't want your life."

Demeter's eyes widened. Hades looked a little startled, too. Persephone tested this newfound power.

She spoke again, and the words floated on a summer breeze. "I will choose, because I am not yours, and not his. I am mine." *Mine.* It was a very satisfactory word.

Demeter's eyes teared. "I can't bear to lose you. How am I to bring you home, then?"

"By inviting me," Persephone said. "I'll bring your grandchild."

Demeter's mouth tightened for a moment, and then she closed her eyes. The rest of her wind fell into stillness.

"Look." Persephone pointed to the figures halfway up the cliff path. "That is a good man. I'm glad you didn't kill him. I'll come to see you both, with the baby."

"Is that a promise?"

"Always. And tell Hermes I forgive him, but being a hero doesn't suit him." She held her arms out, and Demeter clung to her.

Slowly, after a long while, Demeter pulled away. "As soon as the baby comes. Promise me."

"I promise, Mother."

Demeter set out for the cliff path then, and a gentle breeze followed her, smelling of roses.

Persephone looked at Hades. "What did you say to Hermes?" she asked him quietly.

"I told him I would give him to the bones that sleep in the cellars," Hades said. "I meant it, and he believed me."

"Why? He was already half-dead of hunger." His flesh had fallen away slowly as she watched him, the moment they had come out into the sun.

Hades closed his eyes for a moment with a look

of infinite pain. "I thought I had lost you," he whispered. "I was angry. I had to put it somewhere."

Persephone took his arm. "No, you'll have me forever now. I hope you don't change your mind. I don't think this is a choice I can unmake."

"Never." He looked at her solemnly. She stood on tiptoe to kiss him, startling him. His eyes flashed with elation and relief, and she felt his hand tremble as he took her elbow and led her back into the cavern. Cerberus padded at their heels. "You are a mess," he said finally. "I hope that is not your blood."

"No, it's all Hermes's." She looked at his arm a long time but didn't say anything.

"You are wondering about my blood," Hades said. "I do have some, as you can see," he said, turning the words to a small joke.

"Hermes said . . ." She bit her lip.

"Hermes said you have married a monster unwittingly. I know; I was listening."

"Did you hear everything?"

"Enough to see your doubts about the child."

Persephone put her hand over her belly again. "I thought of the story you told me of Minos's monster, about Pasiphaë. That was her child, no matter how she got it. What did she think when her husband chained it up?"

"Well, it was reputed to be violent."

"It was her child."

"It's a story."

"Stories are powerful. That's something I learned here."

Hades smiled then. "Ours is not going to be a

monster. You may examine my head for horns if
you wish."

"Narcissa is dead. Did you know?"

"I did." Hades put his arm around her shoulders.
"I dislike knowing things like that, but we take the
knowledge that comes to us. It is always better
than ignorance."

"Are you sure?" They passed by the corridor that
led to the kitchen garden, and she turned down it.
He followed her.

"If she was dead and you didn't know it, you still
wouldn't have her."

Scylla beamed at them as they came through the
kitchen. "The young hero gone off home, I see."

"Yes, he couldn't stay longer," Hades said, "but
he'll get a hero's welcome up above all the same.
He's been gone a month."

"I told him time was strange here," Persephone
said. "I don't understand it myself."

"Think of it as circular," Hades said. "I do. It
makes things simpler."

Persephone thought that sounded doubtful, but it
didn't matter. It was what it was. She went into the
garden and sat down on a bench under Pomona's
pomegranate tree. The pomegranates were just beginning to form at the blossom ends, round little fruits
like marbles. She picked one and balanced it in her
hand. "The stubborn fool never would eat the whole
time he was here."

"Just as well," Hades said. "I have found there is
some truth to that rumor. One can leave, of course,
but one will come back."

*Everyone has to come back*, Persephone thought. She
laughed. "So when I go to visit Mother, I will have

to come back?" That might be useful. You couldn't argue with fated things.

"True. But she can visit you, too, for that matter. As you can see, the living come here fairly often."

"When the baby comes," Persephone said. She rubbed her fingers over her stomach, feeling the possibilities inside.

Read on for a preview of
Aphrodite's Tale

# FATAL ATTRACTION

Coming from Signet Eclipse in October 2005

Everyone knew she was trouble from the start. Even Zeus knew it the minute he saw her. For one thing, she didn't have that look that newborn babies always had—slightly squashed and slit-eyed as if they weren't quite awake yet. This one's eyes were wide open and she looked like someone who had arrived to take charge. *I am here,* that look said. *Watch out.* And she was beautiful, which newborn babies also rarely are. Her eyes were the color of lapis lazuli, not the slate blue of normal newborns, and her hair was a cloud of rose gold curls just as long as the first joint of his finger. Like everyone else, he fell in love.

The farm he brought her home to was in Argolis, on the fertile plain that lay below the hill fort village of Tiryns. There his family raised cattle, goats, and olives and were a power in the world. The rest of the household took one look at her and knew trouble when they saw it, too. To begin with, Zeus claimed he had found her on a fishing trip off Cythera. He said, casually, that she had been lying in the surf, an exposed baby left to die, as surplus girl children often were.

"And why exactly do we need another one?" Hera inquired. She fixed the baby with steely gray eyes, looking from the child to Zeus and back again, perhaps measuring their features against each other. "We have a daughter."

"A playmate for Hebe," Zeus said jovially.

Hebe looked up from her dolls and smiled at Mama and Papa. Hebe was a biddable child.

"This house doesn't need another mouth to feed," old Rhea said, stumping into the nursery on her two canes.

"Let me worry about that, Mother," Zeus said. His mouth compressed slightly and a tic started under his left eye, the tic that his mother always produced in him.

"Always bringing home your bastard brats." Rhea mouthed the remaining stumps of her teeth. "You'll be putting your poor mother out into the snow next, to make room for them."

"It hardly ever snows, Mother."

"It might as well," old Cronos said, joining her. "Death song for this farm. Going to go under soon the way you and your brothers run it. I might as well die now."

Zeus looked at his father with exasperation. Cronos was nearly as bent as Rhea, they were like two malevolent bears, half crouched over their canes. Hera stood with her arms crossed, tapping her long fingers on the folds of her gown. This was between her and Zeus. Stubbornly, she refused to take advantage of his parents' opinions on the child. Shortly after her marriage Hera had found herself drawn into the ongoing war in which Zeus, his siblings and his parents continually engaged, and from which no one ever escaped.

"If you'd married a woman with some fire to her you wouldn't be out rutting with servingmaids in a hay barn every night," Cronos said, reminding her why.

"I told you, Father. I found the child," Zeus said between his teeth. "In the surf. She was wet and cold."

"No need for another girl," Cronos said. "Waste of resources."

"Should have exposed the last one," Rhea said.

Hebe, playing with her dolls on the nursery floor

beside her brothers, pretended she hadn't heard that. Hebe was seven, quite old enough to understand things. That particular thing she had been hearing all her life, so that she hardly took notice anymore.

"That other one, too," Rhea said. "The deformed one. Ill luck to keep that one. I said so." She pointed a wavering finger at Hephaestus, who sat with his brother and Hebe, pounding a wooden block with his wooden hammer.

"That will do!" Hera turned on her mother-in-law with fire in her eye. "Get out!" She flapped her mantle at Rhea as if she were shooing chickens. "Out! Get out or I *will* put you outside. I'll put your bed in the barn!"

"Zeus! Are you going to let her talk to me that way? She's wicked! She'll freeze me to death! Save your poor old mother!" Rhea sucked her teeth at Hera with a malign glare, tottering on her canes. She sifted both of them to one hand and crossed her fingers against the evil eye with the other, nearly toppling herself over.

"This isn't your business, Mother."

"Ungrateful children come to a bad end, always," Cronos grumbled. He had been tall in his youth, but was bent so nearly double with age that he had to cock his head to look up at Zeus with a mad eye.

"Or yours." Zeus put a hand on each. "Now go and sit down and rest, or I'll call a servant and have you carried."

"It's come to this," Cronos said, stumping along on his cane, closer to his son. "All my children betray me."

"Heracles!" Zeus shouted, and a muscular servant appeared. "Take my parents to their sitting room, please."

"Yes, lord." Heracles scooped up Cronos in his arms and carried him off while Cronos beat at him with his cane. In a few moments he came back, slightly battered, for Rhea.

Zeus let out a deep breath. "Patricide begins to look a more acceptable option, daily."

"You won't, though," Hera said. "You're still afraid of him."

"True, alas." Zeus ran a hand through his coppery

hair, as if combing his father out of it. "Now . . ." He peered into the rush basket where he had laid the baby, and tickled her. She cooed at him. "Abut the child . . . I thought, a playmate for Hebe."

"Hebe has her brothers," Hera said. She and Zeus were united in their opposition to his parents, but only in that. The two boys on the nursery floor eyed them watchfully, with considerably more attention than they had given their grandparents. When Mama used that tone, someone was often sorry quite soon. Hephaestus went on pounding his hammer on his blocks, his odd twisted feet stuck straight out in front of him, but Ares got up from his toy soldiers and trotted over to peer into the rush basket at the baby.

"Pretty," he said. "Can we keep her?" The shrieks of two more little boys outside the window claimed his attention, and he darted out the door, abandoning the baby for them. In a moment they heard louder shrieking.

"We need another girl," Zeus said cajolingly. "With all these boys."

Hera's mouth flattened out. The two boys outside, Dionysus and Hermes, were Zeus's, but they weren't hers. Their mothers were servants on the farm, among the many who had received his attentions.

"Always room for one more. That's my sweet." Zeus slid an arm around her.

"That's generally been your theory," Hera said. She eyed the baby again. "You've been overpopulating the farm for years." She had milky skin and shimmering hair the color of chestnuts. She was the most beautiful woman in the village, maybe even in the city of Tiryns, but the simmering anger she directed at her husband made it a fearsome loveliness, like the statue of some dangerous goddess, that only Zeus had the nerve to approach.

Hebe and Hephaestus watched in silence. When their parents struck sparks, things caught on fire, and it was better not to be in the direct path of the flames.

"What would you like?" Zeus asked. "Some splendid present for being such a good wife? For putting up with troublesome old Zeus?"

"I'll think of something," Hera said between her teeth, because she knew he was going to keep this baby no matter what she said. "I put up with a lot, so it had better be extremely splendid." She swept from the nursery, leaving Zeus with the baby, who began to howl. He shouted for the nursemaid.

So she stayed. Zeus claimed she wasn't his, but he never had a good answer for why he had brought her home. He had never been the best of fathers to the children he had already, male or female, calling them to him to pet them like puppies and dismissing them carelessly when they bored him, and sometimes seeming to forget their names. But he named this one himself. He called her Aphrodite, meaning "Wave Born."

The farm he brought her to was on land that had first been worked by the ancestors of his clan, and handed down over the years to Cronos and Rhea. The rocky hillside supported olive groves and the lower land pastured cattle and goats or was tilled for grain. A terraced vineyard climbed the slope in between. Of Cronos it was rumored that he *had* killed his father for control of the land. The old couple were now too feeble to run the farm themselves, but still able to tell their children when they were doing it wrong. They terrified Aphrodite as she grew, sitting in their armchairs at the center of the great hall like spiders. They appeared to unnerve her aunts and uncles as well. There were four of them besides Zeus—Poseidon and Hades, and the sisters Demeter and Hestia, plus Poseidon's wife Amphitrite—and they all avoided the grandparents' scolding tongues when they could manage it, sending the unfortunate farm servants to care for them, and gritting their teeth through dinner as Cronos expounded on the numerous errors Poseidon made in his training of the young horses, and Rhea complained of Hera's supervision of the kitchen and Amphitrite's lack of children.

Zeus and Hera's children, who ate in the nursery with Zeus's other sons, got most of their information on family matters from eavesdropping on these conversations.

"When I am grown," Ares said, "I will lock them up in a tower, if Father hasn't done it already by then."

"He would have," Hephaestus said, 'but Grandfather threatened to curse him, and Father thinks he can."

"Always another mouth to feed," Rhea's voice came querulously through the wall. "And in these hard times. Likely your poor old parents will starve, for you feeding your bastards all our food."

"What hard times?" Hermes asked. He had never noticed any. His mother was a maid here, but he was petted and spoiled by Zeus.

"Grandmother says it's hard times," Hebe said. She was the oldest, at nine. "She caught me in the garden yesterday and told me I'd never have a dowry, and I'd have to go on the streets."

"Spiteful old witch," Dionysus said.

"She's always saying I should have been exposed. She thinks poor little Aphrodite should too."

"She's afraid because she's old," Hephaestus said. He was well aware of what his grandmother had always said about him. He was eight and Ares seven. Hermes and Dionysus were five and six.

"Lots of people are old," Hebe said, "and they don't tear at each other like jackals."

"Our family does."

Hermes pointed at the baby, now two, banging her spoon on the table. "Maybe Father brought us that one to give them something new to complain about. Keep them off his back."

"Didn't work," Ares said.

"Baby, don't do that." Hebe took the spoon away from Aphrodite before she could smack her cup with it. "Before this one they complained about you," she said to Hermes.

"Do you think she's Father's?" Dionysus asked.

"No!" Ares said. "He found her. He said so."

Hephaestus snorted. "There are enough of Father's children to go around the village twice."

"This one is different," Ares said stubbornly.

Hebe sighed. The only time Ares ever stopped fighting with his brothers or the village boys, or lining up armies of bugs and trying to make them fight each other, was when Aphrodite toddled into the yard to find him. Hebe knew that even at two, Aphrodite was dangerously beautiful. Her beauty wasn't just in the eyes, it was a presence, a force like an overpowering scent. There might be other girl children as beautiful, or maybe even more so, if you painted her picture and showed it to people and asked them to vote on the prettiest. But no one who saw her in person ever saw anyone else to match her. She was going to be more beautiful than Mother, Hebe thought, and that was going to make more trouble yet.

Aphrodite wasn't sure when she had figured out for herself that she was beautiful. She had simply always known it. Wherever she went people looked at her, and they would do things for her without being asked. If she asked, they would do nearly everything. Or the men would. Hera told her not to get above herself, and Hebe told her to be careful. The shepherd boys made her wreaths of daisies when she came out to play with the new lambs, and Heracles carved her a little wooden horse on wheels. Ares pulled her around in his goat cart and uncle Poseidon gave her rides on his shoulders. Animals liked her, too. The goats and Hera's chickens followed her everywhere she went.

When Aphrodite was five years old, a woman who ran a very high class house of hetairae in Mycenae tried to buy her. (Hera would have sold her if Zeus hadn't been there.) Aphrodite wasn't sure what the woman had wanted, but she had promised her beautiful dresses and to teach her to play the lyre, and Aphrodite had wanted to go with her.

"You wouldn't have liked it," Hephaestus said solemnly. But he thought she might have.

When she was seven, two twelve-year-old boys in the village outside Tiryns fought over her and one pushed the other off a wall and broke both his legs. Aphrodite watched them with interest, twining one rose-gold curl around her finger. She yearned for those boys, for both of them, they were so wonderful and strong, and she liked the way they moved inside their skin, like young horses. They gave her an explosive sense of power, rolling in the dirt like that, pummeling each other for her sake.

"You come home!" Ares said, grabbing her by the arm. "You belong to us!"

"Ow! You're hurting me!"

Ares loosened his grip. "Sorry. But you stay away from those louts."

"Why?" Aphrodite demanded. "They gave me a sweet. One of them did."

"You can't take sweets from strange boys," Hephaestus said, hobbling beside her.

Aphrodite looked at him thoughtfully. He always seemed to know things. The boys in the village teased him because of his feet and threw rocks at him because they knew he couldn't catch them. When Ares was with him, Ares caught them instead and beat their heads together. Aphrodite knew Hephaestus didn't like that when it happened, but she didn't understand why. Who would want rocks thrown at them? "Why can't I have the sweet?" she asked.

"Because they will want something for it," Hephaestus said.

"Because you're ours," Ares said.

When she was ten, a group of mothers from Tiryns came to the farm to complain to Hera that Aphrodite had been in a cattle shed kissing boys, each in turn, in exchange for a silver bead or a bronze bracelet, or whatever he could offer her. She was wearing the offending bracelets when Hera turned her over her knee.

"Disgraceful!" Hera's hand came down wielding an ivory hairbrush.

"Ow!" Aphrodite thrashed on her lap as Hera got a good grip on her hair with her other hand.

The brush came down again. "No child of my

household will behave like a trollop! In a shed! With seven boys!"

"Ow! Stop!" Aphrodite wailed, kicking her feet, her face slick with tears.

"Stay! Away! From boys!" The brush came down with each word.

Hebe stood to one side, worried. Hebe was seventeen and she would not until now have thought of kissing a boy until her parents presented her with a suitable husband; then she would kiss him *after* the wedding.

"There!" Hera grabbed Aphrodite by the shoulders and stood her on her feet again. "You are not to go into the village alone again! Do you understand me?"

Aphrodite sniffled, rubbing her backside. Hera's anger sparked out of her gray eyes like lightning but Aphrodite still didn't comprehend why. "Yes, Mother," she said, because it was easier to say that than to argue. But it had been fun, kissing those boys. It had felt very nice in places that Aphrodite hadn't noticed before. She looked sorrowfully at her bare wrists. Hera had taken the bracelets.

"You need work to do," her Aunt Hestia said, taking her by the ear and leading her to the kitchen, where she washed dishes for a ten-day until her hands were raw, snuffling at her misfortune to the household snake, who came out of his basket and wrapped a sympathetic coil about her ankle, his flat head resting on her foot. After that her Aunt Demeter took her into the kitchen garden, where she set out bean seedlings until all the nails on her reddened hands were broken to the quick. The Aunts were not unkind, and said they had her best interests at heart, but dishwater and beans didn't make her stop liking boys.

Hephaestus was sixteen then, old enough to know danger when he saw it, but he couldn't help feeling sorry for her as she mourned her confiscated bracelets. He had begun to take over the forge on the farm by then, sitting on a stool he had built, his lame feet dangling, hammering out bridle bits and sheaths for wagon wheels, spear points for hunting and cauldrons for the kitchen. Sometimes Aphrodite would sit and watch him, her tame hen in her lap, or one of the other farm animals who always came to her hand. Today it was a goat, its knobby head resting on her knees. She looked so sad that on impulse, he said, "If *I* made you something, Mother would let you keep it."

Aphrodite's face brightened. "Would you? What would you make me?"

"I have a little gold. I could make you a girdle to wear with your good gown. Not all gold, bronze mostly, but I could put gold ornaments on it. What do you like?"

Aphrodite's eyes shone. "I like doves. They make such a sweet sound. There's one that sits on my windowsill every morning. Could I have doves on it?"

"Doves it shall be," Hephaestus said.

Aphrodite beamed at him. A ten-day later, when it was finished, she fastened it around her slim hips to admire herself. The girdle was forged of delicate, spiraling links of bronze, with gold rosettes between the links, and the buckle, as promised, was a pair of gold doves, facing each other.

"I made it so you can move the buckle when you get bigger, and you won't outgrow it," he said.

Aphrodite sighed with delight and danced across the yard. "I'm going to go look at myself in the pool!" she called to him. Hera possessed a silver mirror, but just now Aphrodite felt it might be unwise to borrow it. She ran along the wagon road that sloped down from the farmyard into a grove of trees. From the road, the path to the sacred spring branched off and she darted along it.

It was cool and mysterious in the woods by the spring where the Goddess lived. In the heart of the woods an olive tree stood guard over a spring-fed pool and a stone altar, all three so old they had been there in the time of Erebus, the first of Cronos's clan, so Mother had said. Beside the altar sat the omphalos, a round stone shaped by an ancient hand, and nearly as tall as Aphrodite. The omphalos was the navel of the world, older even than the altar and the tree. Aphrodite thought that the Goddess talked to her here sometimes, but she had never said so to anyone. She suspected she would have been spanked for impertinence, as it was common knowledge that the Goddess spoke only to her priestesses in her temple. But Aphrodite had heard her.

This morning she knelt beside the pool and looked into its black water. Her pale face shimmered back at her and around her waist shone the magical, marvelous girdle that Hephaestus had made for her. Aphrodite held her breath, staring at her reflection. The girdle glowed, it sang, it felt warm against her hips and waist.

On impulse she unbuckled it and dipped it in the water. "Make everyone love me," she asked the Goddess. Its bronze spirals flashed like golden fish in the depths. Ares had begun to run after older girls and leave her behind. "Make him love *me*," she told the water and the golden belt.

*Be careful what you wish for,* the water whispered back.

Aphrodite cocked her head, trying to decide if she had really heard that.

No other sound came back t o her except the liquid *plop!* of a frog at the far end. of the pool. Aphrodite shrugged and put her marvelous girdle back on, feeling its still-warm links imprint themselves on her waist. What could be wrong with being loved?